Death and the Librarian

Also by Victoria Gilbert:

The Campus Sleuth Mysteries

Schooled in Murder

The Hunter and Clewe Mysteries

A Killer Clue

A Cryptic Clue

The Book Lover's B&B Mysteries

A Fatal Booking

Reserved for Murder

Booked for Death

The Blue Ridge Library Mysteries

Murder Checks Out

Death in the Margins

Renewed for Murder

A Deadly Edition

Bound for Murder

Past Due for Murder

Shelved Under Murder

A Murder for the Books

The Mirror of Immortality Series

Scepter of Fire

Crown of Ice

Death and the Librarian

A BLUE RIDGE LIBRARY MYSTERY

VICTORIA GILBERT

Books should be disposed of and recycled according to local requirements. All paper materials used are FSC compliant.

This is a work of fiction. All of the names, characters, organizations, places and events portrayed in this novel are either products of the author's imagination or are used fictitiously. Any resemblance to real or actual events, locales, or persons, living or dead, is entirely coincidental.

Copyright © 2025 by Vicki L. Weavil

All rights reserved.

Published in the United States by Crooked Lane Books, an imprint of The Quick Brown Fox & Company LLC.

Crooked Lane Books and its logo are trademarks of The Quick Brown Fox & Company LLC.

Library of Congress Catalog-in-Publication data available upon request.

ISBN (hardcover): 979-8-89242-046-4
ISBN (ebook): 979-8-89242-047-1

Cover design by Griesbach/Martucci

Printed in the United States.

www.crookedlanebooks.com

Crooked Lane Books
34 West 27th St., 10th Floor
New York, NY 10001

First Edition: July 2025

The authorized representative in the EU for product safety and compliance is eucomply OÜPärnu mnt 139b-14, 11317 Tallinn, Estonia, hello@eucompliancepartner.com, +33757690241

10 9 8 7 6 5 4 3 2 1

For my husband, Kevin.
Always my first, and favorite, reader.

Chapter One

The problem with omens is that they're easy to miss. You often don't recognize them until after their predictions have come true.

Dark clouds rolled across the late July sky like a great wave, making me jump up from my lawn chair so quickly that it fell backward onto the grass. "Ella and Nicky, out of the yard, now," I called out.

My six-year-old twins looked up from the fort of old boxes they were building in our backyard. "We're not done yet, Mommy," Ella said, her gray eyes narrowing as she blew a loose lock of dark brown hair away from her face.

"Yeah, we wanna finish," her brother Nicky said, his brown eyes pleading as a puppy's.

I pointed up at the sky. "Looks like a storm. Grab those boxes and come here."

"That's odd. It wasn't supposed to rain today." The tall, broad-shouldered older man who'd been sitting next to me also rose to his feet. I glanced at him. No one would guess that Kurt Kendrick, who was my children's godfather, would

1

turn eighty before the end of the year. He was still fit and handsome, despite the lines on his rugged face, and possessed a full head of thick white hair.

My aunt, Lydia Talbot, paused beside the ironwork table on our flagstone patio. She set down a pewter tray filled with sandwiches. "I think it will pass," she said, motioning to the fast-moving clouds.

Aunt Lydia, who looked petite next to Kurt, was actually a woman of average height. Taller than I was, anyway, which meant Kurt, like most men, towered over me. I wasn't slender like my aunt, though. My curvaceous figure always made me feel larger than my aunt, even though she had a few inches on me.

The dark clouds scuttled away like crabs on a beach, leaving behind a clear blue sky. "You're both right," I said. "It's already clearing, and it is a little odd," I added, casting Kurt a smile.

He flashed a wolfish grin. "Note this moment, Lydia. Amy has admitted I was right about something."

"What foolishness." Aunt Lydia pursed her thin lips and peeled the plastic wrap off the platter of sandwiches. As she turned away, the sun illuminated the few flyaway strands of her short silver hair. "Children, please stop playing for a minute and come grab something to eat."

Ella and Nicky didn't have to be asked twice. Not only were they both growing like weeds, but they also knew that their great-aunt was one of the best cooks in our town of Taylorsford, Virginia. Bounding over the lawn that separated the patio from our garden, they reached the table in record time.

Death and the Librarian

"Hold on," Aunt Lydia said, pointing toward the sink that was part of our outdoor kitchen. "Hands must be washed before you touch the food."

If I had issued the same order there might've been some grumbling, but my aunt's imperious blue-eyed gaze silenced any protest. The twins dutifully trotted over to the sink and followed Aunt Lydia's command, although they did manage to splash water at each other in the process.

"So the speaker tomorrow afternoon is that true-crime author who wrote about the Baron murder?" Kurt asked as he nonchalantly picked up a ham and cheese sandwich. "I thought your Friends of the Library association had originally lined up someone who writes literary fiction."

I grabbed half an egg salad sandwich. "They did, but there was a scheduling problem with that author, so the chair called in a favor from an old friend."

"I didn't realize Nancy Nieman knew any authors. At least, I've never heard her brag about it, which I'd think she surely would." Aunt Lydia checked Ella and Nicky's hands before allowing each of them to grab a sandwich.

"We're gonna eat in the fort," Ella said through a mouthful of turkey and cheese. Nicky, his cheeks plumped out with chewing, nodded in agreement.

"Alright, but try not to feed most of it to the ants," I said, as they dashed back to their cardboard construction site.

The garden beyond the lawn created a lush backdrop of herbs, flowers, and vegetables. It was backed by a frieze of shrubs and trees in all shades of green. The scalloped edges of the Blue Ridge mountains rose up behind the woods, appearing closer than they actually were. A hike to the summit would take hours, even though it looked like I could reach out and touch the nearest ridge.

Kurt stared up into the sky, his eyes equally blue and untroubled. "It appears that the dark clouds were a passing warning. But perhaps it presages a storm to come," he said, sitting down.

"I hope not," I said. "The arts festival starts tomorrow, and our Friends of the Library book sale is supposed to be held outside on the library lawn."

"The weather report said it would be a clear weekend, which is good for all of the festival events." Aunt Lydia plucked an egg salad sandwich off the plate, then stretched the plastic back over the platter.

I righted my chair and sat back down, nibbling on my sandwich. "Anyway, to get back to Nancy and the speaker, apparently she went to college with Maureen Dryden, who is pretty famous, I guess."

Aunt Lydia shrugged her slender shoulders and sat in the chair on the other side of Kurt. "Her true crime book was a *New York Times* bestseller in nonfiction, from what I hear. And there was even a documentary series on one of the streamers a while back."

"That was the Beverly Baron murder case." Kurt appeared lost in thought. "It's still officially unsolved, although Ms. Dryden laid out a strong case against the main suspect."

"Yeah, Allen Cardullo. He was supposed to be one of Baron's most ardent fans." I frowned. "Didn't he commit suicide without ever admitting any guilt?"

Death and the Librarian

"Which just made him look guiltier," Aunt Lydia said, dabbing at her lips with a napkin.

Kurt, who'd finished off his sandwich, wiped his broad hands on his own napkin and reached for a plastic cup sitting on the small table between us. "In the court of public opinion, at any rate." He paused to take a sip of water. "The most vicious court that exists."

Aunt Lydia cut him a sideways glance. She had an ambivalent relationship with Kurt, because she felt he'd been a bad influence in her late husband's life. But their animosity had cooled over the last several years, especially after Kurt had aided our family in various ways, including rescuing a few of us from danger. "I'm still surprised that Nancy could get someone of that caliber to speak at a small-town arts festival, college friends or not," she said.

"I think Dryden may have fallen out of the public eye because that book was published over six years ago. That probably helped Nancy recruit her," I said. "But on the other hand, I suspect the Baron book was popular enough to keep her in cash for quite some time, especially when you consider the television rights and all that." I rubbed my fingers with my napkin. "I did some research on her . . ."

"Of course you did." Kurt cast me a sly smile.

I balled up my napkin and tossed it on the table. "I *am* one of the library directors, after all. It's important for me to know about the background of any speaker sponsored by our Friends of the Library. Also, Ms. Dryden's assistant contacted us about Maureen doing some research in the town archives on Monday. Apparently, the book she's writing now is an anthology covering several cold cases. The focus is on missing persons and murders in small towns like Taylorsford."

Aunt Lydia arched her pale eyebrows. "She's interested in the town archives? Does that mean she's covering a cold case that occurred around here?"

"Yes, although it's nothing I've ever heard about. Which is strange, because when you work in a community gathering place like a public library, you typically hear every scrap of gossip or rumor that's ever plagued the town." I smiled as I watched Ella and Nicky rearrange their collection of boxes to create a taller structure. "Those two have the wildest imaginations."

"Now I wonder where they got that from?" asked a familiar voice from the door to our screened back porch.

I dropped my head back. "They inherited your creative genius, I guess," I said, as light footsteps came up behind me.

Richard leaned over to kiss my forehead. "And your tenacious curiosity," he said, circling around my chair to greet Aunt Lydia and Kurt.

"Help yourself." My aunt smiled as Richard headed straight for the table after a brief hello. "I'm sure you're hungry after rehearsal."

"Always," he replied, flipping up one corner of the plastic wrap to grab a sandwich. As he stood behind the table, I couldn't help but admire the grace inherent in his pose, which made sense considering he was a celebrated contemporary dancer. Although, at forty-four, he was more focused on teaching and choreography, he still practiced in the studio every day and occasionally danced in productions or galas devoted to charitable causes.

Death and the Librarian

"Daddy!" Ella and Nicky rushed Richard like he was the quarterback on an opposing team. It was a testament to his core strength and balance that he wasn't knocked off his feet when they both threw their arms around his legs.

"You see, it isn't even having a Daddy's girl in our case," I told Kurt dryly. "It's Daddy's girl *and* boy."

Kurt crossed his arms over his broad chest. "Ah, but what do you expect? Doesn't everyone adore Richard?"

"True, true." I couldn't help but feel a sensation of warmth in my chest as Richard set down his half-eaten sandwich and lifted up each twin in turn to give them a big hug. "I don't mind when it's the kids. It's just those young dancers who make me nervous . . ."

Aunt Lydia audibly sniffed. "You'd better be joking, young lady. Your husband is as loyal as they come."

"Absolutely," Richard said, setting Nicky back on his feet. "I mean, who would dare do otherwise and face the wrath of Amy Webber Muir?"

"Ha, ha, very funny." I made a face at him, but then smiled. Honestly, I knew I had nothing to worry about where Richard was concerned. Despite many temptations, I'd never seen him show the tiniest bit of interest in any female other than me, unless it was just as a friend.

Ella tugged on his hand. "Come see our fort, Daddy. Nicky and me have been building it all afternoon."

"Nicky and I," Aunt Lydia corrected, causing Kurt to give me a wink.

"Back in a minute," Richard said, his gray eyes sparkling as the twins pulled him toward their pile of boxes.

7

Aunt Lydia turned to me. "You never finished telling us about the lecture, Amy. It's late tomorrow afternoon, right? Zelda and Walt said something about joining me. We thought we'd visit the book sale as well as any of the town merchants' sidewalk sales and then head over to the town hall."

"The author talk is at five o'clock," I said. "There's that community music performance at the Lutheran church right before, so I think most of the crowd will show up at the town hall around five. If you want good seats, skip the music—there's another performance on Sunday anyway."

Kurt stared across lawn, his focus obviously on Richard and the twins. "I think it was a good idea that Richard and Karla decided to hold the premiere performance of their new company the following weekend. It now falls outside the bounds of the actual arts festival, but there's so much going on, people might've felt too tired to attend dance performances this weekend on top of everything else."

I leaned across the side table to pat his arm. "I know that was your suggestion. And I do agree."

He laid his other hand over mine. "Glad to have your approval."

"Well, since you're the primary sponsor, I suppose the Tansen-Muir Company has to dance to your tune," Aunt Lydia said, with a sidelong glance at Kurt.

"Now, Lydia, you know I won't interfere in artistic decisions. Or any decisions concerning the company, actually." Kurt lifted his hand and straightened in his chair. "I'm truly a silent partner."

Death and the Librarian

"Hmm, why do I doubt that." My aunt tapped the arm of her chair with her short but well-manicured fingernails. "I'm just sad Hugh won't be here for the festival or the dance company's premiere. But I'm in good company. Fred's with him, so Sunny will be on her own as well."

My aunt's significant other for the past several years, Hugh Chen, was an art expert called in by collectors and museums, and even the authorities, to aid in tracking down missing art and antiquities and evaluating possible forgeries. Former police detective turned private eye Fred Nash, who just happened to be my best friend Sunny's longtime boyfriend, often accompanied Hugh to help identify and locate the criminals associated with forgeries or thefts.

"Off doing the work of the angels?" Kurt's lips quirked into a smile. As an art collector and dealer, he was well known to both Hugh and Fred, especially since some of his colleagues and acquaintances had already come under their scrutiny.

"Unlike your more devilish dealings." Aunt Lydia said this under her breath, but it was obvious she meant it to be heard.

Kurt's smile broadened. "Indeed."

Richard crossed the lawn and retrieved his half-eaten sandwich before grabbing a lawn chair.

"How was rehearsal?" I asked after he sat down beside me.

"Acceptable. The one piece featuring the younger dancers still needs polishing, but we'll get there." Richard took a bite and chewed before continuing. "Conner is doing great. It's some of the girls who aren't always precise enough. I think they're just nervous. Karla is going to work with them separately tomorrow afternoon."

"So you don't have rehearsals tomorrow?" I asked, surprise tinging my tone. Karla Tansen and Richard, who'd collaborated on running an intensive summer dance academy for several years, had finally taken the steps to establish their own professional company. The premiere performances were set for the weekend following the arts festival, so it was only a week until what Richard jokingly called "hoping not to break a leg day."

Having finished his sandwich, Richard leaned back with his arms crossed behind his head. "No, although I'll be meeting with some members of the technical crew in the morning. But I can accompany you and the kids to the festival events later in the day."

"That's a relief," I said, exhaling loudly. "Allocating one parent per twin is so much easier, especially in a crowd."

Kurt chuckled. "Are you saying my godchildren are hard to handle?"

"You should know, after the infamous zoo incident." Richard cast Kurt a sardonic smile.

Kurt straightened in his chair. "They only slipped away for ten minutes."

"Right, but why did Amy and I receive fifteen phone calls within that short timeframe?" Arching his dark eyebrows, Richard's expression held more than a hint of smugness. "It was you and Scott *and* Ethan. Three to two, and the twins still managed to outwit you."

"You should've listened to me and taken Aunt Lydia along," I said. "Ella and Nicky can't put anything over on her."

Death and the Librarian

"Can anyone?" Kurt asked, shooting my aunt a wicked grin.

Aunt Lydia huffed in displeasure. "You make me sound like some tyrant. I just know how to inspire proper discipline and respect, that's all."

Richard and Kurt and I shared a look, then burst into laughter.

Chapter Two

The sudden gust of wind that swept over the lawn in front of Taylorsford's town hall could've been another herald of things to come, but all I noticed at the time was true crime author Maureen Dryden's notes flying off the table on the performance stage.

It also spun the pinwheels held aloft by Ella and Nicky. Breaking free from my hold on her other hand, Ella dashed toward the stage. Laughing and twirling in a series of pirouettes, Ella used her pinwheel to bat at the pieces of paper as they fluttered to the grass like giant snowflakes.

Fortunately, the audience for Ms. Dryden's lecture hadn't arrived yet, as most of the summer arts festival's attendees were still watching the musical performance at the Lutheran church.

"Elenora Muir, get back here this minute," I called out, running to grab her after sharing an exasperated glance with Richard, who still had a firm grip on Nicky's hand.

Before I could reach her, a lanky young man jumped off the low stage and knelt down in front of Ella. "That's an

Death and the Librarian

amazing pinwheel, and I do like your dancing," he said, in a gentle voice. "But I really need to collect all these papers for my boss. Could you run back to your parents and let me do that? I don't want to get yelled at," he added, with a wink.

"I'm so sorry," I reached Ella and threw my arm around her shoulders. "We don't want to make your job any harder than it already seems to be." I looked him over, observing his pleasant features and shoulder-length light brown hair. "You're Ms. Dryden's assistant, right? I remember seeing your photo in her promo materials."

The young man rose to his feet. Towering over me by at least ten inches, he offered a warm smile. "Yes, Sean Gordon. I'm assuming you're one of the codirectors of the Taylorsford public library?"

"That's right, I'm Amy Muir," I replied, tightening my hold on Ella, who was wriggling under my arm.

"I'm Ella, and I'm a real dancer," my daughter said. "You want to see? I can do leaps and everything."

"Thanks, but I do have to grab all these papers before we get another gust of wind. Maybe another time?" Sean Gordon's hazel eyes sparkled as he gave Ella a little bow. "Excuse me until then, young lady."

"Everything okay here?" Richard asked, stepping up beside me with Nicky in tow.

"No problem at all," Sean said, examining my husband carefully. "You're Richard Muir, right? The dancer?"

Richard grinned. "Yes, but my primary job these days seems to be twin wrangler." He motioned toward the pieces of paper scattered across the grass. "Glad to help collect those if you'd like."

"No, you take this one"—I pushed Ella toward him—"and I'll assist Mr. Gordon." As Richard met my gaze with a quizzical look, I shrugged. "You have a stronger grip."

"True," Richard said, his eyes filled with amusement. "Alright, come on, kids. Let's back off and let Mommy help."

"It's really not necessary." Sean Gordon bent down and began scooping up the typed pages. "But I won't say no."

As Richard led the twins to the front row of folding chairs that had been set up on the lawn in preparation for Ms. Dryden's talk, I noticed that the back rows of seats were already occupied by a few townspeople and visitors, even though the lecture wasn't supposed to start for fifteen minutes.

"The early birds are grabbing their perches," I told Sean as I joined his quest to retrieve his boss's notes. "In the back, of course."

Sean cast me a smile. "Ready to make a quick escape if the talk turns dull."

"Isn't that always the way?" I picked up several pages. "Good thing it's late July and it's been hot and dry." I held up one page. "Don't see any damage."

"Which is a blessing for me. Maureen would be furious if all her notes were waterlogged." Sean grabbed the last two pieces of the escaped papers. "I'll have to put these back in order, of course."

I handed him the pages I'd collected. "I'm surprised your other colleagues ignored your efforts."

Death and the Librarian

Sean glanced up at the temporary stage, where two people—a wiry dark-haired man who appeared to be in his mid-twenties and a young woman with short, bleached blonde curls—were fiddling with some electronic equipment. "Not really colleagues," he said, with a frown. "That's Terrell Temkin, the podcast host, and his assistant, Mindy LaSalle. We don't usually work with them, but Maureen decided to bring them along for this gig. Terry's working with her on her new project. He'll be doing some podcasts to support her book."

"That's right, I read about their collaboration in an article. I guess this book will work better for a podcast since it's going to be a collection of true crime stories, rather than focusing on one case, as she did with the Beverly Baron murder."

Sean looked down at the sheaf of papers in his hands. "Yeah. Maureen claims she wanted to try something different. But just between you and me, I think she just felt it'd be difficult to top *Deadly Desire*."

I didn't doubt his assertion. Maureen Dryden's last book had been such a bestseller that she'd spent the intervening years discussing it on talk shows and in numerous print and online interviews. "She's still doing research for this book, I guess, since she sent the library an email asking to use our town archives on Monday. Will you be accompanying her?"

"Maybe." Sean shuffled the pages. "She hasn't told me her schedule for next week yet, but that's par for the course." He flashed a faint smile. "She may send me out to interview some of the locals. The older ones, I mean. She thinks they may remember more details about the Jaffe case."

"I don't know. I did a little research when I heard that's what she was interested in, and there really isn't much I could find. Of course, I haven't dug too deep yet." I met Sean's inquisitive gaze with a shrug. "It's not a murder case, you know. Edward Jaffe is still considered a missing person."

Sean clutched the papers to his chest. "I know, but Maureen's convinced he's dead and that it was foul play. She says she has her sources and just needs to verify a few things. But I'm not sure if that's true or just wishful thinking. She hasn't shared much about it with me. She's had me researching other cold cases."

"Speaking of your work, I suppose I'd better let you get back to it," I said, motioning toward the papers. "Maybe I'll see you later, or on Monday?"

"Sure thing." Sean bobbed his head and headed back to the stage.

A steady stream of people now filled the rows of chairs where Richard and the twins were already seated. I caught sight of my Aunt Lydia and Zelda and Walt Adams and waved them over.

"Hello, dears." The vibrant crimson print on Zelda's tunic top rippled like a field of poppies as she trotted toward us. Walt and my aunt followed more slowly. Zelda glanced at the stage, where Sean was already seated at the table, rearranging the loose sheets of paper into a coherent order. "This is that true crime writer, isn't it?" She switched her sparkling tea-brown gaze to me. "Are you going to let Ella and Nicky stay for that?"

"No, I'm taking them inside for the storytelling session." Richard calmly confiscated Ella's pinwheel before she could

Death and the Librarian

hit Nicky with it. "I was just waiting for Sunny's announcement."

As if his words had conjured her, a tall woman with long hair that fell over her slender shoulders like a golden veil appeared on the stage. "Hello, everyone," she said after grabbing one of the handheld microphones from the table. "Most of you know me, but for those who don't, I'm Sunshine Fields, the codirector of the Taylorsford Library. I'll be providing a storytelling and craft session for the children during Ms. Dryden's lecture. So if you don't think your child will enjoy a talk about true crime, please take them inside the town hall. Some library volunteers and I will keep them entertained while you enjoy the lecture."

"My cue." Richard stood and took each of the twins by the hand. "Save my seat," he added, leaning over to brush a kiss across my temple before following Sunny inside.

"Good plan," Aunt Lydia said, sitting down beside Zelda and Walt. She turned to me, her blue eyes cool as spring water. "I doubt many parents want their children to hear about crimes, no matter how cold the cases are."

"Actually, I think they might've enjoyed it, up to a point. You know how kids love gruesome stuff," I said. "But Sunny and I thought they'd eventually get restless and cause disruptions."

"True enough. About kids liking scary stories, I mean." Walt stretched out his long legs and leaned back in his chair. He slipped a lanky arm around Zelda's plump shoulders. "My youngest grandchild revels in all things gross and spooky."

Zelda gave a little shudder. "Not to mention anything to do with spiders and snakes." She bobbed her head, bouncing her perfectly tinted blonde curls. Although the same age as my aunt, Zelda refused to allow her hair to go gray. Along with her rosy cheeks and vivacious air, she appeared younger than her seventy-four years.

Not that Aunt Lydia, despite her silver hair and the lines fanning from the corners of her eyes, truly looked her age. As slender as Zelda was plump, my aunt maintained a regal posture and an air of elegance time could not destroy.

"Have you heard anything more from Hugh?" I asked her as I sat down, placing my purse on the adjacent chair to hold it for Richard.

"He called last night from Paris," Aunt Lydia said, lifting her sharp chin. "But I don't think he and Fred are there now. He said they had to head out into the countryside to follow a lead on the latest forgery ring."

"Must be rough," I said, shooting her a sidelong smile. "I still don't know why you don't accompany him on some of these trips. I mean, Paris and the French countryside . . ."

"It's work. I'd only be in the way." Aunt Lydia flicked one fine-boned hand through the air. "Besides, Hugh often has to keep a low profile when he's on these trips."

"And he certainly couldn't do that with you on his arm," Walt said gallantly. He winked at Zelda. "Lydia's hard to miss."

A faint blush stained my aunt's high cheekbones. "What nonsense you talk, Walt. Hasn't Zelda gotten you in line yet?"

"As if." Zelda rolled her eyes.

Death and the Librarian

I smiled, knowing that this banter was common among the three, who'd been friends since elementary school, despite the fact that Walter Adams had been one of the few Black students in their class. A carefully concealed attraction between Zelda and Walt—which had been deemed socially unacceptable in Taylorsford when they were young—had survived both of their marriages and led them, long after their spouses had passed, to finally marry.

"Sunny is certainly brave," Richard said, as he strolled over to join us.

I grabbed my purse so he could sit beside me. "You just figured that out?"

Richard grinned. "I know she's shown her mettle in the many scrapes you've dragged her into, but handling that sugar-fueled batch of little monsters is the real proof."

I wrinkled my nose at him. "She has help, and anyway, what do you mean by me dragging Sunny into anything? She always jumps in on her own."

Before Richard could reply. Aunt Lydia cleared her throat and tapped my arm. "It looks like they're about ready to start."

I turned my attention to the stage. The podcaster Terry Temkin had taken his place behind a stationary microphone, while Mindy LaSalle was seated next to a compact setup of audio equipment. Sean Gordon picked up one of the handheld microphones and rose to his feet.

"Hello, everyone," he said, immediately pulling the microphone away from his lips as reverb rattled one of the speakers. "Sorry about that, and welcome. We're delighted so many people could join us today."

I looked around. There *was* a crowd; all the chairs were filled. Glancing down the front row, I noticed Kurt and, in the row behind him, two other familiar faces—Sheriff Brad Tucker and his wife, Alison. She also worked in law enforcement, as a deputy in a different county than her husband. I assumed they'd dropped off their two children inside the town hall for Sunny's storytelling event.

Since I'd already researched Maureen Dryden and her team, I zoned out on Sean's lengthy introduction of the author. It was only after he finished speaking that a short, stocky woman climbed the steps behind the stage and made her grand entrance.

I knew Dryden was only forty-one, a year younger than me, but she looked older. *Or at least,* I told myself, *I hope so.* The lines on her face, rather deep for her age, I attributed to a heavy smoking habit. She'd said in an interview she'd recently quit, but the damage to her skin remained. She certainly sported a more dramatic style than I did—on one side, her auburn hair was shaved close to her scalp, while the rest fell in a smooth swoop that framed her square jawline. Her dangling gold earrings were reminiscent of intricately patterned Moroccan lanterns.

"Hello, and thank you for the wonderful welcome." Maureen's voice, slightly husky, was a perfect match for her eclectic style. As she took her seat, she tossed an Indian-print scarf over one shoulder of her vivid chartreuse blouse.

Another gust of wind rattled the objects on the table, but Sean was quick to press both hands over Maureen's notes, saving them from scattering again. As soon as the wind died

Death and the Librarian

down, he slid the stack of papers over to Maureen, who only took a quick glance before launching into her lecture, which seemed to be mostly about her own accolades.

Richard leaned in close to me and whispered in my ear, "Not shy of tooting her own horn."

I elbowed him. "Shh. She is a best-selling author."

"For one book." Richard sat back in his chair. "Written six years ago."

"She's working on a new one," I said, although I had to agree with him to a certain extent. From what I'd been able to discover, Maureen Dryden had definitely exploited every shred of fame generated by her book examining the infamous Beverly Baron murder. Baron was a gorgeous young actress who'd won an Academy Award for her third film role. Her death was technically still labeled *unsolved*, but Maureen's book and the subsequent true crime documentary had pointed the finger at fellow actor Alan Cardullo. Since Cardullo had committed suicide not long after Baron's death, most people were convinced he was the killer.

"That's enough about my past endeavors," Maureen said. "What I really want to discuss today is my latest project. It's an anthology of various cold cases, where the crimes occurred in small towns like Taylorsford. In fact"—she rose to her feet, gripping the microphone—"one of the cases I'm writing about actually happened right here."

I already knew this information, but the gasps from the crowd told me that I was one of the few who did.

"It's the mysterious disappearance of someone many of you in the older generation may have known—Edward Jaffe, more commonly known as Eddie." Maureen's gaze swept over the audience, as if searching for some reaction to this name.

Beside me, Aunt Lydia shifted in her chair. Glancing at her, I noticed that Kurt was leaning forward, gripping his knees with his hands.

"Anyway, I'm going to be doing some research in your town archives, and also hope to speak to anyone who wants to share any information." Maureen toyed with one of her earrings. "Anything at all; just let me or one of the people here on the stage know. And even if Jaffe's name doesn't ring a bell, if you're old enough to remember 1966, I'd love to talk to you."

Zelda leaned closer to Aunt Lydia and said under her breath, "What's this, are we supposed to divulge all our teenage secrets now?"

My aunt, her lips pressed into a straight line, waved her off.

"In fact, my research has turned up the names of a couple of individuals I'd love to find," Maureen said, searching the crowd once more before sitting down. "They are people who I think might have some important information on the Jaffe case. Not that I suspect them of being involved, of course"— she flashed a broad smile—"but it appears they might've been in the general area where Jaffe disappeared on that fateful day." She glanced down at her notes. "Yes, here it is. Anyone know a Delbert Frye or Karl Klass?"

Chapter Three

A wave of murmurs rolled through the audience. I assumed this reaction was due to the mention of Delbert Frye. Even though he was a recluse who lived in a cabin in the mountains, he was also Alison Tucker's great-uncle, as well as a locally renowned dulcimer maker and performer.

Fewer people would recognize the name Karl Klass. Even if they did, they wouldn't connect it to Kurt Kendrick. Only a few of us knew he'd lived in Taylorsford as a child and young man before disappearing from the home of his foster father, Paul Dassin, who just happened to have built the house Richard and I lived in now. Karl had not returned to Taylorsford until he was in his early seventies, and then with an entirely new name and profession.

I swiveled in my seat to observe his reaction, only to discover he'd disappeared.

"He slipped out as soon as she mentioned the Eddie Jaffe case," Richard said.

Turning to him, I raised my eyebrows. "Which means he probably knows something."

"Most likely. But apparently Alison had no clue Delbert could've been involved." Richard gestured discretely toward the Tuckers.

Alison was on her feet, gesticulating wildly. Brad reached out to grab her arm, but she swatted his hand and stormed away, leaving Brad slumped in his chair.

"Hush," Aunt Lydia said, cutting us off with an icy glare. "The author is still speaking."

I stared at her, noticing her already pale skin had turned bone white. "Sorry," I muttered, switching my gaze to the stage. Aunt Lydia knew all about the Karl Klass connection, of course. Since Kurt, in his youth, had been her late husband Andrew Talbot's best friend, she was well aware of his murky past.

I refocused on Maureen Dryden, who was describing the Jaffe case in more detail.

"Eddie was only eighteen when he disappeared without a trace," she said, her tone appropriately somber. "He'd been known to dabble in drugs, so at first the authorities thought he might've experienced an accident after a bad trip, but there was also speculation that he could've been murdered during a drug deal gone wrong. According to my research, Eddie dropped out of high school and fled his home in North Carolina when he was sixteen. He was something of a vagrant, but had been living in this area for about a year, working odd jobs, when he vanished. I've uncovered information about Eddie participating in drug parties with small gatherings of young people up in the mountains. I believe he may have attended one of those events the evening he disappeared." She

Death and the Librarian

looked out across the audience, her gaze landing on me. "But I haven't found enough facts to corroborate my suspicions yet, which is why I'm grateful the Taylorsford Library is opening their town archives to me on Monday."

I shifted in my seat, wondering how she knew I was one of the library directors. *Silly*, I thought, stilling my tapping foot, *she probably saw your photo on the library website. Like me, she would've done some preliminary research before this event.*

Maureen continued speaking but shifted her focus to discussing the other cold cases she was including in her new book. When she'd concluded her talk, she once again asked anyone in the crowd who had information on the Jaffe case to speak to her or her assistant, Sean, then turned the program over to Terry Temkin.

He'd been recording the entire talk without speaking, but now jumped into interviewer mode, asking Maureen about her writing process, the making of the television show, and other related enquiries. When he opened up the floor to audience questions, Aunt Lydia rose to her feet.

"I'm going to sneak out before the crowd disperses," she said. "I'll see you later."

"We'll go with you," Zelda said, tugging on Walt's shirtsleeve.

I wanted to leave with them, but knew it wasn't a good look for one of the codirectors of the library to preemptively abandon an event arranged by the Friends of the Library. Sinking down in my chair, I crossed my arms over my chest.

"I know you can't go," Richard said, patting my arm. "Don't worry, I'll stick it out with you."

I leaned into him, resting my head against his shoulder. "We have to collect the kids anyway. It's probably better to wait until most of the audience leaves instead of jostling through a crowd."

"Hmm." Richard slipped his arm around my shoulders. "This isn't so bad."

I snuggled closer. "How about this?"

"Better," he said.

Several minutes passed. I blocked out the questions and answers and allowed myself a moment of relaxation.

"Sorry to interrupt, but Ms. Dryden wondered if you had a minute to talk to her."

I blinked and looked up into Sean Gordon's pleasant face. "Is the talk over?" I asked, heat rising in my face.

"Pretty much. Maureen is still answering some individual questions, but that's it."

Looking around, I noticed the audience filing out of the rows of chairs. A few people were clustered on the stage, forming a ragged line leading to Maureen Dryden's chair. I noticed that most of them were clutching a thick paperback book.

"Getting her signature on copies of *Deadly Desire* too, I see." I sat up in my chair as Richard pulled his arm back.

"Yeah, that always happens." Sean lowered his lashes, shadowing his hazel eyes. "We have to build that into the schedule for each event." I started to stand, but Sean waved me back. "You can just wait here, Ms. Muir. Once she finishes up on the stage, Maureen will come down and talk with you."

Death and the Librarian

"Since it's just Amy she wants, I'll go check on the kids." Richard rose to his feet, He acknowledged Sean with a nod and strode off toward the town hall.

Sean sat down beside me. "Thanks for waiting around. Maureen will be very appreciative of your time."

"It's not a problem. I'm actually a little curious about her research into our local case. I hadn't heard of Eddie Jaffe before this, despite being in charge of the town archives."

"Well, he wasn't actually from Taylorsford, so maybe it didn't make as big an impact."

"He didn't have any family around here?" I asked.

Sean shook his head. "Not that we know of. The only reason Maureen has those two names she mentioned is that she spoke with someone who was married to a deputy who covered the area in the sixties. It was a bit of luck, really. The woman passed away not long after speaking with Maureen."

I thought about Kurt's former life, when he'd been Karl Klass. I knew he'd dealt drugs back when he was a teen and young adult, and had already left Paul Dassin's home a few years before 1966, when Eddie went missing. *But he was still in the area,* I reminded myself. *Or at least he was still around from time to time, to visit Andrew Talbot if nothing else.*

With the line completed, Maureen had a word with Terry Temkin and his assistant before climbing off the stage. She strolled over to us, her tiered cotton maxiskirt brushing the tops of her suede ankle boots. "Thanks so much for waiting," she said. "I just wanted to say hello and check on the best time for me to show up at the library on Monday."

Victoria Gilbert

"We're open eight to eight on Mondays, but I'll only be there until five, so I suggest morning or early afternoon,' I said, meeting her appraising stare with a smile.

"Good to know." Maureen sat down on my other side.

Sandwiched between Sean and Maureen, with both of them gazing at me, I felt a twitch in my fingers. "I do have to warn you that it may take some digging to find anything related to your research," I said. "We haven't been able to digitize all of our holdings, so much of it is still in paper format. We've sorted and labeled the archival cartons by years, though, so at least you can narrow down your search to the proper boxes."

Maureen swept her hand through the air, jangling a stack of gold and silver bracelets. "Don't worry about that. I've crawled through attics and basements to find material before. I'm sure your archives will feel positively palatial compared to that."

Sean, with a glance at the stage, jumped to his feet. "Excuse me, but it looks like Terry and Mindy need some help packing up the equipment. Nice to meet you, Ms. Muir."

"Likewise," I said. "Maybe I'll see you on Monday?"

Sean didn't reply, just gave me a friendly wave and loped off.

As soon as he reached the stage, I clasped my fingers in my lap and took a deep breath. "Actually, Ms. Dryden, I'm curious about those names you mentioned earlier . . ."

"Karl Klass and Delbert Frye." Maureen's light brown eyes brightened. "Do you know them?"

"Well, a lot of people know Mr. Frye, as you could probably tell from the audience reaction. And he is still alive,

Death and the Librarian

although something of a hermit. But he's ninety now, so I can't imagine that he was attending a get-together up in the mountains with a bunch of much younger people back in 1966."

"No, of course not. My source never said he was actually connected with that group. But apparently her husband questioned Delbert Frye about the evening Eddie disappeared because Mr. Frye was spotted exiting the woods near the rumored gathering spot."

"That isn't really much of a clue. Delbert collects fallen limbs and branches to use in his woodworking, so he's often hiking in the mountains. And more so back then, I expect." I frowned. "What trail was this, anyway?"

"Somewhere on the other side of town, from what I can gather. It was simply a path beaten down over time, leading off a field, but now there's a park where the field used to be, and the trail has been upgraded," Maureen said, examining me with interest.

I froze my expression into a pleasant mask. If what Maureen said was true, then this trail was close to my house. That meant the path had branched off a field next to Paul Dassin's house. Tying it back to Kurt again . . . I shook the thought from my head. Since I lived next door to Aunt Lydia, it was also close to her house. But had she been living there at that time?

"What month did Eddie disappear?" I asked. "That might narrow things down."

"Late August," Maureen said.

"Thanks. That will help focus the search in the archives," I said, my mind busy calculating. Yes, Mom and Aunt Lydia would've been living in Taylorsford at that point. They lost their parents in a car crash in early 1966. So, since Eddie had disappeared in the summer, they would've already been residing with their grandmother, Rose Baker Litton, in the three-story Queen Anne Revival home where Aunt Lydia still lived.

"I want to talk to Delbert Frye, of course, but I haven't been able to get in touch with him. Would you have any contact information?"

Observing Maureen's overly eager expression, I decided I didn't want to get involved in connecting her with Delbert, whom I considered a friend. "You might try speaking to his grand-niece, Alison Tucker," I said, knowing full well that Alison was not likely to cooperate with Maureen's request.

"The sheriff's wife?" Maureen pulled a small notebook and a pen from her tote bag.

"Correct," I said, as she jotted down Alison's name.

"That's convenient. I plan to talk to the sheriff's department and see what they might have in their files anyway." Maureen snapped the notebook shut. "You don't happen to know Karl Klass, do you?"

Did I? I knew Kurt, but I was fairly certain that he'd changed significantly over the years since he'd left behind his illegal activities or, at least, any dealings with drugs. "I'm afraid not."

"He's actually the one I really want to find. The deputy's wife told me that he was known as quite a 'bad boy' back in the day. He was suspected of dealing, but the authorities could never pin anything on him. So, you know"—Maureen spread

Death and the Librarian

wide her hands—"he could've been involved in Eddie's disappearance, or at the very least, know who was."

"Sorry, I can't help you there," I said.

"Oh well, perhaps I'll turn up something in the archives," Maureen said airily.

"How long do you plan to stay in Taylorsford?" I asked, mentally planning a trip to search the archives on Sunday, when the library would be closed.

"I'm not sure. Terry wants to collect some background interviews, and I need to talk to the townspeople too." She slid the notebook and pen back in her tote and pulled out a business card. "Here's my contact info. We're all staying at the Taylorsford Inn, so if you think of anything that might help—anyone who might have some knowledge of the drug scene around that time or whatever—please get in touch, even before Monday."

"Okay, sure." I stood up, pocketing the card. "If you don't mind, please excuse me. I see my husband and children coming out of the town hall and I need to join them."

"Of course, of course," Maureen said, rising to her feet to shake my hand. "Nice to meet you, Ms. Muir. I look forward to working with you soon."

I made a noncommittal noise and swiftly pulled my fingers free of her hearty grip. "See you Monday," I called over my shoulder as I hurried across the lawn to catch up with Richard and the twins.

A thud stopped me in my tracks. I turned to see that one of the temporary light poles set up for an evening folk song performance had fallen over.

That was probably an omen too.

Chapter Four

My plans to do some research in the archives on Sunday were thwarted when Richard had to extend his dance company rehearsals from the afternoon into the evening.

Instead, I took Ella and Nicky on a walk to the library. We arrived not long before the sale closed down at three o'clock so they could each choose a book. Nancy Neiman, as chair of the Friends of the Library, was in charge.

"We've done quite well," she told me, as I paid for the twins' books. "I don't have the final tally yet, but I should be able to let you know the total by tomorrow."

"That's fine. And your speaker was actually quite good. Where did you two meet?"

Nancy ran her fingers through her feathered cap of dark blonde hair. "In college. We were in the same sorority."

"That makes sense," I lied. I had trouble picturing Maureen as part of a sorority. Nancy, a petite woman who always dressed impeccably, yes. But Maureen Dryden appeared bohemian rather than preppy. "Anyway, her lecture was interesting. The crowd seemed to appreciate it."

32

Death and the Librarian

Nancy puffed out her chest. "See, I told you it would work. By the way, it will be fascinating to see what turns up in the archives. When we met for breakfast this morning, Maureen told me she was going to visit the library tomorrow to research the Eddie Jaffe case."

"We arranged to meet, but I'm not sure if she'll find anything useful or not." I glanced around to locate Ella and Nicky, who'd grabbed their books while I was handing over my debit card. I breathed a sigh of relief when I saw our full-time library assistant, Samantha Green, sitting beside them on a bench under a nearby oak tree. I knew the twins wouldn't run into the road, but with all the people in town for the festival, I didn't want to leave them alone for more than a minute.

"Still, it's great that we can help her out. Maybe she'll even give the library a shout-out in her acknowledgements."

"That would be nice," I said automatically. "I should scoot out of the way so the line can move. Might as well get all those final sales in before you shut down." I stepped aside but paused before leaving the sales table. "You're going to lock up the library when you're done, right? I remember Sunny gave you a set of keys for today."

"Of course. After the other volunteers and I pack up the remaining books and store them inside the building, I'll be sure to lock the library doors."

"Great. You can just bring the keys back tomorrow. Anytime is fine. Someone will be on the desk all day." I thanked her again and strolled over to the bench. "Let's head home, kids. I'll help you read before I make dinner, okay?"

Ella and Nicky jumped off the bench, clutching their books to their chests. "Me first," Ella said. Nicky's expression turned mulish, but he didn't argue. His dark brown eyes, wide and black-lashed like mine, gazed up at me speculatively. *Judging whether his sister's pushiness would turn the tide in his favor*, I thought with a smile.

"We'll see." I turned to Samantha. "Thanks for keeping an eye on these two," I added. "Did you volunteer for the book sale today? You know that's not required in your job description."

"It's no problem," Samantha said, dabbing the sweat from her upper lip with a tissue. "Shay had a rehearsal with Karla today, so I was at loose ends anyway."

"That's right, she's in the corps for that larger piece Karla choreographed." I took hold of Ella and Nicky's free hands. "Is she excited to be dancing with the company?"

"Definitely." Samantha's deep brown eyes sparkled. "It's great experience for her future career. More useful than most summer jobs, that's for sure. Seeing how Karla handles the younger dancers is an education in itself, Shay says."

I smiled. I'd known Samantha's only child, Shay, since she was a young teen. She'd studied dance with Karla for several years and was now in college, training to be a dance teacher herself. "Alright, I'll see you tomorrow then." I squeezed Ella and Nicky's hands. "Let's march, troops."

"How come Shay gets to dance with Daddy and Karla's company and we don't?" Ella asked, as we wove through the crowd to reach the sidewalk. "Nicky and I were in *The Nutcracker* just like Shay."

Death and the Librarian

"Yes, but that show involves children, and none of the pieces that Daddy or Karla have choreographed this time do." I kept a firm hold on Ella and Nicky as we walked the five blocks to our house. The sidewalks had been restored to their original brick pavers when Sunny had served as mayor of Taylorsford. It was attractive, and historically accurate, but sometimes the uneven surface could be a tripping hazard for children's shoes or women's high heels.

As Ella and Nicky chattered about their books and who could read more words without help, I admired the houses lining both sides of the street. From boxy two-story wooden structures with black shutters and stoop porches, to Craftsman-style cottages, to elegant Victorians festooned with decorative gingerbread trim, there was enough variety to please any taste. *Other than those who preferred something modern*, I reminded myself. But no one moved to Taylorsford expecting that type of house. The most recent buildings were a few brick structures erected in the late 1930s or 40s, but those were clustered in the center of town and housed small eateries and other businesses.

Tall trees shaded the sidewalk, providing a green canopy that rustled like taffeta in the light wind. Walking past my aunt's house, Ella stopped in her tracks.

"Want to show Aunt Lydia my book," she said, slipping free of my hand and flipping open the latched gate in the white picket fence.

"Get back here!" I shouted, but Ella had already traversed the sidewalk that bisected the narrow front yard and reached the short flight of stone steps leading to the porch. Most of the house was built of the fieldstone once prevalent in area fields, but its wraparound porch was constructed of wood decorated with white Victorian-style gingerbread.

Ella rose up on tiptoe to try to reach the heavy bronze knocker on the mahogany front door. The light filtering through the stained-glass sidelights cast a rainbow over her white tank top. "I don't think she's home, Ella," I called out, as Nicky and I followed her up onto the porch. "She said something about having dinner at the Adams' house today."

"Phooey." Ella dropped her heels back down, her expression sullen. "I wanted to read my new book in the castle room"

I shook my head. The "castle room" was the front parlor, which was located on the first floor, where the house bowed out in an attached tower—three-quarters of a circle where it rose with the house, then turning into a full, circular turret above the second-story roofline. "That will have to wait for another day," I said. "Come on, let's go home."

We didn't have far to go, as our 1920s farmhouse was right next door. Our yards were only separated by a short fence laden with climbing roses.

"I'm going the back way," Nicky said, running to the wooden arch that led from Aunt Lydia's backyard into ours. Ella clattered down the steps to chase after him.

I took a moment to latch the front gate before following them. "You have to wait for me anyway," I said. "I'm the one with the keys."

*   *   *

Later that evening, with the twins fed and finally tucked snugly in their beds, I plopped down on the sofa to watch

Death and the Librarian

some television while I waited for Richard. I'd already carried two glasses and an open bottle of red wine from the kitchen and set them on the coffee table as soon as he called to let me know he was on his way home. If it was like most evenings after late rehearsals, Richard would've already grabbed something to eat, meagre as that might've been. Instead of food, he'd be looking forward to a glass of wine as well as watching some mindless TV with me so he could unwind before bed.

Everything was going according to plan after Richard got home, until my cell phone rang.

"Who would be calling at time of night?" Richard asked, his dark brows drawing together.

"Probably my mom. Or yours." I picked up the phone and glanced at the name of the caller. "Nancy Neiman? Why is she calling me so late?"

"The Friends of the Library woman?" Richard lifted the arm he'd draped around my shoulders.

"Yeah. Of course she has my number, but what can't wait until tomorrow?" I leaned forward as I swiped to answer the call.

"Amy! So glad I could reach you," Nancy said in a suspiciously chipper tone.

"Hi, Nancy. What seems to be the trouble?" I shot Richard a *what now?* glance.

"Oh dear, I hate to bother you, but . . ." Nancy's nervous trill of laughter did nothing to calm my own nerves. "I'm afraid I didn't lock the main library door. Or, that's to say, I'm not sure if I did or not. There was such chaos as we were trying to make the last sales while packing everything up and moving the boxes and all that and, well . . . I'm just not sure."

37

"It's so late," I said, rolling my eyes as Richard mouthed, "What is it?"

"I know, I know. I just didn't even think about it until now, and then I realized I really couldn't be certain if I'd locked the doors . . ." Nancy's voice trailed off. After a pause she added, "The thing is, I have Sunny's keys, so of course she can't help, and I can't reach Samantha, and, well, you know I live closer to Harburg than Taylorsford, so it's a bit of a drive for me."

Grinding my teeth, I had to admit she was right. Nancy lived between Taylorsford and Harburg, the larger town that housed Clarion University, where Richard taught a few dance courses. "So you want me to go." I didn't phrase this as a question.

"Go where?" Richard asked.

I waved him off. "Alright, I have my keys and I guess I do live much closer. I'll drive over there and check."

"Bless you," Nancy said. "I really couldn't sleep a wink worrying about this."

Meanwhile, my sleep will be disrupted. I sighed. "It's alright. Now that I know, I have to make sure, one way or the other." I wished her a terse good night and turned to Richard.

"I have to drive over to the library," I said, holding up my hand, palm out, as he tried to protest. "Nancy isn't sure she locked everything up properly, and I can't in good conscience ignore the possibility that the library doors could be left open for anyone to wander in."

Richard raked his fingers through his dark brown hair, still only slightly peppered with gray. "I'll go with you then."

Death and the Librarian

"No, you have to stay here with the kids."

"Oh, right." Richard slumped back against the sofa cushions. "I suppose you have to check, but please simply test the main doors, and lock them if needed. Don't go inside alone. If someone got in, just lock the place down with them inside. You can always alert Brad and have the place searched before any of the staff or patrons enter tomorrow."

"Good thinking," I said, flashing him a smile. "Okay, I'm going to run over there. Fortunately, I've only had a half glass of wine, so I should be good to drive." I leaned in and kissed him. "Save me a glass."

"No promises," Richard grumbled, then kissed me back. "We do have more wine in the house, of course."

I patted his shoulder and rose to my feet. "It's still warm out, I guess?"

"Yeah, no jacket needed." Richard examined me for a moment. "The shorts and tee will work, but you might want shoes."

"Sandals are at the door," I said, crossing to the coat rack next to a tall, narrow table with shoes stored in baskets underneath. I slipped on my sandals, grabbed my keys from a decorative ceramic bowl on the table, and blew Richard a kiss before heading outside.

All was quiet as I drove to the library. Parking on the street, I ran to the front doors, keys in hand. Grabbing the door handles, I tugged.

The doors *were* locked. I swore under my breath and stuffed my keys into the pocket of my cotton shorts. Of course, as one of the library directors, I had to check, but

39

I was seething over Nancy sending me on this unnecessary errand. If only she'd remembered clearly . . .

My mental tirade against Nancy Nieman continued as I walked back to my car, but the wail of sirens cut it short. Leaning against the passenger side door, I stared down the street as the sirens were joined by flashing lights and a growing rumble of voices.

I squinted to locate what was obviously an emergency situation. It looked as if wasn't that far, but as I trotted down the sidewalk, cell phone in one hand, I covered several blocks before I could determine that the sheriff's department vehicles and emergency service vehicles were parked in front of the Taylorsford Inn.

A tall man in running shorts and a T-shirt blocked the sidewalk as I tried to move closer.

"They told me to stay back," he said, pushing his glasses up his rather hawkish nose with his thumb.

I stared up at him, not recognizing him as a Taylorsford resident. Which didn't mean he wasn't, just that he hadn't visited the library or other places I was likely to frequent. He looked to be around ten years younger than me and wasn't wearing a wedding ring, which was probably another reason we hadn't crossed paths. Busy as I was with the twins and my home and work, I didn't tend to hang out in any spots popular with younger singles.

"Do you know what happened?" I asked.

"All I heard was some talk about a death at the inn," he replied, brushing his sandy brown hair away from his sweat-beaded forehead. "I don't know who or how, I'm afraid. The site

Death and the Librarian

is locked down, though." He shrugged. "I'm sure it will all come out on the news, and I suppose it's best if we stay out of the way. I'm going to head back home. You probably should too."

I knew he was right, but something in his tone made me want to stay in place. "Have a good run in the other direction, then," I said, which earned me raised eyebrows and a quirk of his lips. But he did turn and jog off in the direction of the library.

As I watched him leave, I noticed a familiar black Jaguar pull out of a side street as if it were turning in the direction of the inn. But then it backed up and disappeared, obviously using the narrow lane that ran behind the buildings close to the inn to escape the road blocks.

What is Kurt doing in this area at this time of night? I thought as I slowly moved closer to the emergency activity. But my pondering of this peculiarity was cut short when I spotted a slender blonde woman running toward me.

"Amy, what are you doing here?" Sunny asked, yanking up the drooped shoulder of her aqua cocktail dress.

"Nancy called and wasn't sure if she'd locked the library so I had to check," I said, scrutinizing the disheveled condition of her hair and makeup. "The bigger question is, why are you here?"

As Sunny bobbed her head, another lock of hair fell out of her simple chignon and draped over her shoulder. "I was meeting someone at the restaurant. And before you get any ideas that I'm cheating on Fred, this was a team from a company that's interested in distributing organic produce from the farm to restaurants throughout the region."

Victoria Gilbert

"I see. A business meeting." Sunny, in addition to sharing the job of library director with me, managed Vista View, the organic farm owned by her grandparents, Carol and P. J. Fields. "So you were in the inn when whatever happened was happening?"

"I guess. Not sure on the timing." Sunny rubbed her upper arms as if she were cold.

Shock, not cold, I thought, examining her more closely. Her pale skin appeared more tightly drawn over her bones and her lips were quivering. "Wait, was it someone you knew?"

"Not really, I just met her this weekend, but still . . ." Sunny reached up and yanked the clips from her hair, allowing it to tumble free. "They were all there earlier, in the restaurant and then at the bar."

"Who was?" I asked, reaching out to clasp her hand.

"Maureen Dryden and her team. That Terry guy and his assistant or girlfriend or whatever, and Maureen's research fellow, Sean. Hanging around the bar with Maureen, off and on." She looked up at me, her blue eyes wide but unfocused. "I saw a couple of other people I didn't expect too. Alison was there without Brad, and she got into an argument with Ms. Dryden. I think she stormed off after that, but I'm not sure because I was still trying to have a business meeting and I just didn't notice who was coming and going. But even weirder"—Sunny squinched up her face—"was seeing Kurt there. I mean, I don't know why he'd be hanging around the bar at the Taylorsford Inn. Doesn't seem like his scene."

"No, it doesn't," I said, thinking of him driving away.

"I had to go to the bathroom, and when I came out everything was chaos." Sunny cast a glance over her shoulder. "One

42

Death and the Librarian

of the maids was screaming about finding someone dead in their bed."

"Dead? Someone died?" I tightened my grip on Sunny's hand.

"Yeah, that's what I heard. Then everyone was scattering—I followed my group into the lobby and then they said they'd better get going or they'd never get home, because we could already hear the sirens."

I released Sunny's hand so I could move to stand beside her, facing the opposite direction from the beleaguered inn. "But you didn't go with them?"

"No, I stayed in the lobby. I thought maybe the deputies would want to talk to everyone who was there, you know?" Sunny squared her shoulders. "A lot of those people disappeared, including Kurt and Alison and all of Ms. Dryden's team, but the thing is, I don't exactly know when they left. I couldn't tell the deputies whether any of them exited the restaurant and bar area before or after the maid started screaming. I couldn't even name everyone who was present. The restaurant was busy, so it isn't going to be easy for the authorities to contact all the witnesses. Or suspects, I suppose, if this wasn't an accident. I guess I wasn't terribly helpful."

"I'm sure the authorities appreciated whatever information you could provide. Can you get to your car?"

Sunny shook her head. "Blocked off. I'm not sure what to do."

"Okay," I said, sliding my hand through the crook of her arm, "what you're going to do is walk with me back to my car, and then I'll drive you to my house. You can stay there tonight."

"I don't want to put you out . . ."

43

Victoria Gilbert

"Don't be ridiculous," I said, tugging her arm as I stepped forward. "We can sort out your car in the morning. There's no reason for you to stand around here all night, waiting for the first responders and deputies to clear out the scene. Who knows how long that will take."

"Alright." Sunny, keeping pace with me, tossed her loose hair behind her shoulders. "But I might have to borrow some clothes to sleep in. This dress isn't that comfortable."

"Well, all my stuff will be too short, but I'm sure Richard will be happy to lend you sweatpants and a T-shirt. It might be a little big, but at least it'll be long enough." Reaching the car, I made sure Sunny was safely seated in the passenger seat before I climbed in. "By the way," I said, as I made a U-turn to head back to the house, "who died?"

Sunny's reflection in the dark window appeared troubled. "The last person you'd expect, especially seeing how vivacious and healthy she seemed yesterday." She turned to look at me. "It was Maureen Dryden."

Chapter Five

Sunny left early the next morning, determined to walk to her car despite my protests.

"No, you should stay and have breakfast with Richard and the kids." Sunny tugged up the lightweight sweatpants Richard had loaned her. Although Richard was not heavy, he was muscular, and even with tying the drawstring as tight as possible, the pants kept sliding down. Fortunately, the T-shirt he'd also provided was long enough to cover her hips and upper thighs. "I want to get a shower and take care of some things at home this morning. I'll wash these things and return them when I come in for the late shift today."

"No rush," I said, as she headed out the front door, her cocktail dress slung over her arm and high heels dangling from one hand. I'd lent her some open-backed sandals that fit well enough to get her to her car. "I'll see you around one, then."

As codirectors, Sunny and I took turns covering the library, which was beneficial for us both. It gave me more time with the twins and her the opportunity to do work related to Vista View. Sometimes we switched off days and sometimes, when the library was open later, we split the time into two shifts.

I had the morning shift today, which meant I needed to arrive at the library before eight to make sure everything was set up and then unlock the doors. "Hey, guys," I said as I walked into the kitchen, where Richard was making breakfast. "I need to head out soon. Remember, Daddy will be with you this morning, and then he's going to drop you off at Aunt Lydia's house when he goes to his rehearsal."

Ella waved her fork, scattering bits of scrambled eggs across the table. "Daddy said he was going to give us a dance lesson."

I shot Richard a raised-eyebrow look. "Are you sure you're up for that? You got back late last night, and tonight will probably be the same."

"It's fine," he said with a shrug. "I need to exercise and warm up anyway."

Grabbing a muffin from the basket Aunt Lydia had brought over the day before, I ate standing at the counter.

"You don't want any eggs?" Richard asked, as he handed me a white mug emblazoned with *Best Mom Ever* in shaky red letters, a Mother's Day gift from Nicky and Ella.

"No, this will do." I finished off the muffin before swigging my coffee. Noticing Richard checking his phone, I moved closer to him. "Anything about last night's events?"

He cast a quick glance at the kitchen table. "Just an announcement that someone passed away at the inn and the sheriff's office is investigating," he said under his breath.

Death and the Librarian

"I'll probably hear more at the library." I set down my empty mug.

"I'm sure." Richard laid one hand over mine. "Don't worry, I'll try to keep the news from the kids as long as I can. That's one reason I thought it would be best to offer dance practice instead of turning on the television."

"Good idea," I said. 'You know how ghoulish they can be. They'd pester you for details."

"Which I don't have." Richard's smile faded. "I hope it was just an accident or something brought on by the victim's actions, like an overdose. The last thing we need is another murder in this town."

"Yeah. I'm sure Brad is thinking the same." I frowned, remembering Alison Tucker's reaction to Maureen's mention of her great-uncle Delbert. *And Kurt being at the inn last night,* I thought. *Then fleeing the area via the back streets.* "Well, I should go brush my teeth and head out. I want to walk to work today, so it'll take a little longer."

"Alright." Richard leaned in and kissed my forehead before lifting his hand. "You'll pick up the kids at Lydia's around one?"

"A little after, with the walk back." I flashed him a grin. "She'll have already given them lunch."

"Smart thinking," Richard said, turning to face the kitchen table. "Have you guys finished? If so, help me clean up, please."

As soon as Ella and Nicky had deposited their plates and forks in the sink, I leaned over and gave each a hug and a kiss. "Be good for Daddy and Aunt Lydia today and we'll go for a walk at the park after I get home."

Both of the twins squealed in delight at this news. They took after their father in terms of preferring physical activity over sitting down—which didn't really bother me, since they were not yet addicted to television or the internet. As long as they enjoyed reading and would sit still long enough for that, I was satisfied.

After brushing my teeth with the extra toothbrush I'd left in the downstairs hall bathroom for just such quick getaways, I grabbed my lunch and stuffed it in my tote bag along with my small purse and headed out the front door.

Even at seven-thirty, the air outside was already warm and thick with humidity. By the time I'd reached the library, I had to push my dark brown hair away from my forehead to wipe away a sheen of sweat. I walked around the corner of the stone building to enter through the staff door, but stopped short when I saw a tall man standing on the concrete stoop.

"Amy, glad to catch you before the library opens," Brad Tucker said. "Can we talk inside?"

Brad had always been a good-looking man, in the husky-but-toned mold of a former football player. He took off his sheriff's hat as we entered the library and placed it on one of the metal shelves in the workroom. Looking him over, I realized that it was difficult to tell if his short-cropped hair was still blond or had faded to silver. But his eyes were as brilliant blue as ever. "I understand you were outside in the vicinity of the Taylorsford Inn last night."

"I guess you've already spoken with Sunny," I said, setting my tote on the battered wooden table we used for processing interlibrary loans and similar tasks.

Death and the Librarian

"Just a preliminary chat over the phone. She plans to stop by the office to give a more complete statement later this morning."

"But she mentioned I was there."

Brad shifted from foot to foot. "She did, saying something about checking the library doors?"

"Yeah, I had to drive here to make sure the building was locked. The person who was supposed to close up after the book sale yesterday called me late because she suddenly wasn't sure if she'd locked the doors or not."

"The library is several blocks from the inn," Brad said, his gaze never leaving my face.

"True, but it was hard to miss the sirens and lights." I managed a faint smile. "I wanted to figure out what was happening. You of all people know how curious I am."

"That's the understatement of the year," Brad said, looking me up and down. "Which can be useful, if properly directed."

I crossed my arms over my chest. "You want to put it to use, I take it."

"Research is always helpful," Brad said, finally cracking a smile. "Especially in a case like this. But before we get to that, I have to ask if you saw anyone, other than Sunny, near the inn last night."

I gnawed the inside of my cheek for a moment. I'd seen what looked like Kurt's car in the vicinity, but I hadn't actually caught a glimpse of him. "There was a black car on one of the side streets a few blocks away. It backed up when the driver saw the activity at the inn and I guess took the back road to evade the road block."

49

"Did you recognize the car?" Brad asked, his eyes boring a hole into my forehead.

"Maybe. It could've been Kurt Kendrick's black Jaguar, but I can't be absolutely sure." I dropped my arms and turned away. "Excuse me, but I need to go out into the library to bring up the computers and check on other things before I open. You can follow if you want," I added as I walked through the door that opened on the space behind the circulation desk.

While I turned on the computer and other equipment at the desk, Brad leaned against the back wall, covering a portion of a framed American Library Association READ poster. This was one of my favorites, featuring LeVar Burton of *Reading Rainbow* fame.

"One of my deputies dropped the ball on that. He was supposed to shut down the back road immediately, but it was open for a while." Brad cleared his throat. "I imagine Sunny may have told you that she saw Kendrick at the inn a little earlier in the evening."

"Yes, she did. Along with Maureen Dryden and her whole team and many others," I said, testing the barcode wand on a book from the interior drop. I glanced over at Brad. "Is that important? I thought perhaps Ms. Dryden died in some sort of accident."

Brad's expression grew stony. "Unlikely. We still have to wait on tests, but the coroner has a strong suspicion that she was suffocated with a pillow."

"Good heavens, who could do that without causing a ruckus? I didn't know Ms. Dryden well, but my first impression

Death and the Librarian

was that she was pretty tough. I can't imagine her not screaming and fighting back."

Brad trailed me as I left the desk and crossed to the public computers. "It's possible she was drugged beforehand."

"Oh." I paused with my fingers resting on one of the computers' switches and looked up at him. "That's why you need the test results."

"Exactly." Looking over my head, Brad stared down the row between two book shelving units as if focused on the reading room beyond the stacks. "If she was drugged, perhaps by something slipped into her drink at the bar . . ."

Sunny had also mentioned seeing Alison at the inn, but I thought better of mentioning that. Brad already looked troubled. If his wife became a major suspect, he'd have to step aside and appoint someone else to manage the investigation. Not to mention the toll such suspicions would take on their children. "I'm sure you're questioning everyone who was there."

"Yes," he said curtly. Softening his expression, he met my inquisitive gaze. "My deputies will take care of that. I need your help for something else."

I straightened and stepped back from the bank of computers. "Looking into the Eddie Jaffe case? Ms. Dryden planned to use our archives for her research, so I'm guessing you want me to do that now?"

"To be clear, I don't know that it's connected to Ms. Dryden's death in any way," Brad said. "The motive for Maureen Dryden's murder could be totally unrelated to any of the cold cases she was researching."

"But you want to examine all the angles anyway." I looked him in the eye. "I know you too, Sheriff Tucker. You never leave a stone unturned."

His grim smile told me that I was right. He'd do whatever it took to uncover the truth, even if it did somehow involve his wife. "Just see if you can find anything on the Jaffe case in the town archives. People who may have had any sort of connection to the man, or anything like that. I have the department's records, but the file is pretty thin. I'd like to speak with anyone the deputies may have interviewed, or missed, back then."

I glanced at the wall clock. "Oops, I need to grab my keys and open the front doors." I headed back to the circulation desk, calling over my shoulder. "You can go out the side door if you prefer."

"I guess I have to," Brad said, following on my heels. "My hat's back there."

"Oh, right." I scooped my key ring off the desk. "The staff door will lock automatically behind you when you leave, so don't worry about that." I pointed the keys at him. "And never fear, I promise I'll check the archives, and search online, for that matter, for information related to the Jaffe case. If I find anything I'll let you know as soon as possible."

"Thanks, that would be a great help." Pausing near the staff door, Brad turned and cast me a warning look. "I am aware of who was once called Karl Klass, you know."

I waited until he left, then slowly crossed to the interior glass doors. Pushing my way through, I paused in the small lobby for a moment, the keys jangling from my fingers.

Death and the Librarian

Of course Brad knew all about the young orphan who'd been taken in by reporter and author Paul Dassin but had eventually run away from home. He had to be aware of all the stories about Karl being a troublemaker who, though never caught, was believed to have been a lone-wolf drug dealer in the Taylorsford area before he disappeared for decades.

Only to return as a wealthy dealer in another, more reputable field—art and antiques. A man who could buy and renovate Highview, an elegant eighteenth-century estate located up in the mountains just outside of town.

Until now, Kurt had been successful in leaving his past as Karl Klass behind. At least as far as the general public was concerned.

But sadly, I thought, unlocking the front doors and automatically greeting the two patrons waiting outside, *now that could all change.*

Chapter Six

I was alone on the circulation desk until ten, when Samantha was scheduled to arrive, but since the library was fairly quiet, with only a few people checking out materials and no reference questions, I decided to do a little online sleuthing.

There was really nothing about the Jaffe case online, other than brief mentions that it would be included in Maureen Dryden's new book. I switched to searching for more information on Maureen, as well as those who'd accompanied her to Taylorsford—Terry Temkin, Mindy LaSalle, and Sean Gordon.

Despite trying several different search strategies, I found almost nothing on Mindy or Sean. Mindy's social media showed several photos of her with Terry, which appeared to cement her status as Temkin's girlfriend as well as his assistant. A few older pictures showed her with brown hair, confirming my guess that she was not a natural blonde. Sean's limited social media presence was focused on his studies in American history, his current research, and his favorite books, all of which fit my first impression of him.

Death and the Librarian

Terry Temkin, on the other hand, turned up all sorts of information, not all of it flattering. He'd started young, working as a radio DJ while a college freshman before switching to podcasting with Mindy. Their podcast, *On Ice*, had garnered negative attention as well as devoted followers. One man they'd profiled as the most likely suspect in a cold case kidnapping and murder had actually sued the podcast. The matter was settled out of court, but I bookmarked the information to share with Brad. It revealed Terry and Mindy's willingness to push boundaries and take chances, if nothing else.

Of course there was a plethora of information on Maureen, some of which I'd already read. But I dug a little deeper into the furor that had erupted when *Deadly Desire* had been published. Along with its great success had come a good deal of criticism, particularly concerning the guilt or innocence of the primary suspect. Allen Cardullo had been investigated but not yet charged when the book was published, due to a lack of substantiated evidence. But Maureen's conviction that Cardullo was Beverly Baron's killer had resulted in a hate campaign against him that only ended when he committed suicide.

Although Allen Cardullo's family had filed a lawsuit and won an unspecified amount in a settlement, most people were still convinced he'd murdered Beverly. This number increased exponentially when the television series based on Maureen's book became an international hit.

It was interesting background material, and I would share it with Brad, but nothing seemed to point to a connection between the people present when Maureen died and her murder.

When Samantha arrived at ten, I asked her to cover the desk while I headed out to the archives, with the proviso that she could give me a call if someone needed help with a difficult reference question.

I deactivated the alarm on the back door. We'd installed this security measure fairly recently, wanting to keep the door unlocked when the library was open so it could be a fire exit in an emergency, but not wanting materials taken off site without being checked out. I didn't worry too much about leaving it deactivated when I was in the archives, as it was clearly marked and the few instances when someone had tried to sneak items out the back door had resulted in a piercing shriek that had trained our patrons on the consequences.

I crossed the library's gravel parking lot to reach the small stone building that housed the town archives. It was original to the site, having been built as a cottage for the first library directors, but in the fifties, when the archives had outgrown their alcove in the main building, the town took over this space.

Unlocking the door, I flicked on the light switch. The archives were a single room with a large, pitted wood table situated under a dangling fluorescent light. Old filing cabinets and metal shelving stuffed with archival banker's boxes lined the four walls.

I stepped inside, closing the door behind me. The whir of the window air-conditioning units filled the silence as I walked over to the section of shelving that held the boxes of materials from the 1960s. I pulled all the boxes covering 1967 as well as

Death and the Librarian

1966, figuring there might've been articles mentioning the Eddie Jaffe case in the year following his disappearance. Setting all but the box marked July to December 1966 on the floor, I placed that box on the table and popped open the lid. Then I slipped on a pair of white cotton gloves and began a careful perusal of the files.

After an hour, I concluded that there'd been little interest in whether Eddie was dead or alive and, if still living, where he might've gone. There were two short articles written in the weeks after Eddie vanished, and nothing more. The town saw him as a transient, I realized, and without family or friends badgering the authorities for a resolution to the mystery, the case had quickly gone cold.

I moved on to the boxes containing the 1967 files. It was probably a futile task, but I wanted to tell Brad that I'd completed a comprehensive search.

Finally, a newspaper clipping turned up that offered a new angle on the case. On the first anniversary of Eddie's disappearance, some intrepid reporter had located a young woman who claimed to have been his girlfriend at the time he disappeared.

I smoothed the clipping flat and studied the photograph of a girl named Sheryl Abernathy. The article stated that she was twenty, but the hollows under her cheekbones made her look older. Her frizzy dark hair was pulled back in a messy ponytail, and her collarbone jutted out above the scooped neck of her tank top. She looked like she hadn't eaten a decent meal in months, but I had a suspicion that her gauntness was the result of abusing drugs.

Victoria Gilbert

She all but confirmed this in the short interview included in the article. Sheryl said she and Eddie used to party in a clearing in the woods with a variety of people she claimed she didn't really know.

"You didn't ask names," she told the reporter. "Not real names, anyway. 'Cause there was drugs involved, along with the drinking. Eddie always had drugs on him, though he was more interested in selling them than taking them."

I slid back in my hard wooden chair. If Eddie was dealing drugs in the Taylorsford area at that time, he undoubtedly would've run across a twenty-one-year-old Karl Klass. Or, at least, Kurt would've known him. I'm sure he kept tabs on every other dealer in the region, even though he wasn't still living in Taylorsford himself.

The truth was, Kurt had never explained where he'd lived after he'd fled Paul Dassin's home at age eighteen. Since he'd continued to stay in contact, albeit secretly, with Andrew Talbot, he couldn't have been too far away, but no one else in Taylorsford, including my aunt, remembered seeing him after he abandoned his foster father. He hadn't contacted Aunt Lydia or Richard's family or any other local connections until a year or two after he'd purchased Highview.

"But somehow, Maureen Dryden discovered a link between the young man she knew as Karl Klass and Eddie Jaffe," I said aloud. "She must've interviewed someone who knew them both."

I stared down at the clipping, wondering if Maureen had already spoken to Sheryl Abernathy. It seemed likely. Even

Death and the Librarian

though she hadn't yet examined the materials in the Taylorsford town archives, she may have located Eddie's former girlfriend through some other means.

Reading the rest of Sheryl's comments didn't yield much information. She admitted that she'd attended a gathering with Eddie the night he disappeared, but while she said other people were present, she couldn't, or wouldn't, provide their names or any solid descriptions of them.

"Everything's blurry 'bout that night," she said in the article. "Eddie and I had a fight on the way up to the clearing, so I started drinking right away. Popped a few pills too. I remember noticing a handful of people, but I was already blasted by the time they showed up and couldn't tell you who was there or when they left or anything like that. I just remember waking up alone in the clearing and calling for Eddie and getting no answer. So I just stumbled back down the path into town."

The article concluded with Sheryl's assertion that she'd never seen or heard from Eddie Jaffe after that night.

Old casters squealed against the plank floor as I pushed away from the table. I rose to my feet, then slid the clipping back into its manila folder and yanked off my gloves. Leaving that folder on the table, I reshelved the rest of the boxes, my mind racing. Sheryl's claim that she didn't remember anyone else at the gathering rang false to me. *Were they all truly strangers? Or was she protecting the others, or even herself? Did she witness something that would've placed her in danger if she shared what she'd seen?*

I left the archives with the folder, planning to make a copy of the clipping for Brad before returning it to its storage box.

59

Entering the library, I rearmed the back door and headed for the circulation desk. "I'm back if you want to take your lunch break," I told Samantha, who immediately headed for the restroom.

"She should've asked me to watch the desk if she needed to go that bad." Zelda, who was one of our most dedicated volunteers, pushed a book cart out of the stacks. "I was just shelving some returns. Nothing that urgent." She eyed the folder I held as she rolled the empty cart around the desk and lined it up against the wall. "Samantha said you were out searching for info in the archives. I see you found it."

"I found something, anyway," I said, laying the folder on the desk.

Zelda stared at the file with obvious interest. "Are you helping Brad research the Maureen Dryden case?"

"Yes." I looked her over, noting the gleam in her eyes. How could I forget Zelda's uncanny nose for news and gossip? I had another source of information standing in front of me. Zelda knew Taylorsford as well as anyone—all the information worth sharing, and even some that wasn't. "Do you remember anything about the Eddie Jaffe case? You would've been a young teen at the time, right?"

"Fifteen, same as Lydia. Seems impossible I was ever that young." Zelda fanned her face with her hand. "But I remember 1966 all right, mostly because of what happened to Lydia that year. We were already friends, since your mom and Lydia lived just outside of town and we all attended the same schools. But then her parents died in that horrible crash. I tried to stay

60

Death and the Librarian

in touch and be there for Lydia, but she kinda withdrew from everyone for a while."

"Not to mention, Mom and Aunt Lydia had to move in with their grandmother Rose, and from what I understand, she was difficult to live with. So that might've been part of it," I said.

"Yes, lamb, I know all about that. Lydia told me later." Zelda's typically merry expression turned somber. "It was a hard year for everyone. I didn't see Lydia much, but the few times I did, I realized she was trying to deal with her grief by burying it under an infatuation with your uncle."

I fiddled with the stack of bookmarks we kept on the desk. "Didn't she meet Andrew long before that?"

"Sure, when he'd visit Kurt, well, Karl at the time, at Paul Dassin's house. Being right next door to Rose Litten's home, it gave Lydia a lot of opportunities to see Andrew. She and your mom and grandparents visited Rose every Sunday, you know." Zelda narrowed her eyes. "Of course, once Kurt took off, Andrew didn't come around as much, but he still visited Paul Dassin occasionally. And there was another opportunity for her to meet him that summer."

"He would've been around nineteen, so he must've been headed off to college soon," I said.

"That's true, and he'd gotten a scholarship so he didn't have to work full-time in the summer, but he needed some pocket money, I guess. Anyway, he took a job teaching art at the Lutheran church's community building, and somehow Lydia convinced her grandmother to allow her to attend his class."

"Sounds like she was pretty fixated on him," I said, trying and failing to picture my self-sufficient aunt chasing after anyone.

"Oh, lordy, yes. I once caught her trailing him around town after the art class was over. I told her Andrew was too old for her and she was silly to chase him, but she just stuck her nose in the air and said I didn't know anything about anything." Zelda smiled. "You know how imperious she can be. I backed off after that."

"What about Eddie Jaffe? Did you ever meet him?"

Zelda shook her head. "Never did. Heard his name mentioned a couple of times. He had a decent reputation for doing repair work on appliances or handling odd jobs like painting barns and such, but people didn't want their young folks associating with him. I know my parents warned me to steer clear. Rumor had it he was a druggie or drinker or both in his off hours."

"It doesn't seem like there was much of an investigation into his disappearance," I said. "There were only a few articles about it in the archives. Did people just not care?"

"Well, it's like this, dear." Zelda pressed her palms against the well-worn desktop. "In most people's minds, Eddie Jaffe wasn't really part of Taylorsford. He simply appeared one day, pretty much kept to himself, then vanished a year or so later. Everyone figured he'd just moved on. He didn't have any family here, or friends, for that matter. No one who claimed him, anyway."

I flipped open the manila folder. "He had a girlfriend. Someone called Sheryl Abernathy. This is the newspaper interview she did a year after he disappeared."

Death and the Librarian

Zelda glanced at the article and snorted. "Sheryl? Good heavens, I had no idea."

"You knew her?" I asked.

"Not looking like that, but yes. She was five years older than me, so we never hung out, but I knew her from church, until she stopped coming. Rumor was she'd fallen into the drug scene after leaving home, but I never heard she'd hooked up with Eddie Jaffe."

"Do you know where she is now?" I stepped back and took a breath to temper my overeager tone. "Does she still live in Taylorsford?"

"No. According to her sister, Diana, who still attends my church, she married some fella in the navy and moved away. They never had kids and split up at some point. Last I heard, Sheryl was in a nursing home in Smithsburg. Sunny Rest, I think it is." Zelda shook her head. "Diana and her husband are footing the bill, since there's no one else."

I glanced at the work calendar at the desk. I'd be off work the next day, so if I could convince Aunt Lydia to watch Ella and Nicky . . . "I'll let Brad know about that when I share this article with him. I bet he'll send someone to interview Sheryl again."

"Doubt they'll get much out of her. Diana says she's foggy-headed most of the time. Doesn't always remember Diana, much less the past." Zelda shrugged. "Fried her brains with drugs and alcohol, I reckon. Poor thing."

"Still, she told the reporter she was with Eddie the evening he disappeared." I glanced at Sheryl's gaunt face again before closing the folder. "That could be a lead. Of course,

Victoria Gilbert

only if Maureen Dryden's death is somehow connected to her digging into the Jaffe case."

Zelda patted her crisp blonde curls. "That's a big *if.* It's more likely to be something recent, like a love triangle or her owing money to the mob or something, don't you think?

"You could be right," I said, although I sincerely doubted Maureen Dryden was mixed up with gangsters. "I'll just let Brad know and see what he decides."

That was half true, at least. I flashed a smile at Zelda and headed into workroom to make a copy of the article. I would certainly share the article, and Sheryl's whereabouts, with Brad. But if he decided it was useless to question her, I didn't intend for that to be the final word.

I could always do a little interviewing on my own.

Chapter Seven

As it turned out, I didn't have to engage in any clandestine activities to visit Sheryl Abernathy. After I scanned the article and sent it to Brad, he called to thank me.

"I appreciate you taking time to dig into the archives," he said. "It seems there wasn't much on the Jaffe case, though."

"Just a few mentions of his disappearance and the interview I emailed you. I asked Zelda Adams if she remembered anything from that time, but she said she never interacted with Eddie and his disappearance didn't make much of an impact on anyone."

"That backs up the departmental reports. The consensus was that Eddie Jaffe simply left town. They didn't bother to follow up on where he might have gone, though, so I have a deputy working that angle. It may be too late to track his movements, but we'll give it a try."

"Apparently he never contacted Sheryl Abernathy again," I said, lifting the clipping out of the folder to examine her picture once more. "She doesn't look healthy in the newspaper photo, does she?"

Victoria Gilbert

"Pretty washed-up for a twenty-year-old," Brad said. "But that's not uncommon when someone is suffering from an addiction. I suspect she continued to take drugs and drink after Eddie vanished. In fact, she probably fell in deeper if she actually cared about the guy."

"I guess you've seen a lot of people under the influence in your line of work."

"Unfortunately." Brad paused for a moment. "Zelda told you where Abernathy is now?"

"Yeah, in some nursing home in Smithsburg. Sunny Rest, or some such thing."

"I've been to that place. And there's nothing sunny about it." Brad cleared his throat. "Would you be willing to drive to Smithsburg to speak to Abernathy? You still have special deputy status with the department, and I really can't spare anyone on my team right now."

"Sure, happy to," I said, shocked that he'd offered up the opportunity. "I can take notes, but you know nothing I discover can be used as evidence."

"This is a long shot anyway. If you glean anything from her that seems useful, I'll send over a deputy for an official interview. If not, we'll continue to focus on the more recent case."

I laid down the clipping and closed the folder. "You really don't think there's any connection between Maureen Dryden's death and the Jaffe case, even though she mentioned knowing more about Eddie's disappearance and talked about researching possible suspects?"

Death and the Librarian

"To be honest, I think the motive doesn't lie that far in the past. But I don't want to leave any information on the table, so if you're willing to see what Sheryl Abernathy has to say, I'd appreciate it."

"Of course," I said, refraining from mentioning that I'd planned to visit her regardless. "I'll try to go tomorrow. I have the day off; just need to see if Aunt Lydia is free to babysit Ella and Nicky."

"It makes a big difference, doesn't it?" There was a rueful note in Brad's tone. "I'm eternally grateful that Alison and I have mothers who live close by and are always willing to watch the kids when we are called to work at odd hours."

"Did Alison ever cut back on her workload at her department? I know she was thinking about it."

"Yes, she's only working a three-quarters position now. But that means nothing when something big happens, I'm afraid."

"Like a murder," I said.

"Right." Brad wished me a good day and thanked me again before hanging up.

Not long after his call, Sunny arrived for the late shift, allowing me to head home. I walked home, considering the information I'd gathered over the past few days.

After collecting the twins from Aunt Lydia's house, I changed into shorts and a T-shirt and ate an apple and a protein bar while Nicky and Ella played with the cats. "Do you still want to go for a walk?" I asked, as Nicky rolled a small multicolored ball across the living room floor. Fosse, the slightly younger of our pets, wiggled his butt for a moment, then made a flying leap to pounce on the ball.

Ella laid down the wand and dangling feather she was swinging in front of Loie, who simply yawned, displaying her lack of interest along with her sharp white teeth. "I'd rather go to the playground."

"Me too." Much to Fosse's displeasure, Nicky retrieved the ball and tossed it back into the woven basket that held a pile of cat toys.

"Alright, let's do that," I said, grabbing my tote bag and checking their shoes as I ushered them out onto the front porch. "If we were hiking you'd need your sneakers, but I guess sandals will be okay for the playground."

I really didn't mind the change, since it gave me a chance to read my book while they played. Everyone thought librarians got to read books all day, but it wasn't true. We were too busy helping patrons and managing things like the budget, community programs, and interlibrary loans.

It was just a short walk down the sidewalk that ran in front of our house to reach the playground, a recent addition to a park created from farmland donated to the town by Brad's mother, Jane Tucker. Since ours was the last house before the road ended in a turnaround, we had easy access to the playground, as well as a few hiking trails that branched off the park.

While I settled on one of the benches placed around a large circle of shredded rubber mulch, Ella and Nicky clambered all over the playground's main feature—a polished and brightly painted metal construction that included a climbing wall, slides, tunnels, and a swinging bridge. I didn't worry too

Death and the Librarian

much about the equipment on this playground because EMT Hannah Fowler, a colleague of my firefighter brother-in-law, Ethan Payne, had supervised the build to making sure everything was safe.

I'd just pulled my book from my tote bag when a voice called my name. Looking up, I saw Kurt stepping out from the entrance to one of the trails.

Ella and Nicky immediately used one of the slides to reach the ground. They rushed Kurt, who lifted each of them in turn, giving them a hug and a peck on the cheek.

"How are my godchildren today?" he asked, squatting down to be closer to eye level. "Having fun?"

"Yep, want to watch me climb?" Ella said. "I'm the fastest."

Nicky scuffed one of his rubber-soled sandals through the soft mulch. "No, you're not."

"I am, aren't I, Mommy?" Ella's eyes flashed fire like her father's when he was passionate over something.

"Well, why don't we see?" Kurt strolled over to the bench and sat next to me. "You two line up and make a run for the gym set and I'll judge who gets to the top first."

The twins readily agreed, standing side by side with their backs to us.

"Hold on, I'll start the countdown," Kurt said. "Alright, get ready and one, two, three, go!"

Nicky reached the base of the climbing wall first, but Ella, choosing to run up the steps that led to the swinging bridge, met him right as he stood up on the top platform.

"Looks like a tie," Kurt said, earning protests from the twins. He shook his head of shaggy white hair. "If I say it's a tie, it's a tie. You're both excellent, so don't fuss." He cast me an amused smile before calling out to them again. "Now, I want to talk to your mother. Go on and play while we chat."

This last pronouncement, given in a tone that matched Aunt Lydia's air of command, quieted Nicky and Ella. They resumed playing without any more argument.

"Were you hiking today?" I asked, turning to survey Kurt's rugged profile. "A bit far from your property, isn't it?" I looked over my shoulder. "I don't see your car. Where did you come from, anyway?"

"I parked behind the library and walked over," he replied, continuing to watch the twins. "Just wanted some extra exercise today."

"Really? There are numerous trails near Highview—"

"Amy," Kurt turned the full intensity of his icy blue gaze on me, "are you really digging into the Eddie Jaffe case?"

I slid a few inches away from him. "I'm helping Brad Tucker. He wanted me to do some research in the archives, that's all."

"And did you find anything?"

"Not much," I replied. "The only item of any real interest was a newspaper clipping. It featured an interview with Eddie's girlfriend given a year after he vanished."

"Girlfriend?" Kurt furrowed his brow. "Who was that, exactly?"

I studied his stony expression for a moment. "Sheryl Abernathy. Did you know her?"

Kurt looked away. "The name sounds familiar, but I can't really place her."

70

Death and the Librarian

"She told the reporter that she was at some outdoor get-together with Eddie the evening he disappeared. Not too far from here, apparently. Right up that path you were on, as a matter of fact."

"Is that so?" Kurt side-eyed me. "There is a clearing at the end of that trail, and I saw some beer cans scattered around today, so I suppose it's used by local teens or others who want to drink in secret. Which also could've happened in the sixties, I suppose." He focused on the twins, now using the set of swings. "Did she say who else was there?"

"She couldn't remember, or so she claims. She'd been drinking and popping pills or whatever, and says everything was a blur. That's likely to be true, according to Zelda Adams, who knows her sister." I pursed my lips, observing the rigid set of Kurt's broad shoulders. "Did you know Eddie, by any chance?"

"I knew of him." Kurt rolled his shoulders and leaned back, staring up into the mosaic of maple leaves shading the bench. "He was small-time, so I wasn't too concerned about his little side deals. Not exactly competition," he added, flashing me a wolfish grin.

"How magnanimous of you," I said dryly. "So why do you think Maureen Dryden mentioned your name, or to be more exact, your former name, in her lecture the other day?"

Kurt stretched out his long legs, digging his heels into the mulch. "I have no idea, unless she'd connected Jaffe's minor drug operation to other dealers in the area. I suppose there are a few people who still remember my Karl Klass persona, if only the name."

"But Delbert Frye wasn't into drugs back then, was he?" I waved to Ella, who was on the ground, showing off her dance abilities by lifting one foot and holding it up in an unwavering pose.

"He never was, as far as I knew. He was older, anyway. Already in his early thirties by then, I think." Kurt appeared lost in thought. "Dryden probably found references to him wandering the mountains around the Taylorsford area, collecting limbs and branches for his woodworking projects. I did run into him a few times when I was meeting people in some rather secluded spots."

I examined his face, looking for any signs of embarrassment or shame. Finding none, I coughed, hoping to draw his attention. "Brad told me that the original investigation concluded that Eddie had simply left town, but no one ever followed up, which is why the case is still open."

Kurt swiveled his upper body so he could face me directly. "I'm sure that's what happened. You should remember that Ms. Dryden made her living spinning conspiracy theories around murder cases. She may have made numerous enemies in the course of her career, one of whom decided to silence her. There's the team she brought with her too. The relationship dynamics in that group . . ."

"Did they display jealousy or anger or tension?" When Kurt raised his eyebrows, I added, "I mean, I wonder if you noticed any of that at the inn the night she was killed."

"Who says I was there?" Kurt's tone was sharp as a thorn.

"Sunny, for one. She was meeting some business acquaintances at the restaurant and saw you. I'm sure others did too."

Death and the Librarian

I stopped short of mentioning that I'd observed what looked like his car leaving the area. He didn't need to know I'd seen that.

Kurt leaned in and took my chin in his hand. "Leave it alone, Amy. Nothing good will come of you involving yourself in this matter."

Meeting his cold stare with a glare of my own, I yanked my chin away and slid to the end of the bench. "Are you threatening me?"

He crossed his arms over his chest. "Of course not. But you're rummaging through some old garbage that rotted away long ago. There's no point to it."

"Then there's no harm in digging it up, either, is there?" I straightened and squared my shoulders. "If it all is, as you claim, basically an archeological excavation, it can't possibly hurt anyone in the present."

Kurt's nostrils flared. "I've cut you a lot of slack in the past, Amy, but I'm warning you—the Jaffe disappearance has nothing to do with Ms. Dryden's death. You're going to be poking a hornet's nest if you insist on trying to link the two cases."

I stared at him, struck dumb by his expression. Knowing something of his past, I'd always assumed Kurt could be dangerous, but I'd never truly feared him.

Not until now.

Chapter Eight

Kurt stood up first. "I think I'll go. Tell the children I had to run to a meeting."

I opened my mouth but snapped it shut again when I realized I really didn't know what I wanted to say. Kurt turned and stalked away, his long stride taking him out of sight within a few minutes.

Sitting on the bench with my book open in my lap, I pretended to read while not turning any pages. Kurt's aggressive demands that I cease and desist any investigation into Eddie Jaffe's disappearance made me question not only his possible involvement in that case but also whether he'd had anything to do with Maureen Dryden's death.

"This is nuts," I said, chiding myself for such thoughts. But I couldn't ignore the red flags fluttering like butterflies in my brain. "Kids," I finally called out, "let's go."

For once they didn't whine, probably because they were more tired than they wanted to admit. Dutifully following me back to the house, they questioned why "Grandpop Kurt" had left without saying goodbye.

Death and the Librarian

"He had a meeting," I said, as I unlocked the front door. "You know how Daddy is often busy with classes and rehearsals? Well, Kurt has a lot of meetings with people who want to buy or sell things."

"Art and antiques," Ella piped up. "Like all the stuff in his house."

"That's right." I glanced down. "You know the rule. Outside shoes off in the house. You both already broke that rule earlier, so let's get it right now."

We all slipped off our shoes and dropped them into one of the baskets under the table. Although Richard and I complied in order to act as role models, the no-outside-shoe rule was primarily directed at the children, mainly to prevent them from damaging the dance floor that covered one half of the large front room of our house. When Richard had renovated his great-uncle's house he'd removed the wall between the original living room and dining room and turned part of the resulting space into a home dance studio, complete with mirrors and a barre on one long wall.

"What do you guys want for dinner?" I asked, sliding my feet into a pair of open-toed slippers.

"Macaroni and cheese!" they shouted in unison.

"Alright, but why don't you wash your hands and help me make it?" I pointed a finger at them. "And we are having vegetables as well, so don't turn your noses up." Spying their grimaces, I added, "Dancers need good nutrition, remember?"

After dinner, I supervised baths, aided by Fosse, who had a strange fascination with water for a cat. He liked to perch on the edge of tub and take a swipe at any bath toys floating by.

We snuggled on the sofa after that, accompanied by both cats, and watched a baby animal documentary from one of our streaming services. It wasn't long before the twins were nodding off, so halfway through the second episode, I turned off the television and herded them upstairs to their bedrooms.

Once they were asleep, with Loie at the foot of Nicky's bed and Fosse cuddled up against Ella, I grabbed my cell phone and sat back on the sofa to search for the exact location of the Sunny Rest nursing home. I also texted Aunt Lydia to ask if she could watch the twins for a few hours on Tuesday.

Richard came home about an hour later, after I'd confirmed my plans for the next day.

"Kids asleep already?" he asked, sitting on the sofa next to me.

"They were when I last checked." I set my phone on the cocktail table. "How'd it go today?"

"Good, good." Richard slumped back against the sofa cushions. "But I'm exhausted. I can't keep up the pace like I once could. I tell you, sweetheart, it's terrible getting old."

"Better than the alternative," I said, rubbing his arm. "How does a good back massage sound?"

He turned to me, his eyes brightening. "Fantastic. But let me grab a shower first. I'm way too sweaty right now."

I leaned in and sniffed. "You don't stink. Or maybe I'm just used to your smell," I added, sitting back.

"Are you now?" Richard pulled me into a close embrace. "I think I'll still get that shower," he whispered in my ear. "Then I'll let you work your magic."

Death and the Librarian

"Magic, huh?" I patted his back. "Is that what you call it?"

"Every time," he replied.

* * *

On Tuesday, I used the morning to take care of laundry and clean the kitchen—not my favorite tasks but necessary. Piles of dirty clothes seemed to manifest in the hamper overnight, and while I encouraged Ella and Nicky to help prepare meals, their efforts resulted in a lot of spills and crumbs.

After lunch, with the twins safely left in the care of Aunt Lydia, I drove over to Smithsburg to talk to Sheryl Abernathy.

Smithsburg, a thirty-minute drive from Taylorsford, was much less quaint, but it offered more services. There was the renovated Art Deco cinema that had been turned into a performance space for local and touring theater companies as well as other performing groups, and an urgent care facility along with several doctor and dentist offices. It was no surprise that the Sunny Rest nursing home was located close to these medical facilities.

Parking in a visitor space, I collected the sunflower bouquet I'd picked up at the grocery store just outside of Taylorsford and entered the sprawling two-level brick building. The older woman at the reception desk asked me to sign in. As she took my temperature to ensure I wasn't bringing in anything contagious, she glanced at the resident's name I'd scrawled on the roster.

"Ms. Abernathy? That's nice. She gets so few visitors. Her sister and brother-in-law are the only ones who ever stop by."

Victoria Gilbert

I smiled and asked for Sheryl's room number. "It's my first time visiting," I explained, when the receptionist gave me a questioning look.

"It's 204. Take the elevator to the second floor and turn right."

I thanked her and crossed the lobby, which included a gleaming black baby grand piano and several standing urns filled with silk flowers. The perfume of air fresheners couldn't quite cover the acrid tang of antiseptic blended with the sharp scent of commercial cleaning products.

Walking down the second-floor hallway, I nodded greetings to the patients sitting in wheelchairs outside their rooms. A few smiled and said hello, but several of them appeared to be lost in their own worlds. It was a sobering sight. *Everyone gets old*, I thought, *and we all hope we won't end up in a place like this, no matter how nice it might be. But sadly, sometimes that's out of our control.*

The door to room 204 sat slightly ajar. I peeked in. It was a single room, which meant Sheryl's sister was generous enough to pay to avoid Sheryl having a roommate. I knocked on the door before entering.

"Who is it?" Sheryl Abernathy's voice was soft and featured a definite quaver.

Entering the room, I brandished my bouquet, hoping the bright flowers would buy me some goodwill. "Hello, Ms. Abernathy. I'm Amy Muir, one of the library directors at the Taylorsford public library."

The head of Sheryl's bed had been raised and pillows had been used to prop her up in a sitting position. She stared with

Death and the Librarian

narrowed eyes, the lines bracketing her thin lips deepening as she surveyed me. Her once voluminous curly dark hair had turned white and was cropped so close to her head that I could see patches of pink scalp.

"I don't know you," she said, her gaunt fingers plucking at the bedspread.

"You're right, we've never met before." I crossed to the bank of metal-clad windows. Grabbing an empty vase off the sill, I turned to face Sheryl. "But I know your sister."

That was a lie but a useful one. Sheryl's taut lips relaxed slightly. "You're friends with Diana?"

"Not exactly friends, but I've met her. She attends the same church as my friend Zelda Adams." I walked into the small attached bathroom, calling over my shoulder. "Excuse me, I need to put these in water."

As I stepped out of the bathroom, I could see Sheryl puzzling over this name. "She used to be Zelda Shoemaker before she married," I said, setting the vase of flowers on the windowsill.

"Oh, Zelda. Yeah, I remember. Her family used to sit in the pew behind us. She was always too loud, and my mother had to turn around and shush her." Sheryl scrunched up her face as I pulled one of the guest chairs up near the bed and sat down.

"Zelda said you don't get many visitors, so I thought I'd stop by." I crossed my hands one over the other in my lap.

"She was younger than me. Just a kid." Sheryl grimaced. "She had a friend who tagged along with her. A skinny blonde kid who always acted like she was better than anyone else.

Stuck-up little thing. She lived in that fancy house with her crazy grandmother."

Aunt Lydia, I thought, forcing a smile. "You must've known a lot of people in Taylorsford."

"Can't remember most of 'em." Sheryl turned her watery blue gaze on me. "Long time ago."

"Of course." I considered my next words carefully. "The thing is, I was doing some research in the town archives . . ."

Sheryl rubbed her wrinkled neck. "Why'd you wanna do that?"

"Well, like I said, I'm a librarian. People ask me to find information for them, and recently someone was interested in an event that happened in the past." I took a deep breath. "It was the disappearance of Eddie Jaffe."

The mention of that name froze Sheryl's expression. Her eyes appeared to glaze over and the hand lying on the bedspread twitched like a dying fish. "Don't know much about that."

"I realize it was a long time ago, but you did give an interview to the paper a year after he went missing." I shifted in my chair. "You said you were with him the day he vanished."

"He just abandoned me." Sheryl's voice faded into a whine. "Left me up on the mountain. I was knocked out, lying on the ground, and he didn't care."

I gazed at her, realizing I had to tread carefully if I wanted any answers. "You mean you woke up and no one was there with you?"

80

Death and the Librarian

"That's right. I was alone. All of 'em gone. Had to stumble down the trail by myself in the morning."

"All of them? There were other people there besides you and Eddie?" I asked.

Sheryl slumped back against her pillows. "Yeah, it was always like that. We had these gatherings where we'd party, you know. Up the trail, in that mountain clearing. Did some drinking and"—she shot me a sly glance—"other things."

"In the article you said you didn't really remember who was there that evening." I pressed my palm against the edge of the bed. "Whoever they were, they weren't very polite, leaving you like that."

"Should've known better. They weren't friends, really. Just people who wanted to party." Sheryl gnawed at her chapped lower lip. "I was young and pretty then, so lots of guys made moves on me, but Eddie protected me from all that. He was okay, was Eddie. I missed him when he was gone."

"He never contacted you after that night?"

"Nope. Not a call or note or nothin'." She lifted her bony arms and waved her hands. "Went poof, like one of those magicians."

I sat back, a pang of sadness twisting my stomach as I examined her wasted frame. She was only five years older than Zelda and my aunt, but appeared ancient compared to either one of them. "What about the people that were there with you two that night? They never gave you any clue as to where Eddie might've gone?"

81

Victoria Gilbert

Sheryl hugged her arms close to her chest. "Like I said, I don't remember who was there. Some young guys, that's all I know." She lowered her sparse lashes over her pale eyes. "But there were a couple other people I saw that night. Yeah, two others. Only they weren't with us in the clearing."

"Where did you see them?" I asked, sliding to the front edge of my chair.

"Down the trail." Sheryl released her grip on her upper arms and used one hand to wipe her brow. "Yeah, that's it. It was before I fell asleep. Had to pee after all the drinking, and didn't wanna do that around those guys, you know?"

"That makes sense," I said.

"So I stumbled down the trail a bit. That's when I saw the guy. He was older than us and had this canvas thing with handles that was full of branches and stuff." Sheryl's eyes brightened. "He asked me if I was okay. I thought that was nice. But then he disappeared into the trees."

It must have been Delbert Frye, I thought, digging my fingernails into my palms to keep from squeaking with excitement. "You said two others. Who else was there?"

Sheryl's expression suddenly crumpled, sunken as a fallen soufflé. "That girl," she said, in a hollow voice. "That horrible girl. Caused all the trouble, that little witch."

"What girl? Someone else on the trail that night? Maybe another attendee at the gathering, coming late?"

"No, no." A bubble of spittle flew from Sheryl's mouth. "That girl. I told her to stay away. Left her there, after warning her to head back down the trail. Don't know what she did after that. Maybe Eddie ran off with her. That's what I always

Death and the Librarian

wondered. He left me for her. For that awful girl." Beating her fists against her temples, Sheryl leaned forward and made a keening noise that rose into a wail.

I jumped to my feet as the door flew open and a nurse and aide ran into the room. They cast me angry looks as I backed away from the bed.

"Why'd you go and upset her? She's been doing so well, but now . . ." The nurse turned to the aide and barked out an order for a sedative. "I think you should leave," she added, glaring at me.

"Sorry, sorry." I scuttled past the foot of the bed and dashed into the hall just as the aide pushed a small cart into Sheryl's room. She slammed the door in my face before I could apologize again.

I leaned against the wall of the hallway, breathing heavily. A tug on the hem of my blouse made me glance down.

An elderly gentleman looked up at me, his dark eyes twinkling with mischief. Despite his age, it was clear that he'd once been quite handsome. "I should've warned you, miss. That there old lady is a real hellcat." He tapped his forehead with one gnarled finger. "Too many drugs when she was young, you know. Fried her brain."

"It appears so," I replied, with a smile. "I don't think I'll be coming back to see her anytime soon."

"You can always come and see me," the man said, with a trace of flirtation in his tone.

"I don't know," I said, my smile broadening. "I'm afraid I might not be able to resist your charms, and being a happily married woman . . ."

83

Victoria Gilbert

His guffaw filled the hallway. "You must come back, little lady. I'm Randy, by the way."

"I bet you are," I called over my shoulder as I turned away, earning another loud burst of laughter that followed me down the hall.

Chapter Nine

On Thursday, Aunt Lydia called me early in the morning.

"I assumed you'd be up, even though you're off work today," she said.

I glanced over at the kitchen table, where Ella and Nicky were eating cereal under the supervision of the cats.

"Don't give any of the leftover milk to the cats, no matter how much they beg," I told them. "Milk isn't that good for grown-up kitties."

"Ah, yes, I was right. The twins get you up early, no matter what," Aunt Lydia said.

"Usually. Unless they were totally exhausted the day before." I swirled my spoon through my coffee. "What's up? I was just going to hang out with the kids today, so don't worry about having to watch them."

"I never mind that," Aunt Lydia said, with a sniff. "Actually, I wanted to invite you and the children to accompany me to the art exhibit at the inn. If you remember, I loaned the art committee a few of Andrew's paintings."

"Oh, right, we were going to go earlier in the week, but then the inn was shut down for a few days." I rinsed my spoon and stuck it in the dish rack. "I assume visitors are allowed in again?"

"Starting today. Apparently, according to Zelda, the authorities have completed their investigation of the public areas, although I think Ms. Dryden's room is still off limits."

"That makes sense." I took a sip of my coffee. "What time would you want to leave home?"

"Around ten? Then maybe we can stop at the diner for lunch on the way back. The weather is supposed to be nice today, so I thought we could include a walk rather than take the car."

"Hold on just a minute." Fosse was inching closer to Nicky's bowl. I strode over to the kitchen table and shooed him away. Loie, who was sitting on the windowsill, feigned innocence by turning her head to stare out the window. "Want to go with Aunt Lydia to see some art and then have lunch at the Heapin' Plate?" I asked Ella and Nicky.

Nicky nodded enthusiastically. He enjoyed anything related to art and had, according to his preschool teacher, an aptitude for it.

"Sure. Can we have French fries?" Ella gazed at me with a hopeful expression. I knew she wasn't that interested in paintings, but the opportunity to eat food we rarely had at home would convince her.

"We'll see." I turned my attention back to the phone. "Okay, we'll meet out in front of your house around ten. See you then," I added, before ending the call.

Death and the Librarian

I put on white cotton slacks and a rust-red blouse and had the twins exchange their pajamas for shorts and sleeveless shirts. While we waited for Aunt Lydia just inside her front gate, I texted Brad, letting him know what I'd found out from Sheryl Atkinson.

Thanks. Looks like we need to officially interview her, Brad texted back. *And, just so you know, since you're helping with this investigation, we have confirmed that Ms. Dryden's drink was spiked with Rohypnol, which probably allowed her killer to smother her while she was knocked out.*

I frowned. If Maureen had made it to her room and fallen unconscious into her bed, anyone could've murdered her. It wouldn't require that much strength. *It could've been a woman, or even,* I thought, *an elderly man.*

As expected, Aunt Lydia showed up in more formal attire—a short-sleeved pale blue linen jacket and matching skirt. *She wants to make a good impression as Andrew Talbot's widow,* I thought, hiding a smile behind my hand. Aunt Lydia took her role as the guardian of Andrew's art seriously. Even though she was in another committed relationship, she'd never relinquished her devotion to her former husband's artistic legacy.

When we arrived at the inn, it appeared that everything was back to normal, although there was still a sheriff's deputy in the lobby. I didn't recognize him, which made me think he was a new recruit.

"The exhibit is in the ballroom," Aunt Lydia said, leading the way down a short hallway.

Nicky ran ahead of us into the large hall, which was rented out for receptions, banquets, conferences, and other events, almost none of which included dancing. The ballroom moniker was more of a marketing ploy, meant to tie in with the age of the historic inn, which had once been a mill.

Transfixed in the middle of the room, Nicky didn't even flinch when Ella dashed over to him and knocked the side of one of her sneakers against his.

"There's your future artist," Aunt Lydia said. "He's always drawn to paintings and sculptures and such, isn't he? It reminds me of Andrew as a young man. Of course, they aren't related by blood, but I still see a lot of Andrew in him."

I studied my son, who had walked over to stand in front of a vivid painting of seashells that was almost abstract in its execution. "He does have an artistic eye. Maybe that comes from Richard."

Aunt Lydia cast me an amused glance. "What do you mean? You were always good at art and even majored in art history as an undergrad."

"Okay, so both of us." While Aunt Lydia took Ella by the hand and led her to one of Andrew's paintings, I crossed the room to stand next to Nicky. "Do you like this one?"

Nicky bobbed his head. "It's cool. You can see light through the shells."

I examined the painting more closely. He was right—the painter had created the illusion that the shells were back-lit by sunlight. "Yes, you certainly can. The artist is showing a lot of skill, don't you think?"

"I want to paint that good someday," Nicky said, his gaze never leaving the painting.

Death and the Librarian

I gave him a side hug. "You have to study and work hard for a long time. But it's possible."

"But I like dancing too." Nicky looked up at me, his dark eyes wide. "Can I do both?"

"Of course. Especially now. You don't have to decide on anything until you're much older. Don't let anyone tell you otherwise."

"Okay." Nicky slipped free of my arm. "Can we see Great-uncle Andrew's paintings now?"

"You've seen a couple of them before, at Aunt Lydia's house."

"But that's not like in a gallery." Nicky trotted off to join Ella and my aunt.

I followed him to the wall where the curators had hung four Andrew Talbot landscapes. They were recognizable scenes from around Taylorsford and the surrounding area, but as in all of his works, Andrew had infused the realistic depictions of meadows and mountains with a sense of mystery and magic. It was something in the quality of the light that gave these typical rural landscapes an almost mystical feel.

"I'm hungry," Ella said, while Nicky gazed at the paintings with wide eyes.

"We'll eat soon enough," I said, patting her shoulder. "Don't you like to see your Great-uncle Andrew's artworks?"

Ella wrinkled her nose. "They're okay, but I like cat pictures better." She pointed at another wall of the ballroom, where watercolors featuring kittens and cats playing in a garden had been hung.

Aunt Lydia visibly winced. "Alright, let's go look at those more closely, shall we?" She grabbed Ella's hand and marched her over to the other wall.

Nicky and I trailed them. Standing in front of one of the cat paintings, Ella declared that it "looks like Fosse, only not as cute."

I leaned closer to Aunt Lydia. "I need to go to the restroom. Can you keep an eye on these two until I get back?"

She nodded, then herded the twins to the next section of paintings.

Slipping out into the hall, I looked around for a nearby bathroom but didn't see any. I wandered down the hall to the restaurant and bar. There had to be something in that area.

I found the restrooms that served the restaurant and hurried inside. Washing my hands after, I noticed a woman in uniform at the farthest end of the sink counter.

"Alison," I said, drying my hands on a paper towel. "what brings you here?"

She straightened and yanked an excessive number of towels from the dispenser. "Some of our department's deputies were pulled in to help Brad's team with the Dryden case."

"Really? I thought they'd pretty much wrapped up the investigation, at least here at the inn."

Alison looked down as she wiped her hands with the wad of towels. "We're double-checking information. I just talked to that podcaster and Dryden's research assistant again. They gave statements before, of course, but Brad asked us to pose the same questions again to see if there's any variation."

"They're still here?' I asked.

Death and the Librarian

"Can't leave town until we tell them," Alison balled up the paper towels and tossed them in the trash can. "I mean, until Brad's department gives the okay."

I threw away my own used towel. "You must've been caught off guard when Maureen Dryden called out your great-uncle like that. Not that I suspect Delbert of anything, of course, but it was a surprise, even to me."

Alison's eyes narrowed. "I don't know what she was up to with that announcement. It was totally uncalled for. It upset my great-uncle when he heard about it. He was very angry, and I don't blame him."

The flash of fire in Alison's eyes told me she was angry as well. "I think Dryden might've heard that Delbert was in the woods the night Eddie Jaffe disappeared. But I understand that he used to roam around that area, looking for supplies for his woodworking projects, so . . ."

"It's just ridiculous." Alison grabbed her deputy's hat off the counter and clutched it against her chest like a shield. "Now all these rumors are flying around about Uncle Delbert. Totally unsubstantiated, but people have always thought he was a bit strange because he's such a hermit. He just likes to keep to himself, but you know as well as I do he wouldn't hurt a fly."

"Hmm." I wasn't so sure about that, since my first encounter with the man had been when he'd brandished a shotgun at me because I was trespassing on his property. While I couldn't see him committing a crime at his age, I also couldn't rule him out as a suspect in the Jaffe case. Delbert would've only been in his thirties then, and he'd always been protective of the mountain environment. If Eddie and his pals were trashing the clearing Sheryl had mentioned . . . "Sunny said something about seeing you here on Sunday evening. Did you notice anything odd?"

Color rose in Alison's cheeks. She slammed her hat down onto her head, so low in front that the brim shadowed her face. "No, and for your information I was just here to pick up some takeout from the restaurant. It was pretty crazy that night, as I'm sure you're aware. Now, if you'll excuse me, I need to get back to work. Have to talk to the bartender again and a few other staff."

She strode out of the bathroom without a goodbye. I waited a moment before I exited, puzzling over her defensive attitude. *Almost like she's hiding something*, I thought.

Walking back through the restaurant, I caught a glimpse of Terry Temkin and Sean Gordon at one of the high-backed booths lining an exposed stone wall. They appeared to be in the midst of an argument, which naturally piqued my curiosity. I moved closer, standing behind the tall back of their booth. Sometimes being short was an advantage.

"I heard you told the deputies that Maureen left the bar after you did, but I don't remember it that way," Sean said.

"I'm surprised you could remember anything, the way you were throwing them back." Terry's voice was laced with sarcasm. "While your memory might be fuzzy, I assure you that Mindy and I fled to the outdoor patio not long after that dark-haired woman confronted Maureen. Did you know she was the sheriff's wife?"

"You don't mean the one who was accusing Maureen of slandering her great-uncle?" Sean asked.

Death and the Librarian

"Yeah, that's the one. Alison Tucker—also in law enforcement, apparently, although she wasn't acting like a law-abiding citizen that night." Terry's bark of laughter held no trace of humor. "But that isn't the point of this chat. What I want to know is why you told the authorities that Maureen and I argued that evening."

"Didn't you? I'm fairly certain I overheard the two of you fighting over some research you claimed she was stealing from you," Sean said.

A waitress, noticing me standing in the passageway between the booth and the kitchen, shot me a questioning look. I slid my phone from my purse and fiddled with it as if reading texts.

"Because she did," Terry said. "The entire section on the Campton murders was something I was going to use as an exclusive on my podcast, until Maureen convinced me that she'd give me credit, and a percentage of her advance and royalties, if I let her have all of my research for her book. But I've never received the agreement she promised, and then I found out last week that she'd never included any mention of that in her contract, which she'd already signed with her publisher."

"Well, you're in luck, then," Sean said in a cold tone. "Since there won't be any book, I suppose you can leverage your *exclusive* on your podcast." Sean cleared his throat. "Interesting timing, that."

"What are you implying?" Terry's question was accompanied by a rattling of silverware.

The same waitress walked by me, balancing a tray filled with empty glasses. "Can you check your phone somewhere else?" she asked. "You're kinda in the way here."

I apologized and scurried away, my thoughts consumed with Terry and Sean's conversation. If Terry truly felt wronged by Maureen's uncompensated use of his research, perhaps he had a motive to kill her. Although I had to wonder if a podcast, no matter how popular, could generate enough money to drive someone to murder.

People have killed over lesser things, I reminded myself as I returned to the ballroom.

"Aunt Lydia was wondering if you fell in," Ella said, earning a sharp glance from my aunt.

"No, something came up that I had to investigate," I said. "You know how Mommy sometimes helps Sheriff Tucker and his deputies?"

Ella and Nicky nodded, while Aunt Lydia frowned. "That's all very well, but the twins and I have already seen all the paintings and now they're famished, or so they claim. I'm afraid you won't get to see the entire exhibit today, Amy."

"It's okay. I can come again once I'm back at work. It'll be easy enough to pop in during my lunch hour."

My aunt gave me a sidelong look. "That won't be until next week, right?"

"Yeah. Sunny, bless her heart, gave me a three-day break because of Mom and Dad coming into town tomorrow and the dance company premiere and all that."

"Good. You can attend the premiere tomorrow night and then rest on Saturday when Debbie and Nick and I take the twins to the matinee."

Death and the Librarian

"That will be nice," I said. "What do you think, kids? Do you want to go see Daddy's show with Aunt Lydia and Grandma and Grandad?"

"Sure." Ella looked up at me. Her gray eyes were so like her father's that it always warmed my heart. And, of course, she knew it. "But right now I want French fries."

"Let's head to the Heapin' Plate, then," Aunt Lydia said. "To be honest, I'm a bit hungry myself."

As we strolled into the lobby, with Ella and Nicky arguing over who would get to order first at the diner, I noticed Terry Temkin's assistant, Mindy LaSalle, huddled in one corner with her cell phone plastered to one ear.

"How could you do that?" she said in an agitated tone. "You'd better watch what you say from now on, or we'll all be in trouble."

I paused in midstride, interested in hearing more, but had to move forward when Nicky tugged on one of my hands and Ella on the other.

"Come on, Mommy, we want lunch," Ella said.

Aunt Lydia glanced back over her shoulder, her fingers curled around the handle of one of the glass front doors. "Put down the sleuthing hat, Amy, and let's just enjoy the day."

I almost retorted that I enjoyed what she called *sleuthing*, but thought better of it. "Alright, forward march," I told the twins, who complied with the exaggerated steps they'd learned while dancing in *The Nutcracker*.

"I didn't ask for a parade," Aunt Lydia said as Ella and Nicky marched ahead of us.

Victoria Gilbert

I shifted my purse strap to my other shoulder. "Don't knock it. It just means they might wear themselves out and actually take a nap when we get home."

My aunt's trill of laughter instantly punctured that dream. "Who are you kidding?"

"I know, I know," I said glumly. "That's the impossible dream."

"And no Don Quixote for miles around," she replied with a wicked smile.

I sighed. "That's the sad part about reality—those fictional characters are never around when you need them."

Chapter Ten

I thought I was well prepared for the premiere of the Tansen-Muir Company, but I'd underestimated the strain it would place on Richard.

"It's going to be wonderful. You're going to do great. Everyone in the company will exceed your expectations," I said, perched on the edge of our bed as Richard paced the bedroom.

"I feel like my head is going to explode," he said, raking his fingers through his short hair until it stood up in spikes. "Last night's dress rehearsal was such a mess. Everything that could go wrong did go wrong."

"Yeah, but you always say a bad dress rehearsal means a great opening night." I patted the bed. "Come, sit."

He crossed the room and sat down next to me, putting his head in his hands. "I'm just worried I'll let down Karla and the company."

"How could you think that?" I asked, rubbing his back. "You polished the choreography to a fine shine. I'm sure of that, since you've spent hours in the dance studio, here and at the theater. And you worked with the dancers from the first steps to the finale. I mean, you've overseen so many rehearsals that the children have almost forgotten what you look like."

Richard lifted his head and cast me a rueful glance. "That bad, huh?"

"It's fine. You spend plenty of time with them, and I know getting the company off to a great start is essential. But really, honey, you have to trust your own dedication and talent. Not to mention the abilities of your codirector and handpicked dancers. This company has been a long time coming, so of course you're feeling the pressure. But I believe it's going to be a fantastic premiere and soon you guys will be so inundated with opportunities to perform that we'll have to buy a camper so the kids and I can follow you around the country."

Turning to pull me into a hug, Richad declared, "All around the world. So we might need a jet or boat too."

"Fine." I laid my head on his shoulder. "We'll travel the globe. Although we will have to figure out what to do about the cats."

"They'll have to come along," Richard said. In response, Loie, who was curled up at the foot of the bed, opened one of her emerald eyes and stared suspiciously at us.

I wrapped my arms more tightly around him. "Feeling better now?"

"Not quite yet," he replied, adjusting his position so he could kiss me. "What would I do without you?" he said when he finally sat back and released his hold on me.

Death and the Librarian

"That's definitely not something to worry about." I laid my palm against his jaw. "I'm here for good and forever."

Richard took hold of my other hand. "My favorite words, other than . . ."

"I love you," I said, finishing his thought. "And yes, I do."

"You'd better." Richard grabbed my arms and pushed me down on the bed. "Speaking of reducing stress . . ."

"The kids will be up soon."

Richard brushed a kiss against my temple. "That's why we trained them to never enter this room without permission if the door is closed, remember?"

"And they always follow our instructions?" I asked, arching my brows.

"Point taken." Richard released me and sat up.

I stayed flat on my back, staring up at the white beadboard ceiling. "Don't fret. This isn't *the end*; this is just *to be continued*."

"Ah, a cliffhanger." Richard pulled me up to a sitting position. "Well, that does build the anticipation. Gives me something to look forward to despite all the anxiety over the show."

I smiled. "See—I knew I could make you feel better."

"You're great at that," Richard said, tapping my lips with one finger. "Among other things."

* * *

My parents arrived by midmorning, stopping by Aunt Lydia's house first to say hello and drop off their luggage. Since our three-bedroom home didn't have a dedicated guest room,

Mom and Dad always stayed with my aunt when they visited. There were plenty of extra rooms in the large family home that Aunt Lydia had inherited from her grandmother, Rose Baker Litton. Fortunately, after some years of avoiding the house due to unpleasant memories, my mom had finally gotten comfortable with staying there.

When Mom and Dad showed up at our house, Ella and Nicky ran to them to receive a shower of kisses and hugs. Aunt Lydia, who'd accompanied my parents, pulled me into the kitchen.

"Debbie and Nick had some questions about this latest murder, particularly whether you were going to be involved in helping the sheriff's department again," she said, keeping her voice low. "Perhaps you should reassure them that you're just doing a little research and nothing more. Debbie's already anxious over your brother, who's out in the field heaven only knows where."

I frowned. My parents and I had always known that my younger brother, Scott, worked for a top-secret government agency, but we'd believed he was a computer expert who didn't venture out into the field. This belief was proven to be false a few years ago, when we'd discovered that he was indeed a field agent, often sent on missions overseas. The fact that his husband Ethan also worked in a dangerous profession as a firefighter didn't make things easier. My mom, who'd been a marine biologist before she retired, had done her share of risky work, including diving in less-than-optimal conditions, but this only seemed to increase her anxiety.

Death and the Librarian

"I know how quickly things can turn catastrophic," she'd once told me.

"I'll reassure them, don't worry," I told Aunt Lydia. I took a quick peek out onto our screened back porch to make sure Fosse and Loie were safely ensconced on two wicker chairs before I followed her into the living room.

"Grandad is going to take us to the park," Ella said. "And then we're going to have pizza for dinner!"

"You lucked out, it seems. Poor Mommy has to eat a cold sandwich and drive to Daddy's show," I said, with a warm smile for my dad, Nick Webber, who at sixty-nine had finally cut his shoulder-length brown hair, losing the low ponytail he'd worn when he'd worked as a computer programmer.

"Alright, kiddos, let's go," he told the twins, who didn't have to be asked twice.

"I think I'll head back over to the house and do some prep for dinner," Aunt Lydia said. "Although with pizza for lunch, I'm not sure anyone will be that hungry."

"We'll let the kids eat most of the pizza," Mom said, laying a hand on her sister's arm. "I'd rather eat what you make, Lydia."

After my aunt followed Dad and the twins outside, my mom sank down onto the sofa. "Come and chat with me, Amy. We hardly get a moment to talk anymore."

"Okay, I'll just grab a couple of glasses of water and be right back," I replied, heading for the kitchen.

When I returned, Mom had placed two coasters on the coffee table.

"Thanks, but as you can see, it already has rings," I said, sitting down and handing her one of the two water glasses. "We've tried to get the kids to use coasters, but they always seem to forget."

Mom rolled her eyes. "No use worrying about furniture when you have young children. You might as well just wait until they're older and replace it all."

"Are you speaking from experience?" I asked. "I don't remember Scott and I being that destructive."

Mom saluted me with her glass. "Here's to selective memory." She smiled, crinkling the lines fanning out from her dark brown eyes. Everyone said I took after her, while Scott more closely resembled Dad. That was true, and sometimes I felt like looking at Mom was a glimpse into my own future. Which wasn't bad, really. While only a few dark brown strands were threaded through her now white hair, she didn't have many wrinkles for a seventy-year-old. If I grew old gracefully like her or my aunt, I'd be thankful.

"Aunt Lydia said you were a little worried about Scott. I guess he hasn't been able to get in touch lately? I know I haven't heard anything from him." I sipped my water as I waited for her reply.

"Oh, you know how it is. He gets sent on these missions and has to go dark. He can't even contract Ethan most of the time. It's something we're used to," Mom said, setting her glass on one of the coasters.

"Doesn't make it any easier." I placed my half-empty glass on the other coaster.

Death and the Librarian

"No, it doesn't," Mom said, with a rueful smile. She leaned back against the sofa cushions and stared up at the rotating ceiling fan. "What's this I hear about another murder in Taylorsford? The news has been a little short on details."

"A woman died at the Taylorsford Inn Sunday night. The authorities think her drink was spiked with something that knocked her out enough for someone to smother her with a pillow. Anyway, that's the theory."

Mom lowered her gaze and turned to me. "Did you know the victim? I heard it was a true-crime author."

"I only met her once, after the lecture she gave Saturday afternoon as part of the arts festival." I slid to the edge of the sofa and gripped my knees with my hands. "Her name was Maureen Dryden and she was famous for writing about the Beverly Baron murder."

"Oh, that's where I heard her name before. Your dad and I watched the miniseries about that case." Mom shook her head. "Such a young, beautiful, and talented actress. It was a terrible shame."

"I never saw that, but know it was wildly popular when it came out," I said. "Anyway, she was friends with our Friends of the Library chair, which is how she got invited to speak during the festival." I grabbed my glass and took a long swallow of water. "Ms. Dryden talked about the new book she was writing—sort of an anthology of stories about cold cases in small towns. She was actually researching a missing persons case that took place in Taylorsford in the summer of 1966. I know that's not long after you and Aunt Lydia moved in with Great-grandmother Rose—"

Victoria Gilbert

Before I could finish my sentence, Mom snapped her fingers. "The Eddie Jaffe case."

"That's right. Do you remember much about it?" I asked, giving her a searching look. "You were pretty young then."

"I was ten, not two. Of course I remember it."

Setting my water glass back down, I swiveled on the sofa cushions, pulling my legs up and crossing them in a pretzel pose. "Exactly what do you recall?"

"Are you back helping the sheriff's department, Amy?" My mom's disapproving tone told me I needed to tread carefully.

"Yes, but just with research. The library houses the town archives, you know, so Brad Tucker asked me to check the archival materials for any background information. That's all, really." I tightened my lips, realizing that wasn't exactly the whole truth. I'd also interviewed Sheryl Abernathy.

"This is how you get in trouble," Mom said. "It starts out with research and then escalates."

"Cross my heart, I'll be careful," I said, making the gesture. "But I don't think I have to worry about anything you might say, so if you remember Eddie Jaffe—"

Mom cut me off with a wave of her hand. "I never met him, although I saw him around town a few times. He was a decent-looking young man, in a lean and hungry sort of way. Very thin, with long dark-blond hair that always looked like it needed a wash." She picked up her water glass and took a sip. "His eyes were very arresting. Even though he was fair, he had eyes so dark they looked black. It was an unusual contrast and made him hard to forget."

Death and the Librarian

"What did you hear people say when he went missing?" I asked. "I'm sure you probably picked up on some of the gossip, even if you were a kid."

"Well, sure. Adults always think children are oblivious, don't they? But Lydia and I heard almost everything Grandmother's friends said when they came to visit." Mom circled her forefinger around the rim of her glass. "Most people in Taylorsford believed Eddie had skipped town. According to the older folks, he disappeared just like he appeared, out of the blue and with no fanfare."

"It was listed as a missing persons case, though," I said.

"Only because he didn't take his clothes or other belongings with him." Mom stared out over the living room. "He had a set of tools he used for the odd jobs he picked up here and there. Some people thought it was strange that he would leave those behind, and his extra clothes were left in the room he rented over the diner too. On the other hand, his truck vanished on the day he disappeared, so there was talk that he was fleeing in a hurry."

"He was apparently dealing drugs, or so I've heard."

"Maybe. Rumor had it he was using, but whether he sold anything or not was never really established." Mom cast me a wry smile. "It's not like his buyers, if he had any, were going to come forward to help the authorities."

"I guess not." I leaned back on the pillow pressed against the sofa arm. "Was there anything else about that time that sticks in your memory?"

Mom arched her dark eyebrows. "Other than my parents dying in a car accident and having to move in with Grandmother?"

105

"Oh, sorry. I wasn't thinking. I know that was a tough time for you."

"Not as tough as it was for Lydia." Mom's gaze turned inward, as if she was visualizing scenes from the past. "She was fifteen, which is a difficult age anyway. Then losing our parents and having to deal with our grandmother." Mom sighed. "It was all too much for her. I blocked out the negativity by reading books and getting involved in 4-H and cycling around town with my friends from school. But Lydia closed herself off from everyone, even me. She did get involved in some art classes, but that was only because . . ."

"She had a crush on Andrew? Yeah, I heard that much from Zelda."

"It was honestly more like an obsession." Mom shook her head. "It wasn't healthy, but Grandmother didn't seem to notice what was going on, and Lydia wouldn't listen to me. Or Zelda, or anyone else. I guess it was her way of escaping the reality of our situation."

"What do you mean, obsession?" I uncrossed my legs and swung them around so I could sit facing the black rectangle of the television mounted on the opposite wall. "I can't imagine Aunt Lydia acting like that. She's so calm and collected most of the time."

"These days," Mom replied. "Not then. She used to follow Andrew around like a puppy."

"Zelda mentioned that too. Was Andrew irritated by that at the time?"

"I don't believe so. At least, I never saw him treat her badly. He was very tolerant, now that I think about it." Mom looked

Death and the Librarian

over at me. "The one who tried to shoo her away was Kurt, or Karl as he was called then."

"But he wasn't living here at the time, was he?"

"No. He'd left home before Lydia and I moved in next door. But we knew him from when we used to visit Grandmother with our parents. I didn't pay him, or his friend Andrew, much attention. To me, boys still had cooties." Her smile faded as she continued speaking. "But Lydia was always trying to hang out with them while we were visiting Grandmother, and then when we moved in, well, she watched like a hawk to catch sight of Andrew every time he visited Paul Dassin. Then she found out about the art class Andrew was teaching and convinced Grandmother to allow her to attend." Mom crossed her arms over her chest. "I have no idea how Lydia did that, except that she may have appealed to Grandmother's conviction that young ladies should have some genteel hobbies."

"How'd she run into Kurt, though? He was living somewhere else, like Smithsburg, and trying to keep a low profile in Taylorsford from what I understand."

"Honestly, I don't know. I guess he and Andrew met up from time to time, and since Lydia was keeping such close tabs on Andrew, she occasionally encountered Kurt as well. All I'm sure of is that there were a few times when I caught Lydia crying and she'd say Kurt—that is, Karl—had been mean to her and she hated him and stuff like that." Mom held up her hand. "We should change the subject."

"I agree." The clatter of shoes on our wooden porch floor had alerted me as well.

Victoria Gilbert

As the front door opened and the twins burst into the room, trailed by my dad, Mom leaned in closer to me. "Don't mention any of this to Lydia. I'm not sure how she'd react."

"I won't," I told her. "Because I am sure."

Chapter Eleven

Later on Friday, the children and my parents used the rose-vine entwined archway that separated our backyard from Aunt Lydia's extensive gardens to head over to my aunt's house. I took the opportunity to shower and get ready for the dance company's premiere performance.

I'd even bought a new outfit for the occasion—a full-skirted, short-sleeved dress in polished cotton. It was a burnt-orange color that I knew complemented my dark brown hair and eyes, and had a scooped neckline that showed off a little décolleté. *Just the sort of outfit Richard will appreciate*, I thought, as I surveyed myself in our full-length mirror. I'd swept my hair back with a gold clip and added the amber necklace Richard had given me for our third anniversary. It achieved the simple but elegant look that had been my goal.

Slipping on a pair of tan sandals, I lifted my ivory crochet purse from the top of the dresser and headed downstairs. I had plenty of time before the performance, but knowing the traffic on the two-lane road between Taylorsford and Smithsburg could be busy, especially on a Friday evening, I wanted to leave the house early. If I had to wait, I'd just sit and read one of the books I'd downloaded to the app on my phone.

Stopping by an upholstered armchair in the living room to pet the cats, who were curled up so closely they resembled a yin and yang symbol, I heard my phone buzzing inside my purse.

I need to silence that before the show starts, I thought, as I glanced at the screen.

It was Kurt's number. Slightly baffled, I answered.

"Good, you haven't left yet," he said. "I saw Sunny at the library earlier. She was on the phone, obviously talking to you, and she said something about a last-minute meeting with a produce buyer at the farm possibly delaying her. I assumed she was driving you to the theater. Knowing you don't want to be late for this performance, why don't you catch a ride with me instead? I can swing by and pick you up in ten minutes since I'm already in town."

"Actually, I told her I would drive myself and meet her there. Richard has our car, but there's still the car I share with Aunt Lydia, and she's staying home tonight with my parents and the twins."

"Ah, your parents are visiting? They can come too, if you want."

"No, they have tickets for tomorrow's matinee. They're taking Ella and Nicky, along with Aunt Lydia. It's just me tonight."

"Then that's perfect. I can drive you to the theater, and you can ride home with Richard. Wouldn't that be preferable to you both driving home separately?"

Death and the Librarian

I had to admit he was right, although I was still a little leery of him after our last encounter. *Don't be ridiculous*, I chided myself. *You know Kurt won't hurt anyone he considers family.* "That does make sense. I'll send Richard a text so he knows what's going on."

"Excellent," Kurt said. "I'll be there soon."

I decided to wait on the front porch. After texting Richard the new plans, I received a quick *okay* in response.

Kurt's black Jag pulled up in front of the house. He got out to open the passenger side door for me. "You look quite lovely," he said, as he helped me into the car.

"Thank you. And thanks again for the ride. It will be nice to be able to go home with Richard."

Kurt's bushy eyebrows rose up to touch the thick lock of white hair that had fallen over his forehead. "Nicer than riding there with me?"

"I'm afraid so. I hope you don't mind," I said, unable to resist smiling.

"Of course I mind. It hurts, right here." Kurt pressed his free hand to the left side of his chest.

"Are you sure that's where it hurts? I thought your heart was pretty inurned to any damage. I think it simply hurts your pride," I said, adjusting my skirt over my knees.

"Et tu, Brute?" Kurt splayed his fingers across his chest and groaned.

I turned to study his rugged profile. "I'm still a little ticked off with you over our last meeting, in case you're wondering."

"Sorry about that. I was overly concerned for your welfare, that's all," Kurt said, keeping his gaze fixed on the road.

"I know the kind of danger you've gotten into before when you were trying to help the authorities solve a case. I don't want to see you fall into that trap again."

I stared out the side window. We'd already left the outskirts of town and were driving through an area of rolling fields and clusters of trees. "It seems you were more concerned about what I might discover in your past than anything about the Dryden case." I shot him a sharp glance. "Or are the two cases connected?"

"Why would they be?" Although Kurt's voice was perfectly calm, he was gripping the steering wheel so tightly his knuckles had turned white.

"I don't know—Maureen Dryden digging up dirt on people who were around when Jaffe disappeared, maybe?"

"Which is all nonsense." Kurt met my inquisitive gaze and held it for a moment before turning his attention back on the road. "Eddie Jaffe was a transient who moved from place to place, from what I understand. A rolling stone, if you will. When he supposedly went missing, his truck vanished too. That tells me he simply fled the area for some reason."

"He left behind other possessions, though, like some clothes and his tools. Why would he do that?"

"As I said, rumor had it that Eddie was a two-bit dealer. Perhaps he angered the wrong people, received threats, and decided to fly the coop. It's quite possible that another dealer might not have taken kindly to him encroaching upon their territory."

Like you? I thought, fiddling with the strap of my purse. "Maureen Dryden knew your former name."

Death and the Librarian

"Apparently. But she didn't know me. Not the person I am now. And I doubt she would've figured it out. A lot of people from the time Jaffe disappeared would've heard of Karl Klass." Kurt shot me an icy glance. "But I left all that behind decades ago. Even people in Taylorsford haven't made the connection, except for those I've told, or a few, like your aunt, who still recognized me."

I wrapped the soft purse strap around my hand. "Speaking of Aunt Lydia, my mom told me something interesting today. About how my aunt used to follow Andrew around, long before they ever dated, and how sometimes she ran into you at the same time. Mom said Aunt Lydia didn't like you much."

"An understatement, I'm sure." The lines bracketing Kurt's lips deepened.

"Mom said Aunt Lydia claimed you were mean to her." I leaned against the smooth leather seat. "I assume that means you tried to chase her away."

"For her own good." Kurt's taut tone matched his grip on the steering wheel. "Like you, my dear, she didn't always know what was in her best interest."

"You didn't like her back then, did you?"

Kurt frowned. "I didn't care, one way or the other. But I knew a fifteen-year-old girl had no business hanging out with boys four or more years older. Andrew was too tolerant, which was actually crueler to Lydia than anything I ever did or said to her."

"Because it encouraged her infatuation?" I adjusted my hair clip as Kurt pulled into the theater parking lot. "But they did end up together. Maybe he already had feelings for her, only she was too young. He could've liked her too, only he had to wait until she was older to express his interest."

Turning off the engine, Kurt sat back, the keys dangling from his fingers. "Lydia was beautiful. You know how attractive she is now, just imagine her as a young girl. Exquisite. And Andrew always loved beautiful things." Kurt turned to me, his expression unreadable. "That's all I'll say on the matter."

"Well, thank you for the ride," I said, unbuckling my seatbelt. "It's early, though. You'll have to wait a while before the opening curtain."

"I'll just take a walk," he replied. "I haven't gotten all my steps in today, so it's a good opportunity. I suppose you're going to see Richard before the performance?"

"No, I never do that. He needs time to focus and prepare. I'll sit in the lobby and read until they open the auditorium doors." I held up my cell phone. "One advantage of reading apps."

Kurt grimaced. "I refuse to give in to that. It's print or nothing."

"I didn't know you were such a Luddite," I said as I opened the car door.

"There are a lot of things you don't know about me, Amy," Kurt said, in a surprisingly serious tone. "Never forget that."

I stared at him for a moment before stepping out of the car. "Trust me, I never have," I said, shutting the door behind me.

Despite his assertion that he was planning to take a walk, Kurt remained in the Jag as I strode away. Stopping for a moment at the back corner of the theater building, I glanced

Death and the Librarian

toward his car. Kurt's head was down, resting on the arms he'd stretched over the steering wheel.

That's odd, I thought while I circled around the building to reach the front entrance doors. *I don't think I've ever seen Kurt in distress before.*

I paused on the sidewalk in front of the theater. One of the older buildings in Smithsburg, it had been renovated a year of two before the twins were born. It could still be used to show movies, and a local film society held an annual festival there, but it was primarily used as a venue for live performances of various kinds, from Richard and Karla's dance productions to touring theater productions and plays put on by the area's community theater troupes.

As I admired the large posters advertising the Tansen-Muir Company that filled the glass-fronted frames flanking the front doors, I pondered Kurt's unusual behavior. He seemed intent on blocking any investigation into a possible connection between him and Eddie Jaffe. *What if he did murder Maureen Dryden?* a little voice in my head whispered. *He's told me in the past that he never killed anyone, except in self-defense. But what if he felt her research into Karl Klass threatened his current life? Wouldn't all bets be off, then?*

I crossed the vivid tile mosaic that mimicked the floor medallions of ancient Rome. Above me, a multitiered chandelier dripping with crystals cast rainbows of light across the marble columns that decorated the perimeter of the lobby. A seating area set beneath one of the arches connecting the columns offered me a spot to wait for Sunny's arrival. Since Richard had gotten us seats together, I had her ticket.

I'd just sat down and pulled my phone from my purse when another person entered the lobby. A plump young woman of average height, she was wearing jeans and a T-shirt with flip-flops. I wasn't sure what she was doing in the lobby, as she didn't look like an audience member, usher, or part of the backstage crew.

"Hello." She trotted across the room to greet me, her blonde curls bouncing against her shoulders.

Oh, it's Mindy LaSalle, I realized. "Hi, are you here for the show?"

"Yes, but I came early because I wanted to check out the theater ahead of time. Terry was curious if the lobby would be a good venue for one of our podcasts. We're stuck in the area right now, you see. Fortunately, we were able to rent a couple of cars that Sean, Terry, and I have been sharing. That's allowed us to travel around a little, but we're not supposed to venture too far yet."

"You can't leave the area because of Maureen Dryden's death?" I asked, quickly adding, "My condolences."

"No need. Maureen and I weren't close." Mindy plopped down in the chair next to me. "You're one of the library directors, aren't you?"

"That's right." I extended my hand. "Amy Muir. Nice to meet you. I saw you on the stage at Ms. Dryden's lecture, but we were never actually introduced."

Mindy flexed her feet, displaying her yellow flip-flops and magenta-painted toenails. "I guess you know that I'm Terry Temkin's assistant. Well"—she wiggled her toes—"actually, we're partners. In life as well as work."

Death and the Librarian

I blinked, wondering why she was sharing this personal information with a stranger. "I see."

"Yeah, he likes to pretend that I just help him with the podcasts, but we're more than that." Mindy's eyes widened. "Amy Muir? So are you related to the guy who runs the dance company?"

"He's my husband," I said, sliding my phone back into my purse.

"Really?" Mindy's gaze swept over me. "I bet you're excited for tonight, then. Seems like it's a pretty big deal."

I met her artless expression with a smile. "It is. This is the premiere performance of the Tansen-Muir Company. My husband and his dance partner, Karla Tansen, have been working toward this goal for years."

"Oh, wow. Yeah, that is big," Mindy said, sitting up straighter in her chair. "Terry and I have been working on something like that. Well, not dance, but the next step for our podcast."

"What might that be?" I asked.

"A television adaption," Mindy said, pride shining in her eyes. "Terry's been approached by a really great producer and studio. They're interested in creating a true-crime documentary-type show based on Terry's research into the Campton case."

"Really?" My smile froze as I remembered where I'd heard that case mentioned at the inn's restaurant, in the argument between Sean and Terry. "I'm not familiar with that, I'm afraid."

"It's a little obscure, because it happened back in the eighties. Not many people know all the details. Anyway, an entire family was killed, shot dead in their home. The authorities labeled it a murder-suicide, committed by the father, but Terry always believed someone else murdered them. He and I have done a ton of research, interviews, and all that, and we have a pretty compelling alternate theory." Mindy pressed two fingers to her lips for a second. "Which I can't tell anyone, of course. That might screw up the deal."

I nodded, my mind racing with thoughts about Terry claiming Maureen was planning to steal his idea. "I understand. You want to keep that information a secret until it's revealed in your podcast or on the TV show."

"Exactly." Mindy squinched up her face. "Argh, I really talk too much sometimes. Terry would be angry with me if he knew I was chatting about this, but we just found out about the possible television option a few weeks ago and I've been bursting to tell someone. You won't mention it to anyone else, will you?"

No one except Brad Tucker, I thought, offering Mindy a bright smile. "Of course not."

"That's good." Mindy rose to her feet. "This place would be great for a podcast, but I hope I can convince Terry to move on. Once we're allowed to go, I really want to leave this area behind. It's got bad vibes now, you know?"

"Of course." I watched as she paced across the floor mosaic. She appeared hyped up, as if she'd had too many cups of coffee.

Or maybe something else? I leaned forward in my chair. Had Mindy decided to speak to me because she wanted to

Death and the Librarian

share an exciting future prospect, or was she simply putting on a show? If she truly was Terry's partner, she stood to gain as much as he did from any use of the Campton case. And lose as much if Maureen Dryden had taken their research and refused to adequately compensate them. *But why would she implicate herself, unless . . .* I sat back. *Unless she's trying to muddy the waters, or throw Terry to the wolves. Perhaps she wants to protect herself by betraying him.*

Mindy stopped short in front of me. "Of course, we'll probably have to come back sooner or later, if only to give evidence against Maureen's killer. We have a hunch, you see."

"Really? Is this based on something you observed that night?" I asked, forcing myself to remain calm.

"Yep. There was a woman at the restaurant who came up to Maureen and gave her grief about something she said in her lecture. It was related to one of the old guys Maureen thought could be connected with the Eddie Jaffe case." Mindy narrowed her eyes. "Seemed like the woman was a relative or something."

"Did this woman actually threaten Maureen?"

"Not in so many words. But she looked like she wanted to take a swing at Maureen, that's for sure. And then"—Mindy fixed me with an intense gaze—"Terry and I saw that woman again, a little later, when we were outside on the patio. She came sneaking out of what looked like an emergency exit. Seemed as if she really didn't want anyone to notice her. She hurried off toward the road behind the inn, like she wanted to escape the area without talking to any of the deputies."

Alison, I thought, swallowing a swear word. *If Mindy's telling the truth, it's testimony that could certainly move Alison Tucker's name up the suspect list.*

"Nice talking to you, but I'm going to pop outside for some fresh air before the show. See you later," Mindy said, as she headed for the front doors.

One of the volunteer ushers, arriving for work, held the door open for her as she left the building.

I slipped my phone back out of my purse and texted Brad, sharing the gist of the conversation I'd overheard between Terry and Sean, as well as Mindy's possible motive to remove Maureen from the picture.

We'll look into all of them, Brad texted back. *By the way, give Richard my good wishes for tonight. Alison is coming, but I'm afraid I have to miss out. Too much going on.*

I thanked him and turned off my phone. The rest of the ushers were arriving, which meant the auditorium would open soon. Standing, I smoothed the wrinkles from my skirt and headed to the restroom. Fixing my hair and makeup in the mirror, I contemplated this new wrinkle in the Dryden case.

There was a growing list of suspects, including Terry Temkin and Mindy LaSalle, but I knew I couldn't rule out Delbert Frye, or more likely, Alison working on Delbert's behalf. Of course, I hadn't mentioned Alison to Brad yet, but I was certain he wouldn't overlook that possibility, devastating as it might be.

Then there was Kurt, who had a possible connection to Eddie Jaffe's disappearance, as well as more than enough

Death and the Librarian

reasons to want to keep such a connection quiet. I didn't want him, or Alison, to be involved, and I knew from past experience that pursuing the truth might take me down a path that would end in heartbreak.

But whatever the end result, if there was one thing I couldn't ignore, it was the truth.

Chapter Twelve

I returned to the lobby just as Sunny walked through the main doors. She waved and hurried over to me.

"Oh good, I'm not as late as I thought I might be," she said, adjusting the scooped neckline of her turquoise silk dress. "I may have driven just a teensy bit over the speed limit, but it was for a good cause." As she flashed a bright smile, I admired her sleek appearance, from the shimmering dress to her simple but polished makeup and gleaming fall of golden hair.

I handed her the ticket. "Yet you still manage to look perfectly perfect in every way, despite any rushing around."

"You don't look so bad yourself." She set a fast pace, heading for the auditorium doors. "Has Richard seen this dress on you?"

"Not yet. I was saving it for this occasion," I said, trotting after her.

"I'm sure he'll be appropriately impressed," she said, with a wink.

Death and the Librarian

I passed my ticket to the usher, who glanced at it and handed me a program. "It is one of his favorite colors."

"On his favorite person." Sunny tapped my arm with her brochure as we walked down the aisle. "Of course, I think he'll be more interested in removing the dress later . . ."

I side-eyed her. "Please behave. This is a classy event, remember?"

Sunny's laugh turned heads. The gazes of a few of the audience members followed us, some strangers obviously admiring Sunny, and some friends acknowledging us both. I waved hello to Alison, but she was staring so fixedly at her program she didn't see me. Or, if she did, she didn't respond.

Once we took our seats in the auditorium, I tried to clear my mind of all thoughts of murder, sleuthing, and suspects. I wanted to enjoy Richard and Karla's creations without distraction.

Looking around, I couldn't help but appreciate the renovation that had turned an abandoned movie theater into a viable performance space. The stage, which had been expanded from its original size to cover a small orchestra pit, could easily accommodate the demands of live theater and dance performances, especially since the original movie screen had been replaced by a retractable version. Midnight-blue velvet drapes, behind an elaborate pseudo-Roman frieze whose plaster decorations gleamed with touches of gilt, were pulled closed to cover the stage.

The orchestra filed into the pit and began the slow process of tuning their instruments while Sunny and I perused our programs. The list of dances was evenly divided between Richard's and Karla's choreography, although one duet and the final piece were a collaboration.

"Richard's only dancing in the duet, with Karla?" Sunny asked, in a whisper.

"Yes," I said, keeping my voice equally low. "He and Karla wanted the focus to be on the other dancers, that's why most of the works are being performed by members of the company. He'll also be in the finale, though, along with Karla."

Sunny tapped the cast list with one finger. "Connor Vogler—I remember him. I'm guessing he's in his early twenties now?"

I nodded. "You'll probably recognize Tamara Hardy too. She's worked for Richard and Karla on a contract basis before. They're both dancing solos, and from what I saw at a rehearsal several weeks ago, they should be spectacular."

Someone behind us made a hushing noise.

"The dastardly duo, always getting into trouble," Sunny murmured, casting me an amused glance.

I smiled in return, but also pressed a finger to my lips as the lights in the chandeliers twinkling overhead blinked and faded. I placed the program in my lap and settled back against the sapphire velvet upholstery of my seat as the curtains parted to reveal a bare stage.

At the back of the stage, fabric screens lit up with images, creating scenery that didn't interfere with the open expanse of the floor. Sound swelled from the small pit orchestra.

As soon as the first dancers appeared, I gave myself over to the beauty of the human body expressing stories, thoughts,

Death and the Librarian

and emotions through movement alone. The music, some commissioned for the individual pieces, and some familiar melodies, perfectly conveyed the theme or story behind each work. I was particularly impressed with Connor's solo. Connor, now twenty-three, had grown tremendously since I'd first seen him dance as a teenager. His solo, choreographed by Richard and set to the haunting melody of Pietro Mascagni's "Intermezzo from *Cavalleria Rusticana*," was so moving it brought tears to my eyes. It somehow evoked sorrow, longing, and hope in equal measure.

Karla's piece that included the special-needs young dancers from her studio was another standout, but it was Richard and Karla's duet that brought the house down. They were perfection in motion—fully human and yet somehow something more. Set to John Barry's "Somewhere in Time" from the film of the same name, their choreography captured the sense of time passing and the feelings associated with growing older while still suggesting a sense of eternity.

"Aww, they're the perfect couple," whispered a woman seated behind us, and I had to agree. Still, I'd never felt any jealousy over Richard and Karla's closeness, since I knew it was entirely platonic and involved a synchronicity that transcended sex or gender.

After the applause for the duet finally died away, the entire company returned to the stage for a finale that was a celebration of energy and the company's collective talent. At the end of this piece the audience was again on their feet and several bouquets went sailing onto the stage amidst a shower of *bravos* and *bravas*.

Victoria Gilbert

I was choked up, but it wasn't until Richard stepped forward and blew me a kiss that the tears welling in my eyes spilled over and drenched my cheeks. Sunny pulled a wad of tissues from her purse and passed them to me. I pressed them to my face, certain my carefully applied eye makeup had washed away, making me look like a raccoon. But I honestly didn't care. This evening was the culmination of years of planning, fundraising, and rehearsals. It was Richard and Karla's long-desired dream come true.

My only regret was that realizing their dream would probably take Richard away from me and the twins for months at a time. But I also knew I could never stand in his way. I understood the need to accomplish something that mattered; something that could express the artistic vision that burned bright in both Richard's and Karla's hearts.

I nudged Sunny. "I'm going to head to the restroom and try to clean up a bit," I told her. "One upstairs, since those in the lobby will undoubtedly be crowded."

"I'll meet you later, then." Although Sunny's eyes glistened with unshed tears, she'd managed to maintain her flawless appearance. "But I want to talk to a few people in the auditorium first, so wait for me in the lobby, okay?"

I nodded and slipped out of our row to reach the side aisle. Pushing through the exit doors close to the stage, I entered a small vestibule and climbed a staircase that led up to the theater's costume shop and offices. Having been in the building many times, I knew how to access the restrooms on other floors. As expected, the upper floor was quiet and I was the sole occupant of the ladies' room. At the bathroom mirror,

Death and the Librarian

I washed my face, scrubbing away the mascara streaks and other makeup smudges. Looking at my bare skin I shrugged and simply applied a tinted lip gloss.

The dressing rooms were located on the bottom floor of the building, along with rehearsal studios of various sizes. I wanted to see Richard, of course, but knew he, Karla, and the rest of the company would be overwhelmed with well-wishers for some time. So I walked down to the auditorium level and took a side hallway back to the lobby.

I recognized several people in the crowd, including Mindy and, to my surprise, Sean Gordon and Terry. *They must've decided to come since there isn't that much to do in Taylorsford in the evenings. Mindy said they had another rental car, so they could easily have arrived after her,* I thought, acknowledging them with a nod. As my gaze swept over the lobby, I noticed Alison Tucker standing next to the table that held dance company merchandise. I tried to catch her eye, but if she saw me, she once again ignored me.

Sunny walked out of the auditorium, deep in conversation with Kurt. I took a few steps forward, planning to talk to both of them, but at that moment Martin Stover, who was the administrator in charge of all arts programs in our county high schools, approached me.

"Amy, so glad to see you. Please tell Richard and Karla the performance was spectacular. I'm afraid I'm not about to fight the crowds near the dressing rooms, so I don't think I'll get a chance to talk to them in person." Marty was about Richard's height but thinner. He had a wiry build and a narrow face overshadowed by his full head of curly gray hair.

I clasped his outstretched hand. "I'll be sure to let them know."

"Good. Having the Tansen-Muir Company based in the area is going to be a boon for all the arts."

I knew from Zelda that Marty, who was in his mid-sixties, was expected to retire soon, which was a shame. He'd been a great promoter of the arts in schools and had also spearheaded the effort to renovate this building. "We have you to thank for this perfect venue," I said. "There really wouldn't have been anywhere appropriate for Richard and Karla to form the company without it."

Marty swept one arm through the air, encompassing the beauty of the lobby. "It was my dream to create a place like this. I'm just happy your husband's company can take advantage of it." His hazel eyes narrowed behind the lenses of his tortoiseshell glasses. "I'm sorry to hear there was another unfortunate event in Taylorsford recently. Are the authorities calling it a murder?"

"I'm afraid so, but of course Sheriff Tucker and his team are on top of things. I'm sure they'll find the culprit soon." I tucked a loose strand of hair behind my ear.

"Are you assisting with the investigation?" Marty, who was well aware of my former association with the sheriff's department, eyed me with curiosity.

"I'm just doing a little research to help out. Background stuff, you know," I said.

Someone in the milling crowd jostled me, their hand connecting with my hip with enough force that I stumbled forward.

Death and the Librarian

Marty reached out and gripped my shoulder to steady me. "Goodness. You'd think people would watch where they're going. Or at least excuse themselves." He glanced around the crowd. "I didn't see who it was, or I'd give them a piece of my mind."

"It's alright." I straightened, shaking off his hand. "No harm done."

"Well, still." Marty looked me over with a critical eye. "You sure you're okay? Your face has gone quite white."

I almost said something about having to scrub off all my makeup, but before I could get the words out, Marty was pulled aside by Nancy Nieman, who started bombarding him with questions about a book festival she and the other members of the Friends of the Library had discussed at their last meeting. I slipped away from them, looking for Sunny and Kurt.

I found Sunny, but Kurt had already disappeared. "Thanks again for coming," I told Sunny after giving her a hug. "I needed the moral support. I think I might have been as anxious as Richard and Karla and the other dancers."

Sunny tossed her silky hair over her shoulders. "Of course, and you should know I wouldn't miss this performance for the world. I just wish Fred could've been here, but he's still overseas with Hugh. Somewhere in Switzerland now, I think."

"A tough job, but someone has to do it." I rolled my eyes.

"Yeah. He gets to gallivant all over the world while I stay here," Sunny said with a wry smile. "But seriously, it is a tough job," she added, her expression sobering.

129

"I know. Neither he nor Hugh is on vacation." I glanced around. "Did Kurt leave already?"

"Yeah, it seemed like he had to dash." Sunny slid her arm through the crook of my elbow. "Shall we head downstairs and offer our congratulations to the company? I've seen a bunch of people exiting the stairwell that leads down to the dressing rooms, so I think some of the well-wishers have departed by now."

"Sounds like a plan," I said.

As we crossed the lobby, Sunny looked down at our linked arms and frowned. "What's that?"

"What do you mean?" I paused in midstride.

"There's something sticking out of your pocket," Sunny replied, pulling her arm free and pointing toward the skirt of my dress.

"Probably a tissue or something," I said.

"No, it looks like a folded piece of copy paper." Sunny leaned over and tugged the paper from my pocket. "Did you bring this with you?"

"No." I took the paper from her slender fingers and unfolded it. Computer-printed words spelled out a simple message:

Stop investigating or harm may come to your friends and family.

The piece of paper slipped from my fingers and fluttered to the ground. As Sunny knelt down to retrieve it, I wiped the shocked expression from my face. "Someone bumped into me earlier," I said in a hollow voice. "They must've shoved that in my pocket without me realizing."

Death and the Librarian

Sunny's eyes widened as she read the short message. "A warning, then," she said, in a low voice.

"I suppose so." I surveyed the lobby, which was quickly emptying. "I don't know who it's from. There was a crowd here at that point, and my back was to whoever it was."

Folding the note, Sunny handed it to me. "Put this away somewhere safe and contact Brad."

I tucked the paper in my purse. "Okay, but I don't want Richard to know just yet, so let's keep it on the down-low."

"Sure. As long as you promise to alert Brad later." Sunny looked me over. "But I suspect Richard will know something is wrong, just by how jittery you look."

Taking a deep breath, I leaned against one of the marble columns flanking the door that led to the stairs. "You go on ahead to congratulate Richard and Karla and the others. I'm going to try to compose myself."

Sunny nodded. She gave me a pat on the shoulder before heading downstairs.

I fished my phone out of my purse and called my mother's cell phone. "Hi, the performance finished a little while ago. Everything went great," I said, cursing the slight quaver in my voice. "I thought I'd check in before we drive home, to make sure the twins went to bed properly and there weren't any other problems."

"Everything's fine here." My mom's voice was edged with suspicion. "Why would you think otherwise?"

"Oh, no reason," I replied, as relief washed over me. "Thanks. We'll be home soon and then you can head back over to Aunt Lydia's and get some sleep yourselves."

Victoria Gilbert

"No rush. We aren't that old, you know," Mom said. "We can stay up past eleven."

"Sure, sure. I know that." I offered her a hasty goodbye and concluded the call.

After a few more deep breaths, I tossed my phone into my purse and headed downstairs. There were still several people loitering in the basement hallway, but most of them were dancers in the company. I congratulated each of them as I hurried past. At the end of the hallway, I found the dressing room marked with Richard's name and knocked on the door.

"It's Amy," I called out, before walking inside.

Sunny, perched on the edge of the makeup table, eyed me with concern while Richard, wearing gray sweatpants and a white T-shirt, draped the towel he was using to dry his hair around his shoulders and held out his arms.

I ran into his embrace. "It was fabulous, you were fantastic, everyone was amazing," I said before Richard leaned in and silenced me with a lingering kiss.

"Couldn't have done it without your love and support," he said as he stepped back, sliding his palms down my arms to clasp my hands.

"All the dancers did a superb job, but of course your duet with Karla was a standout," I said, entwining my fingers with his.

Sunny pressed her palms together. "It really was."

"Thanks," said a familiar voice.

I released my grip on Richard's hands and turned around. "You're quite welcome." I crossed the small room to face Karla Tansen. "And of course your choreographed pieces were"—I touched my lips and then threw out my hand—"chef's kiss."

Death and the Librarian

Karla, who was tall and toned and could serve as a model for a statue of a Greek goddess, engulfed me in a hug. "Thanks again," she said as she stepped back. "But I still think Richard's choreography has an edge over mine."

"Nonsense." Richard tossed the towel over the makeup table mirror.

Sunny jumped down off the table. "Everything was wonderful, although I did love your duet with Richard the most. Anyway, I'm going to head out and let the three of you chat. Call me," she said, casting me a significant look as she walked into the hall.

Karla strolled over to Richard and thrust out her hand. "Good job, partner."

"Oh, come on," Richard said, before pulling her in for a hug.

"I hope you thanked Amy for her support properly too," Karla said, as she extracted herself from his embrace.

"Before you got here," Richard said. "But that was just the first act, of course."

"You have more planned?" I asked, arching my brows.

Richard grinned. "Much more. But maybe we should discuss that in the car."

"Yes, please save that for when you two are alone," Karla said, her eyes crinkling with amusement. "Honestly, you've been married for how long now?"

"I have to think about that for a second." I slid my arm around Richard's waist.

He put his arm around my shoulders and pulled me closer. "Not long enough."

Chapter Thirteen

By the time we got home and shared a celebratory glass of champagne with my parents, I'd almost forgotten about the note. Almost. It began to fill my thoughts again as soon as my parents left for Aunt Lydia's house.

Upstairs, I peeked in on Ella and Nicky, who were both sleeping peacefully, then headed into the master bedroom. Richard was already in the bathroom brushing his teeth as I slipped into our walk-in closet to change my clothes.

I debated whether I should share the threatening note with Richard tonight or wait until morning. It seemed a shame to ruin his triumphant evening, but I knew he'd be equally upset by me withholding such information. Besides, I had a plan I wanted to discuss with him before I broached it to my parents.

Richard was already in bed by the time I completed my nightly rituals. I padded over to the dresser, where I'd dropped my purse, and pulled out the note.

"What's that?" he asked, adjusting his pillow so he could sit up comfortably.

Death and the Librarian

"It's a note someone slipped into my pocket this evening," I said, throwing back the coverlet and sheet so I could crawl into the bed next to him. "After the performance, I waited in the lobby to allow most of your fan club to clear out of the dressing room area. I was actually talking to Marty Stover when someone bumped into me. I felt their hand on my hip, but didn't think much of it. But then Sunny noticed that a folded piece of paper had apparently been shoved into my pocket."

Richard took the note from my hand and opened it. His face paled as he read the short message. "It's a threat," he said, his eyes turning glassy as he looked at me.

"Yes, I suppose it is," I said, biting my lower lip.

"Suppose? There's no suppose about it." Richard dropped the note onto our chenille bedspread as if it was on fire. "Do you have any idea who might have given you this?"

I shook my head. "There was too much of a crowd milling about at the time. Marty didn't see who jostled me, either, so I have no idea."

"Well, we do have one clue—it was someone who attended the performance."

"That doesn't narrow it down much." I picked up the paper and laid it on my nightstand.

Richard gripped my upper arm. "Have you spoken to Brad about this?"

"Not yet. I'll drop the note off at his office tomorrow." I pressed my left hand over his fingers. "The thing is, I was wondering if maybe we should ask my mom and dad for a favor."

Searching my face, Richard's puzzled look quickly morphed into understanding. "You want them to take Ella and Nicky home for a visit?"

"Just for a week or so." I lifted my hand and sat back against my own pillow. "I wanted to mention the idea to you before I talked to my parents, but I feel it would be for the best. If they're several hours away, they shouldn't be in danger, especially if whoever wrote this warning doesn't know where they've gone."

"It's a good plan." Richard sighed and released his grip on my arm. "I thought we were done with this sort of thing."

"So did I, but when Brad asked me to do a little research to help his investigation, I felt I should agree. I had no idea that simply collecting information from the archives could lead to threats. Which makes me think"—I pressed a finger to my lips for a second—"there really could be a connection between the Eddie Jaffe cold case and Maureen Dryden's murder."

"There you go again," Richard said, exasperation sharpening his tone. "Even with a warning you refuse to give up your amateur sleuthing." He slid under the covers, pulling the pillow down with him, and rolled over.

I tapped his shoulder. "So you're going to turn your back on me?"

"Are you going to tell Brad you can't help with this investigation anymore?" Richard muttered.

"No. I'm already in too deep." I rolled over so we were back to back. This wasn't the way I'd envisioned this evening ending, but I couldn't really blame Richard for being upset. He always worried about me when I was involved in an

Death and the Librarian

investigation, and now my participation was inspiring threats against our children. "But that's why I want the twins to go home with Mom and Dad. It makes perfect sense for them to visit before school starts, and since my parents have a pool, Ella and Nicky can practice what they learned in swimming lessons this summer."

"I said I agree with that. But that doesn't solve the whole problem." Richard's voice was muffled by his pillow. "You could still be in danger, as well as Lydia and some of our friends."

"And you." I rolled back over and hugged his tensed shoulders. "The thing is, this case may involve family and friends anyway. Maureen Dryden's mention of both Kurt and Delbert made them suspects, not just in the Jaffe disappearance, but also . . ."

Richard turned, breaking free of my embrace to face me. "You think Kurt or Delbert Frye could've murdered Maureen Dryden?"

"There is a slim possibility. Although in Delbert's case, it was more likely a family member, determined to protect him."

"You don't mean Alison?" Richard propped himself up on one elbow and stared at me in bewilderment.

"She was at the lecture, and Sunny saw her at the hotel the night Maureen was killed. I also noticed her at the theater tonight." I flopped onto my back and stared up at the ceiling. "And two other people who were at the inn when Maureen died apparently saw Alison actively avoiding law enforcement and sneaking away by the back road. I know it seems impossible, but Alison isn't a civilian who's never dealt with danger or encountered murder scenes—she's a trained law enforcement officer. She's also extremely protective of her family and has always been close to Delbert."

"Sometimes I worry about that mind of yours, Amy," Richard said, tapping the top of my head with his fingers. "You'll be suspecting me next."

"Of course not. You were in rehearsals Sunday evening," I said, turning off the light on my nightstand. "So you have an alibi."

"Alibi, my foot." Richard dropped down on his back and gazed up at the ceiling as well. "I suppose if I didn't have one, you'd put me on your suspect list?"

I turned to snuggle up against him. "No, I wouldn't." When Richard expelled a gusty sigh, I added, "You also don't have a motive."

"Now you're just teasing me," he said but didn't pull away.

"I'm trying to lighten the atmosphere." I turned my head to look at him, a little smile tugging at my lips. "Is it working?"

"Maybe. We'll have to see," he said, before taking me in his arms.

I kissed him first. "How about this?"

"That works," he said. "But I think there's room for improvement."

"Only if you help."

Even in the dim light, I could make out his grin. "Happy to oblige."

* * *

Richard and I and the twins joined my parents and Aunt Lydia for breakfast Saturday morning. In between bites of

Death and the Librarian

Aunt Lydia's delicious pancakes, I floated the suggestion that Ella and Nicky leave with my parents Sunday afternoon.

"What a great idea," Dad said. "We should've thought of that ourselves."

Mom nodded. "No better time. We're already here, and it's just a few weeks until school starts. A longer visit would be wonderful. What do you think, kids?"

Ella and Nicky enthusiastically agreed to this plan. "We can practice swimming," Ella said. "I can already swim across a pool."

"I know, your mom sent us the video," my dad said. "And as long as the weather is good, your grandma or I can help you improve every day."

"The teacher said my back float was the best already," Nicky said. "We learned how to tread water too."

"Excellent." My mom, who'd always loved anything to do with the water, smiled brightly. "You'll be learning all the strokes before you know it."

Richard nudged my foot under the table. "The idea just occurred to us last night. Amy thought a weeklong visit would be fun for you as well as Ella and Nicky."

"Of course." Mom cast an inquiring glance at Aunt Lydia. "You don't mind, do you, Lydia? I'm sure you'll miss these imps since you see them almost every day."

Aunt Lydia dabbed her lips with her napkin. "Which is why I approve. I do get to spend a lot more time with them than you do, so why not take advantage of the opportunity? Anyway, I need to give my house a good deep clean and keep up with the garden, so I'll be busy."

I looked around the dining room. My aunt's house always appeared spotless to me, but maybe that was simply in comparison to my own rather messy abode.

Relieved that Nicky and Ella would be safely out of town for at least for a week, I was able to relax the rest of the morning. Even the demands of getting the twins ready to attend the dance company's matinee performance didn't dampen my spirits.

"I want to wear my ballerina dress," Ella insisted. The full-skirted white dress, with its built-in layers of petticoats, had been a gift from Richard's mother, Fiona Muir.

"Okay, but you'll need to carry a sweater. It's often cold in the theater." I brushed Ella's thick dark brown hair back into a ponytail.

"Can I just wear this?" Nicky asked, holding up a pair of sweatpants.

I shook my head. "Not to the theater. Wear those khaki pants with the elastic waist instead, and your green polo shirt."

"Okay," he said, scuffing his shoe against the hardwood floor. "I guess it's like church."

"Absolutely. You have to dress up a little for Daddy's show. It'll let him know it really matters to you." I tied up Ella's hair with a white scrunchie.

"'Cause it's an important thing, right?" Ella piped up.

"Definitely. Now, let's finish getting you dressed so you're ready when Grandma and Grandad come by to pick you up."

"Then we have to pack later," Nicky said.

Death and the Librarian

"Yes, we'll do that, even though you won't be leaving until tomorrow afternoon." I pulled Ella's dress off its hanger and handed it to her. "Run along and change in your room, Nicky."

A half hour later, the twins headed off to the performance with Mom, Dad, and Aunt Lydia, and I was left alone in the house. Due to the matinee and evening performances of the dance company, Richard would be gone most of the day. As I sat on the sofa, with Loie in my lap and Fosse curled up beside me, I considered my next move.

I should stay home and take advantage of this golden opportunity to rest. But despite Richard's disapproval and the warning I'd received, I was still thinking about the current investigation.

After all, I need to drop off the note at the sheriff's department and talk to Brad, if he's available, I told myself. *So why not take a little detour after that and visit someone who might have more information, at least on the Jaffe case?*

I gently removed Loie from my lap. She expressed her dissatisfaction with this turn of events, but soon settled down next to Fosse. Slipping on a pair of sandals, I grabbed my purse and my keys from the side table and headed outside. Fortunately, with my parents driving the twins and my aunt to the matinee performance in their vehicle, I could use the car I shared with Aunt Lydia.

At the sheriff's department, I was informed that Brad was out in the field. I jotted down a message for him and left it and the warning note with the deputy at the front desk.

Driving up into the mountains to reach Delbert Frye's isolated cabin, I admired the majestic trees and thick foliage lining both sides of the gravel road, while cursing the bone-jarring potholes. I was happy that there was no traffic on the narrow road, which wasn't surprising since there were very few houses this far up the mountain. But I knew I still had to be alert to oncoming cars. Right beyond Delbert's cabin, the road ended at a small parking area for hikers who wanted to take on the nearby trails.

I cast a glance at the ski-chalet style home I passed before turning into Delbert's driveway and couldn't help but notice its overgrown yard and the broken railings on the front porch. *Abandoned*, I thought, with a sigh. It had been a beautiful home at one time.

The chinking on Delbert's hand-hewn log cabin was tinted green by moss. Since it was summer, no smoke spiraled up from the ivy-draped fieldstone chimney, and each end of the steps leading up to the front porch held flowerpots full of orange and yellow marigolds. *I bet that's Alison's work*, I thought, as I crossed the front porch and rapped on the weathered wooden front door.

A quavery voice sailed through the door. "Who's there?"

"Amy Muir," I replied loudly, knowing Delbert wouldn't welcome a stranger.

"Oh, Amy. Okay, just a minute." A bolt slid back and the door swung open.

Delbert Frye was a short, wiry man who'd turned ninety just a few months earlier. The few russet streaks in his bushy gray beard bore witness to its original color, while only a few

Death and the Librarian

sprigs of white hair fringed his bald head. That, and the loose white shirt he wore over a pair of faded jeans, lent him the appearance of a medieval monk. He was slightly hunched over, but still appeared physically sound, and the light in his eyes had never dimmed over the years I'd known him.

As I stepped into the cabin, I felt, as always, that I was walking back in time. Limited light spilled through the small windows set into the exposed log walls, so the corners of the main room were sunk in shadow. The only additional light came from standing lamps that cast amber ovals over the worn plank floor.

I followed Delbert over to the stone fireplace and sat down on a pine settle draped in a woven wool blanket. I knew most of the furniture that filled Delbert's home was handmade, either by him or by Walt Adams, who claimed woodworking was his hobby but who created professional-looking pieces.

I glanced up at the shelf that ran along the top of all four walls. It was set far enough below the timbered ceiling to accommodate stringed instruments of all shapes and sizes. There were fiddles and banjoes and, of course, a wide variety of dulcimers.

Delbert sat down in an old armchair covered in a thin quilt. "What brings you here today?" he asked, adjusting the quilt to cover a bare patch on the chair arm. "Alison's been checking in on me every other day, even though I've said there's no need."

"I suppose she told you about your name being mentioned in the lecture Ms. Dryden gave last Saturday," I said.

Delbert clasped his callused hands in his lap. "She did indeed, and she was hopping mad over it too. I told her it was nothing to worry herself over, but that didn't calm her down much."

I filed away this information in my mind. If Alison was that angry around her great-uncle, how furious would she have been when she ran into Maureen Dryden?

"Too bad that writer got herself killed," Delbert said, settling back in his chair. "If I'd had a chance to talk with her, I could've cleared up all the confusion."

"You were in the woods the evening Eddie Jaffe disappeared, weren't you?"

Delbert fixed me with an unwavering stare. "Who told you that?"

"It was part of the sheriff's department report, and I also heard it from Sheryl Abernathy."

"Who?" Delbert's bushy eyebrows came together over his nose.

"She was one of the people at a gathering in a clearing in the woods that evening. Up the mountain trail off the park near my house."

"Well now, I remember I ran into some skinny, curly-haired gal, wearing a tank top and tiny little shorts in the mountains. Just flip-flops too. Foolishness." Delbert snorted. "She seemed like she wasn't feeling any pain, though. Under the influence of drugs or drink or something, I reckon."

"That was Sheryl. I talked to her recently, at a nursing home in Smithsburg. She's gray now, but had dark hair at the time you would've run into her."

"Yeah, yeah, I remember. We didn't exchange names. I guess I startled her when I walked out of the woods as she

Death and the Librarian

was stumbling down the trail. She hollered and ran past me." Delbert shrugged. "Not like I was going to follow her. I was just crossing to the other side of the trail. Looking for fallen branches and such, so I needed to tromp through the woods."

"You didn't see anyone else?" I asked, wrapping one edge of the blanket around my hand.

"Nope. Heard some noise, like folks was partying. That happened too much back then. I chased off a few of them, but that night I couldn't be bothered." Delbert frowned. "I went back a few days later, though, to check out the clearing where I'd heard drug activity often happened. Took a sack to collect up any trash, and I was sure glad I did, because those fools had left beer cans and liquor bottles and cigarette butts all over the clearing."

"Did you give that trash to the sheriff's department?" I asked.

Delbert shot me a puzzled look. "No, why ever would I do that?"

"Well, it might've been evidence in the Eddie Jaffe case. The authorities could've gotten DNA off the cigarettes or bottles . . ." I shook my head. "Not back then, I guess."

"Nope, they didn't have all those tests yet. I suppose they could retest stuff now, but at the time I just figured I should throw out the trash," Delbert said with a grimace. "Wish I could've found out what human trash was up in that clearing that night, but I never saw anyone other than that girl."

"So you didn't see another young woman?" I asked. "Sheryl mentioned something about another girl."

145

Victoria Gilbert

"Saw no one else." Delbert slid forward in his chair and gripped his knees with his hands. "I don't know why that Dryden woman thought I had anything to do with Eddie Jaffe's disappearance. I confess I didn't mind seeing the back of him, but I wasn't involved in him vanishing or whatever."

"I believe you," I said, meaning every word. It was clear to me that Delbert had nothing to do with Eddie's disappearance. I didn't think he could sit across from me and lie that convincingly. Besides, it seemed he had no motive to harm Eddie.

Although, you've been fooled before, murmured the devil on my shoulder.

I rose to my feet. "I won't bother you any further. I just wanted to see how you were doing and also get your side of the story." I lifted my hands. "I'm helping the sheriff's department track down information, you see."

"Thank you for your concern, Amy," Delbert said, standing up to face me. "But there's really nothing to worry about. I'm fine, and as long as the truth is exposed, I'm not concerned about any investigations."

"That's good," I said, thinking, *I only hope your grand-niece feels the same way.*

Chapter Fourteen

When I got home, I was surprised that my parents' sedan wasn't in the driveway, then remembered that there was an ice cream shop across the street from the theater. Sure enough, when I checked my texts, my mom had sent a message to let me know they'd be later than expected because they were going to "visit a few shops in Smithsburg."

I decided to take the opportunity to hike up to the clearing that figured so prominently in Eddie Jaffe's story. Texting my mom back, I let her know that I was out running errands and they should simply hang out at Aunt Lydia's house if they returned before I did.

Not wanting to be attacked by ticks or brambles, I changed into long pants, socks, and sneakers along with a loose, long-sleeved gauze blouse.

I had to walk a block past the main section of the park, then cut across the playground to reach the head of the mountain trail. *It's certainly close to Aunt Lydia's house,* I thought. *I wonder if she or my mom ever joined any parties at the clearing when they were older teens?*

A couple of cars were parked in the small lot just off the end of our road. *Hikers*, I thought, not seeing anyone on the playground as I strolled over to the trail. I stared at it with some trepidation, hoping my old sneakers were sturdy enough to make the climb. The trail was beaten down to the dirt and narrow. Tree branches arched overhead, filtering the sunlight, and shrubs and wild grasses encroached upon parts of the trail until there was only space for one person to walk. As I climbed higher into the mountain, the path was studded with embedded rocks and roots. I had to watch my feet so I wouldn't stumble.

By the time I reached the clearing, my blouse was damp with sweat. I plucked it away from my skin and flapped the fabric to cool off. Looking around, I noticed that the ground of the clearing was beaten smooth like the trail. This was obviously a spot that had been well used over the years.

I could see why it would be a good choice for a clandestine gathering. Trees and undergrowth screened the site from view from everywhere but the narrow end of the trail. Several large stones and fallen tree limbs ringed the center of the circle, creating natural seating. I walked the perimeter of the clearing, stopping when I reached a section that bordered a cliff. It hadn't been apparent from the trail, but there was a sudden drop along the far side of the clearing. I cautiously stepped closer and peered over the edge.

"Oh, hello," said the young man climbing up the sharp-edged rocks below.

I jumped back. "What are you doing?"

Death and the Librarian

"Examining the last place Eddie Jaffe was seen, just like you, I suspect," Sean Gordon said. "Hold on—I'll join you up there in a minute."

I waited to speak until he clambered up and hoisted himself onto one of the stones rimming the clearing. "But why were you climbing around in that deep gully? It looks dangerous."

"It is." Sean brushed back the hair that had fallen into his eyes. "But I'm an experienced rock climber, so I knew I could handle it."

"What did you find down there?" I asked.

"Nothing," he said ruefully. "Well, more rocks and stones, but nothing of importance."

I examined his flushed face. "What did you hope to find? Bones or some other proof that Eddie Jaffe was killed here?"

Sean's hazel eyes narrowed. "I see we had the same thought." He strolled over to a boulder and sat down on the ledge that had been naturally carved out of the granite.

Crossing to join him, I took a seat on a nearby tree stump. "I hadn't really thought of that, until I saw the drop over there. Someone could easily be shoved off and fall to their death against that sharp jumble of rocks."

Sean pulled his hair back and held it with one hand to allow the breeze to cool his neck. "Absolutely, but I didn't find anything that would confirm such a theory."

"I would've thought you'd have left Taylorsford by now," I said. "I know you have to remain available for further questioning about Maureen Dryden's death, but the authorities surely wouldn't hold you here. They'd just want to know where you'd gone."

"That's true." Sean dropped his hair back down against his shoulders and wiped his hands against his well-worn jeans. "They said we could go, as long as we'd come back, or at least answer their calls, if necessary. But Terry and Mindy are still here, along with me, although for different reasons."

I pulled a tissue from my pocket and blotted my forehead and upper lip. "Let me guess—the other two are staying to collect sound bites and other information so they can do a podcast about Maureen's murder?"

"Exactly." As Sean stretched out his legs, his hiking boots plowed lines through the dirt. "They're turning the situation to their advantage."

"So why are you here?" I cast him a questioning look.

"Taking advantage in another way, I suppose." Sean rested his broad hands on his thighs. "I am, or rather was, Maureen's research assistant, so I know the details of almost everything she was working on. It occurred to me that perhaps I could complete the book. I would give her coauthor credit, of course," he added, after a brief pause.

"I see. So you're checking out this spot as research for the Eddie Jaffe portion of the book."

"Yeah. I wanted to be able to accurately describe the scene." Sean turned to look directly at me. "Do you think that's wrong, what with Maureen barely cold?"

"Not really. I mean, some people might think that, but I can see why you'd want to continue your research, and also why you hope to eventually publish the book." I shoved the

Death and the Librarian

damp tissue into my pocket. "It will honor her memory, right?"

Sean looked down at his hands. "Something like that."

"You should speak with Sheryl Abernathy before you leave. She was with Eddie the evening he disappeared. She's in a nursing home in Smithsburg, so it wouldn't be difficult for you to see her. Although"—I brushed some dust from my pants—"she isn't totally coherent and her memory seems to be failing. But maybe you can get more out of her than I did. I suspect she'd respond more positively to an attractive young man than to me."

Flushing slightly, Sean straightened and stared out over the clearing.

"What do you think happened?" I asked, studying his finely honed profile. "To Maureen, I mean, not Eddie Jaffe. Did she have enemies?"

"Yes, quite a few. That's what happens when you accuse people of murder or other crimes." Sean's unreadable expression made me wonder if he was considering possible assailants in his head.

"Like who, for instance? I know some people have the idea that the people Maureen mentioned during her lecture could be involved," I said.

"Delbert Frye and Karl Klass." Sean's expression turned thoughtful. "I've located Mr. Frye, but so far, he's refused all requests for an interview. The other man seems to have vanished as thoroughly as Eddie Jaffe."

I shifted on the hard surface of the tree trunk. "The thing is, if Maureen had other enemies, her killer wouldn't necessarily have had anything to do with Eddie Jaffe."

151

"I know." Sean expelled a deep sigh. "They had to be clever as well as careful, though. It seems they spiked her drink and then, when she'd fallen unconscious in her room, smothered her. That would take a pretty cool customer."

Recalling the conversation I'd overheard in the restaurant at the inn, I decided to take a gamble. "What about Terry Temkin? Did he and Maureen get along?"

Sean fixed me with a steady stare. "You seem to know they didn't."

"I sensed something, that's all," I said, breaking the lock of his gaze.

"Then you're very perceptive. From what I've heard, they never had any problems until Terry accused Maureen of stealing his research on another case she planned to include in her book." Sean rolled his shoulders. "Well, it wasn't exactly stealing—it's just that Maureen had promised Terry compensation and credit for contributing to the book, but it seemed she wasn't going to fulfil her promise."

"I can see why he'd be upset over that," I said.

"It really isn't clear to me how angry he was. Angry enough to kill?" Sean shrugged. "Who can tell? I didn't have a dog in that fight, so I didn't give it much thought."

"The thing is, I spoke with Mindy yesterday evening, before the Tansen-Muir dance company show," I said.

"Which was great," Sean said, flashing a brief smile. "I really enjoyed it."

"Thanks, I'll let my husband know," I said. "Anyway, I'm sure it was more entertaining than sitting around the Taylorsford Inn. But what I was going to say was that Mindy shared

Death and the Librarian

some interesting information with me. I'm not sure if you were aware of this or not, but Terry and Mindy have been approached by a producer about the case you mentioned. They're hoping for a television docu-series or something. I guess that would make getting the rights to the case back more important." I decided not to mention Mindy's comments about Alison. There wasn't any point in throwing more suspicion her way, especially when I didn't know if Mindy was being truthful or not.

Sean's eyes widened. "The Campton case? It certainly would." He sat back against the smooth granite of the boulder. "Makes one wonder, doesn't it?"

"You mean, whether Terry or Mindy could be involved in Maureen's death?"

"Hmm." Sean stood up and began pacing around the clearing. "It could certainly be a motive. I know Maureen didn't want to budge on her decision, despite Terry's pleas, but with her out of the picture . . ."

"Terry would be able to reclaim his story on the Campton murders," I said, finishing his thought. "So Maureen's death could benefit both Terry and Mindy."

"Which means they could've been in on it together." Sean paused to turn and look at me, his hazel eyes sparkling.

"Maybe." I glanced at my watch and jumped to my feet. "Oh dear, I'd better head back down the trail. My parents and aunt took my twins to see the dance performance this afternoon, but even with stopping by some shops, they should be home by now."

"I'll accompany you. I think I've done all I can do here," Sean said.

153

Victoria Gilbert

We set off down the trail, Sean walking behind me since so many sections only accommodated single-file hiking.

"So, where do you come from, Sean? Your accent is hard to place, but I think maybe the Midwest?" I called back to him after a few minutes of silence.

"That's right. Indiana, to be precise. My father was a professor at Indiana University in Bloomington."

"Ah, did you decide to become a researcher to follow in his footsteps?" I asked, batting aside a curving limb of bramble.

"Not exactly. He was in the sciences. I preferred the humanities."

"I see. How did you hook up with Maureen? Were you a fan of her work?"

"Actually, I wasn't. I'd just finished my master's in history which, as they say, could be combined with a dime to get a cup of coffee."

"These days, coffee requires a decent amount beyond the dime," I said.

Sean laughed. "True enough. But it's still not enough to live on. So I decided to use my research skills in a different way. I was looking for Maureen, I mean, someone like Maureen. A writer who needed an assistant. Fortunately, I found her."

"You two got along?" I asked, keeping my tone light.

"We did, professionally. We weren't close, but then, I didn't want a relationship with my boss. I had other things in mind." Sean cleared his throat. "Once I'd proven myself working for Maureen, I hoped to get into a doctorate program. On a free

Death and the Librarian

ride, since I couldn't afford it any other way. That's why I wanted the experience working with an author, you see."

"Makes sense." We had reached the end of the trail. I turned to Sean with a smile. "My house is just over there. Did you walk? I can give you a ride to the inn if you want."

Sean shook his head. "I'll just walk back. It's not that far. I'm sure you want to meet up with your family as soon as possible."

Squinting, I spied my parents' car in Aunt Lydia's driveway. "Yeah, they're back. And it's my parents and aunt who will want to see *me*, after taking care of a pair of hyped-up twins this afternoon."

"Ah, twins."

There was a wistful note in Sean's voice that made me cast him an inquiring glance. "Twice the fun," I said, with a smile.

"Right. Well, I'm going to walk on ahead, if you don't mind. Thanks for sharing your thoughts with me today, Amy. It was very helpful." Sean took two long strides until he was ahead of me.

"You're welcome," I said to his back. "Have a good evening."

He waved his hand over his head in a silent goodbye before striding off down the sidewalk.

155

Chapter Fifteen

On Sunday, Aunt Lydia hosted a midday dinner at her house before my parents and the twins left. There were some tears amid the hugs and kisses as we told Ella and Nicky goodbye, but I knew I'd made the right choice. Whatever the validity of the warning I'd received, I felt relieved knowing the children would be out of town until, hopefully, the problem was resolved.

Entering our house, both Richard and I paused in the living room.

"It's too quiet," he said.

"I know. Sometimes you think that's what you want, but . . ." Tears welled up in my eyes again.

Richard slung his arm around my shoulders. "We've been separated from the twins before, when we took the trip to England and Scotland earlier this summer."

"Yeah." I sniffled. "But then we were the ones away from home, and Ella and Nicky had Mom, Aunt Lydia, and your mother taking turns to watch over them here. This feels different."

156

Death and the Librarian

"It does, but you and I know it's for the best." Richard hugged me to his side. "Sorry I have to leave you today. Maybe try to enjoy some time alone. You never get a chance to read as much as you'd like, so take the opportunity."

"Sure, sure." I wiped my eyes with the back of my hand. "Don't worry about me. You still have the final performance tonight and I don't want you anxious before that."

"It'll be fine. I'm looking forward to dancing off some of my stress." Richard dropped his arm from my shoulders and turned to look at me. "One thing I meant to ask—have you spoken with Lydia about that threatening note yet? She is part of the family."

"I talked to her while we were alone in the kitchen, doing the dishes. She wasn't terribly concerned. She said she doesn't think it's serious—just a way to get me to back off my research into the Jaffe case," I said, using one finger to remove any remaining moisture from my lashes. "To be honest, she thinks Kurt slipped me that note. It's possible, since he was at the performance and is strong enough to practically knock me off my feet. He probably knows how to surreptitiously slip a note in a pocket too."

Richard took a step back and examined me with wide eyes. "Kurt? Sure, maybe he had some involvement in Jaffe leaving town or whatever, but he'd never threaten us or the twins. You can't possibly believe he'd do something like that."

"If it was just to get me to stop looking into Eddie's disappearance, as Aunt Lydia suggested, I can." I lifted my chin and met Richard's gaze squarely. "I don't believe he'd actually hurt us or the twins, but he might use such a tactic as a bluff."

Richard lowered his thick black lashes, shadowing his eyes. "I'd hate to think so, but I suppose it's within the realm of possibility. Anyway, you warned Lydia, so she knows to stay on her toes. What about Ethan?"

"He's out of town. Mom said he'd called to tell her and Dad that Scott was flying back from his assignment and Ethan was going to meet him at the Baltimore airport. Then they're going to take a short vacation in New England. So they're both removed from any threatened danger, at least for now."

"Good." Richard moved closer and kissed me on the temple. "I need to pack my dance bag and leave for the theater shortly, but I'll be back tonight, and then next week it's just the company's normal training and rehearsals. We don't have to leave for our regional tour until next month, so I'll be able to be at home a lot more over the next few weeks."

"That's definitely a positive." I looked up at him. "Just remember you need to stay alert as well. Hopefully, that note is just a ploy, but my family includes you as much as anyone."

"I know, and I promise to stay on my . . . well, you know." Richard rose up on the balls of his feet, holding the position without wavering before dropping his heels back down.

"Very funny," I said, unable to suppress a smile. "You'd better go get ready."

Richard made it halfway up the stairs before pausing to lean over the railing. "One more thing—have you talked to Brad about all this yet?"

Death and the Librarian

"It's fine. He has the note and he also texted me this morning and said he might stop by later this afternoon," I replied. "Stop worrying."

"Like that will happen," Richard said before heading up the stairs.

* * *

After Richard left for the theater, I grabbed one of the books from my towering "to be read" pile and settled on the sofa with the book, a glass of wine, and Loie and Fosse.

"You think it's weird too, don't you?" I asked the cats, who kept gazing around the room as if looking for the rest of their family. "I realize you both like to know where everyone is at all times. Sorry, the twins won't be here for a little while, but they're safe and sound. They're safe," I repeated, more to reassure myself than the cats.

I was deeply involved in reading when the doorbell chimed.

As usual, the cats jumped off the sofa and scattered—Fosse flew up the stairs and Loie headed for the kitchen and the pet door that opened onto the screened back porch. I laid aside my book and walked over to the front door. Peeking through the peephole, I saw it was Brad and opened the door.

"Come in," I said, offering him a welcoming smile. "Glad you could fit this visit into your busy schedule."

"No problem." Brad was wearing a polo shirt and faded jeans.

"No uniform? Is this your day off?" I asked as I closed the door behind us.

Victoria Gilbert

"I really don't have days off," Brad said with a wry smile. "They show up on the department's calendar, but that's usually just wishful thinking."

"I'm sorry. This could've waited until tomorrow." I trailed him over to the living room space.

"No, I don't think so." Brad sat in the overstuffed armchair that sat catty-corner to the sofa.

I paused. "Would you like anything to drink? I mean, if you aren't really on duty . . ." I gestured toward my half-empty glass of wine.

"That's not necessary," Brad said. "Please sit down, Amy. We need to talk."

I settled back on the sofa. "In case you're wondering, Ella and Nicky went home with my parents for a weeklong visit."

"Smart idea." Brad's clear blue eyes fixed me with a stare. "I guess Richard already headed to the theater?"

"Yes. It's the final performance in Smithsburg tonight. Then next month the company will embark on a short tour."

"Glad to hear they already have invitations from other venues. I'm sorry I missed the performance, but with everything going on . . ." Brad shook his head. "But Alison was there opening night and she said it was great."

"Yes, I saw her there." I bit my lower lip to stifle any other comments about Alison.

Brad leaned forward, gripping his knees with his hands. "Anyway, you know why I'm here."

"The note," I said.

160

Death and the Librarian

"Right. You really don't know who shoved it in your pocket?"

"I didn't even know anything had been slipped into my pocket; not until Sunny noticed it later." I sank back against the sofa cushions. "I simply felt someone bump into me. It was a strong jolt, and I thought I felt a hand on my hip, but figured that was the person trying to help me keep my balance."

"And Marty Stover didn't see who it was, either?"

"No, he said there were too many people clustered together at that moment." I picked up a decorative pillow and hugged it to my chest. "What do you think about the threat? Is it legit? Aunt Lydia suspects it was simply a warning without any teeth behind it."

"I wouldn't assume that," Brad said. "We've been investigating everyone who was at the Taylorsford Inn the night Ms. Dryden died, and I understand from one of Smithsburg deputies that some of the same people were also at the performance this past Friday."

I tightened my grip on the pillow. "Like Terry Temkin, Mindy LaSalle, and Sean Gordon? I was somewhat surprised to see them at the theater."

"And Kurt Kendrick," Brad said, straightening in his chair. "Kurt was mentioned in Ms. Dryden's lecture as possibly having a connection to the Eddie Jaffe case. Under his old name, of course."

Alison was both places too, I thought, my fingernails digging into the suede fabric of the pillow. "Delbert Frye was mentioned as well," I said, keeping my gaze locked on Brad to catch his reaction.

Brad shifted his position on the plush seat of the armchair. "Yes. Alison was quite upset about that, as you may have seen. Of course, Delbert was not at the inn when Ms. Dryden was killed, nor was he at the dance performance."

"I wouldn't have expected him to be either place, since he doesn't like crowds," I said. "But . . ."

"Alison was at both." Brad's bleak expression conveyed his struggle over this fact. "I realize her outburst at the lecture, coupled with her being at the inn and the theater makes her a suspect, just as it does Kendrick. Fortunately, she isn't a major suspect, just a person of interest, or I'd have already been taken off the case."

"I really don't think Alison would harm anyone," I said, dropping the pillow into my lap.

"Nor do I. But I have to investigate every possibility." Brad's deep sigh hung in the air. "Allie does have a temper and has been known to take impulsive actions. And then there are a couple of witnesses . . ."

"But could you say the murder was impulsive?" I asked, throwing him any lifeline I could think of. "If Maureen Dryden's drink was spiked to render her unconscious when she went to her room, the killer must've planned that murder ahead of time. Why else would anyone be carrying around a knockout drug?"

"True, true." Brad's expression brightened. "I keep reminding myself about that. It does look like premeditated

Death and the Librarian

murder. Not to mention the fact that it seems Ms. Dryden either left her door unlocked or opened the door to someone she didn't fear."

Which isn't to say Alison couldn't have planned it, I thought, forcing my expression to remain neutral. *She may have had access to confiscated drugs at her department, and Maureen would've been more likely to open the door to a sheriff's deputy than any other stranger.*

"While we're talking about Maureen Dryden's death, I do have some more information to share," I said, anxious for the subject to veer in another direction. "You know I spoke to Sheryl Abernathy. Well, I also talked to Delbert Saturday afternoon and their stories match. Sheryl mentioned running into a slightly older man who was carrying something like a canvas log tote. She said it was when she was at the clearing the night Eddie Jaffe vanished. She apparently walked down the trail to take a pee and ran into Delbert who was coming out of the woods. Delbert confirmed her story."

"We've questioned Ms. Abernathy again, but she isn't very forthcoming." Brad frowned. "I don't think she's quite as addled as she seems, but she swears she doesn't know who else was at the little drug-and-drink party that night, other than Eddie, of course"

"Did she mention running into Delbert to your detectives?"

"She described the man to the point I'm pretty sure it was Delbert, and if he told you the same story, it seems likely to be a fact." Brad ran his fingers through his short, pale hair.

"Did she say anything about a girl?" I asked, remembering that confusing aspect of Sheryl's story.

"No, she didn't say anything about another young woman being at the gathering or in the area. So I'm afraid we've drawn a blank on that information so far."

"I'm not sure she wasn't simply babbling at that point," I said. "Is there any other new evidence? I mean, information you might want me to research to verify?"

"Anything more you can find on Terry Temkin and Mindy LaSalle would be useful." Brad tapped the chair arms with his fingers. "We have discovered that not all was rosy between Temkin and Dryden. Some sort of falling out happened recently."

"Oh, I do know more about that." I filled Brad in on what I had learned from eavesdropping on Terry and Sean, as well as the possible television series deal Mindy had mentioned. "It seems like both Terry and Mindy may have had motives to get Maureen out of the picture," I said as I finished my spiel.

"Could be." Obviously lost in thought, Brad rubbed his chin. "We'd uncovered the rumor that Terry Temkin was furious with Ms. Dryden for supposedly stealing his work on the Campton murders, but I hadn't heard about the possibility of a television series. That would mean more was at stake if Ms. Dryden refused to allow Temkin to freely use his research for that purpose, or at least, refused unless *she* was adequately compensated." His expression brightened.

Probably because the more suspicious Mindy and Terry look, the less their testimony against Alison will matter, I thought.

Death and the Librarian

"I'm sure it isn't a rumor," I said. "I ran into Sean Gordon yesterday and he pretty much confirmed the animosity between Temkin and Dryden, and the reason behind it."

Brad shot me a sharp look. "Where did you see Sean Gordon?"

"In the clearing where Eddie and Sheryl and whoever else partied," I said, placing the pillow against the chair arm and giving it a good chop to indent the top edge.

"Why the heck were you there?" Brad stood up and took a few steps to stand at the arm of the sofa. "You received a threatening note and still wandered off into the woods by yourself?"

"The trail is really close by, so I thought I'd just take a look and get a better sense of this clearing everyone talks about," I said, sinking down into my seat cushion. "I mean, that path and clearing may be connected to Jaffe's disappearance, but I didn't think it would necessarily provoke anyone linked to Maureen Dryden's murder."

Brad leaned forward, his palms pressed against the sofa arm. "You didn't think? No, you certainly didn't. You know someone may have it out for you, yet head to an isolated area on your own. Anyway, that clearing is dangerous, with or without anyone there."

"I did notice the drop-off at that one edge," I said. "Actually, that's how I first realized Sean was there. He was climbing back up from the bottom. He's a rock climber, so he knew how to do it without getting hurt."

"Did he say why he was there and what he was looking for?" Brad asked.

I squirmed on my seat, intimidated by the way he was looming over me. "He wants to complete Ms. Dryden's book, if at all possible. He apparently did a lot of research for it and doesn't want that to go to waste. He also said he'd like to publish the book to honor Maureen. He'd make her the coauthor, or something like that."

As if sensing my unease, Brad stepped away from the sofa. "So he was looking for evidence on some old as dirt case? What could he possibly find after all these years?"

"Bones, maybe?" I rolled my shoulders to release the tension in my back. "It isn't impossible, is it, that Eddie Jaffe actually fell to his death during that clandestine gathering?"

Brad shook his head. "Unlikely. Once he was declared a missing person the sheriff's department would've scoured that area and the woods around it for evidence. If his body was there, they would've found it."

"Someone could've moved the body, though."

"They'd have to be a professional hitman or something to remove a body and any traces of evidence that it had been located there."

"Or had help?" I realized I was nervously wiggling my foot and stilled my leg.

"I don't know, it seems unlikely. Anyway, there's nothing there now. Some of my deputies checked over the clearing, trail, and that gulley several days before your friend Sean conducted his little exploration."

"I wouldn't say he's my friend. I barely know the guy. I mean, he seems nice enough, but that's no guarantee of anything." I glanced up at Brad. "Have you discovered any

Death and the Librarian

motive that could've driven Sean to murder Maureen Dryden?"

"Not yet. But he's still on our suspect list, if only because he worked with her so closely. Who knows how she treated him? When he was interviewed, he seemed pretty reticent to discuss their relationship." Brad glanced at his watch. "I'd better get going. Promised Alison I'd bring home some take-out for dinner."

"And the note?" I asked, rising to my feet.

"No hits with the fingerprints, other than yours, Richard's, and Sunny's." Brad cast me a tight smile. "They're in the system from other cases, you know."

"Right." I followed Brad to the front door. "Should I be worried?"

"Of course, but knowing you, it won't stop you from researching both cases." Brad paused in the open doorway. "It's good the children are out of town. Did you alert other family members?"

I nodded. "Aunt Lydia knows, and Ethan and Scott are on vacation, so they won't be around for a week or two."

"Good. Now if you'll stop running off into the woods, we may be able to find whoever threatened you and your family before they can do any harm." Brad patted my shoulder. "Be careful, and call for help whenever you feel uneasy. Don't worry about false alarms. I'd rather you be safe than sorry."

"I will." I watched him walk away before closing and locking the door.

Returning to the sofa, I finished off my now warm wine in one gulp and headed to the kitchen for more. Loie, hearing

167

Victoria Gilbert

me, pushed her way through the cat door and strolled over to stand near my feet. "I think the thing that's needed is more research," I told her.

She blinked her emerald eyes and meowed.

"You're right," I said. "More wine and then more research."

168

Chapter Sixteen

I was glad to be back at work on Monday. The house was far too quiet.

The library was fairly quiet as well, but I had plenty of work to do behind the scenes. While Samantha covered the desk, I caught up on processing interlibrary loans, ordering books and other resources, and creating a few statistical reports to present to the town council at their next meeting.

Around ten, Samantha poked her head around the workroom door. "Hey, do you mind keeping an eye on the desk while I escort a patron out to the archives?" she asked.

"No problem." I stood up, stretching my arms over my head. "I need to move a little anyway." When I walked out of the workroom, I noticed Samantha leading Sean Gordon toward the back door.

"He's thinking about completing that poor woman's book," Zelda said, as she rolled an empty book cart behind the desk.

"Yes, he told me that when I saw him the other day." I bent down and pulled a few items from the book drop at the desk.

"Well, look at that. Both of our copies of *Deadly Desire* were checked out recently."

"Of course." Zelda brushed a spot of dust off her electric-blue tunic top. "Everyone gets ghoulish when there's a murder in their backyard. They probably wanted to read Maureen Dryden's book so they'd have more to talk about with their friends and neighbors."

I picked up one of the books. "I've actually never read this. Have you?"

"Oh, sure. I watched the series when it came out, and then wanted to go back and read the book, to see what had been changed or left out of the television show," Zelda said. "You know the death of Beverly Baron was never solved, right? This book claims to offer the definitive proof about who killed her, and why."

"Did you believe Maureen Dryden's thesis?" I asked, flipping through the pages to a section of photographs in the middle of the book.

"I'm not sure." Zelda brushed her fingers through her springy curls. "Even though she puts forth a pretty compelling argument, I wasn't entirely convinced. Especially since the case never went to trial."

"Because the primary suspect committed suicide," I said, staring at the pictures of Beverly Baron, who had been a gorgeous young woman. There were several photos of her in costume for her first major role, which was as a spy in an action thriller. Her shiny chestnut hair, bright green eyes, and sleek figure were a perfect match for the character, a mysterious woman whose actions skirted the line between good and evil.

Death and the Librarian

"Sadly, yes. The poor boy was hounded day and night by Baron's fans and the media." Zelda shook her head. "He was convicted in the court of public opinion without a chance to defend himself."

"Sounds like you sympathized with him," I said, turning the page to gaze at a photo of Allen Cardullo. He was equally good-looking, in a boyish sort of way. Tall and slender, he had wavy brown hair and wide dark eyes that held a mesmerizing glint of mystery. With his high cheekbones, patrician nose, and chiseled jawline he looked like a high-fashion model. "He wasn't very old at the time, was he?"

"If I remember correctly, he was about twenty-one. Beverly Baron was twenty-three, so they were close in age." Zelda moved closer and tapped another photo with her forefinger. "There's his family. You have to feel sorry for them if nothing else. They were treated horribly at the time."

The photograph showed the Cardullo family standing in front of a crimson-leafed Japanese maple. A tall man with curly brown hair had his arm around the waist of a sandy-blonde woman nearly his height. Allen stood beside his mother, while two older teenagers, a boy and a girl, posed in front of them. Like Allen, the younger siblings had their father's dark hair and eyes. I leaned in to read the caption. "It says one member of the family is missing from the photo."

"A half-brother, I think. He was from Mrs. Cardullo's first marriage, which ended in divorce. He was older than Allen and went into the navy right out of high school and was out at sea, so he wasn't around when the rest of the family was dealing with the murder investigation." Zelda tapped the page.

Victoria Gilbert

"There should be an index if you want to research specific background info."

"I think maybe I'll check this out myself," I said, sliding the book over toward the desk computer. "I might as well see if there's any possibility that someone connected to the Baron case had a motive to kill Maureen."

"The entire Cardullo family, I'd think," Zelda said. "They brought a civil suit against Maureen Dryden after Allen died. It was settled out of court, so that doesn't really prove his guilt or innocence, I guess."

"Hmm." I slid *Deadly Desire* under our new hands-free barcode reader, then used my credentials to check out the book. "I guess I need to read this, although it isn't exactly what I'm in the mood for right now."

"You and me both." Zelda glanced across the desk, toward the stacks. "Isn't that the podcaster at the computers? I wonder if he's researching for his next episode or something."

I gazed over at the bank of public computers. Sure enough, Terry was sitting at one of the workstations. "That's him. I think he's capitalizing on Maureen Dryden's death for his true-crime podcast. That's what I heard from . . ." I paused, reminding myself that Zelda, although one of the sweetest women in the world, was also quite fond of sharing gossip. *No use mentioning Sean in this context*, I thought, clearing my throat. "That's what I heard, anyway."

Zelda audibly sniffed. "Make hay while the sun shines, I guess, but I don't think it's very nice to exploit your colleague's death like that."

172

Death and the Librarian

"I don't think they were close, but yeah, I agree." As I stared at the back of Terry's head, his brown curls reminded me of the Cardullo family portrait. I narrowed my eyes, wondering how old he was. He didn't look to be more than thirty, but he certainly could be even younger. If he was in his mid-twenties, he'd have been an older teen during the Baron murder case. *Like Allen's younger brother in the photograph, although if he is that boy, he must've changed his name. But it would explain his fascination with true crime, and his willingness to work with Maureen, if only to get close to her. Close enough to kill?* I shook my head. My thoughts were running away with me. Similar hair to a boy from six or seven years ago was not evidence. I'd have to do more research before I presented that theory to Brad or anyone else.

Terry stood up and strode toward the lobby doors. As he passed the desk, he glowered at Zelda and me.

"He didn't seem very happy with us. We must've been talking too loudly," Zelda said, as Terry exited the building.

I swallowed back a comment about his possible anger over the content of our conversation. "Maybe. I guess we should be more careful in the future."

Since Samantha had not yet returned, I asked Zelda to keep watch over the desk and carried *Deadly Desire* into the workroom. Shoving it into my tote bag, I resolved to read it the following day, when I would be off work and Richard would be rehearsing with the dance company. It'll give me something useful to do, I told myself as I sat back down in front of my work computer.

173

I knew I should continue working on my reports, but I was too intrigued by the possibility that Terry Temkin was actually part of the Cardullo family. Switching into research mode, I looked for any information on what had happened to Allen Cardullo's younger brother.

There wasn't much. I discovered that the boy, named Duncan, and the young woman in the photo were twins, and her name was Daria, but that was about it. The entire family appeared to have gone off the grid after the civil trial ended in a settlement, the financial results of which were not disclosed. I tapped a pen against the desktop. *Perhaps they left the area, or even the country,* I thought, as I scrolled through a long list of useless hits.

There was plenty of information on Allen, of course, most of it couched in negative terms. He'd been an actor as well, although unlike Beverly, he hadn't gotten his big break. According to some of the articles, Allen had always idolized Beverly, who began her career as a preteen model before going into acting. He'd hung posters of her in his bedroom and had made a concerted effort to meet her once he moved to Hollywood to pursue his own career. Some of his friends said he'd taken a bit part in Beverly's last film, rather than a larger role in another movie, just to get close to her. It was typical stalker behavior, but that alone didn't make him a murderer.

Zelda popped into the workroom to let me know that Samantha had returned from the archives. "She left Mr. Gordon out there after helping him pull some boxes and files," she said.

Death and the Librarian

"Tell her that's fine," I said. "I may check on him later, to see if he needs anything else, but I think we can trust him not to take anything out of the building."

I turned back to the computer and closed out my browser. It was time to get back to my real work. I'd save any further investigation for later. Maybe after I'd read Maureen Dryden's take on the Baron case, I'd discover more avenues for research.

When my lunch break rolled around, I decided to kill two birds with one stone and carried my packed lunch out to the picnic table near the archives building. Sean had left the door to the archives ajar, perhaps to allow more air to circulate. Even though we had window air conditioning units, it could still get stuffy in the enclosed space.

Setting my lunch bag and bottle of water on the table, I crossed to the archives, but stopped in place when I heard voices resounding against the stone walls inside.

"Now you're going to be a problem?" said a voice I recognized as belonging to Terry Temkin.

"No, I told you I'm willing to work something out," Sean Gordon replied in an exasperated tone.

"Oh, really? Well, let me tell you, Sean, you'd better not get any ideas about finishing and releasing the book before my deal is settled." The anger radiating from Terry's voice was palpable.

"You mean your hypothetical television deal?" Sean let out a bark of laughter. "If I have to wait for that I might as well plan on putting the book off for twenty years."

"What do you mean by that?" There was a razor edge to Terry's tone.

175

I took a step back. This wasn't a conversation I wanted to walk into.

"You know as well as I do that most of those *maybe* offers from producers or studios blow away like leaves in the wind. Until you sign a contract, it means nothing, and even then, the project may linger in development hell and never get produced."

"My contacts are solid." Terry's voice slid into a whine.

"Don't count on it. At any rate, I'm happy to work out a compromise with you so that we all benefit," Sean said. "I'm not Maureen. I won't dig my heels in and reject a reasonable solution."

"You'd better stick by that." The door flew open and Terry stormed out. Seeing me, he stopped short and shot me a glare. "You again," he said.

"Excuse me, I came out to eat lunch"—I motioned toward the picnic table—"and then help Sean if he needed it."

"Oh, he needs help." Terry looked me up and down. "But not the kind you can give. Psychiatric help is more like it. Thinking he knows it all. Just another narcissist."

I resisted the urge to say something about therapy not being much use where narcissists were concerned. "I'm afraid you're right about that. I can assist with his research, not his mental state."

"Too bad." Terry hmphed and stalked off in the direction of the lane that led to the main road.

Sean moved into the doorway. "Sorry about that. As you saw, Terry's rather prickly, especially now. It seems something's ramping up his everyday anxiety to a fever pitch."

Death and the Librarian

Like the fear of being discovered to be a murderer? I thought, forcing a bright smile. "I'm sure it's been a difficult time for all of you who worked with Ms. Dryden."

"Of course. Although, I rather expected Terry to be happier about her demise. It benefits him, you see."

I couldn't tell if the gleam in Sean's eyes was disdain or amusement. "I assume you mean because he may now be able to get back all rights to his research so he and Mindy can pursue the television project."

"Right. Because I'm much more agreeable than Maureen was on that issue, although Terry doesn't seem to realize that yet."

"How's the research coming?" I asked, thinking it best to change the subject.

"Fine, although I didn't find much in your archives. In fact, I was about to head into the library and ask your assistant to lock up behind me when Terry showed up."

"I can do that," I said, sliding my key ring from my pocket.

"Do you want me to put the boxes back first?" Sean asked as he stepped out onto the stoop. "I already refiled the folders."

"No, that's okay. Someone on the library staff will take care of that later." I walked to the door and locked it while Sean stepped down onto the back lawn. "I wonder if I could ask you a few more questions," I added, as I joined him.

"Sure. Why don't we sit at the table so you can have your lunch," Sean said, striding toward the picnic table.

After we were sitting across from one another, I decided to see what Sean might know about Terry Temkin's background. "How well do you know Terry?"

Victoria Gilbert

Sean drummed his fingers against the wooden tabletop. "Not well at all. We didn't meet until a few days before Maureen's lecture. She'd talked to him and Mindy previously, of course, but I didn't have anything to do with their negotiations."

"How old is he, do you think?" I asked, sliding a bag of apple and celery slices and a small tub of peanut butter out of my lunch bag.

"Mid-twenties, I'd say. I know he and Mindy started their podcast when they were in college. They've only been doing it for a few years, so I assume they're both under thirty." Sean stilled his fingers and clasped his hands together on top of the table. "They've done pretty well, from what I can tell. Their podcast has been successfully monetized, with numerous patrons and sponsors."

"So it wouldn't be impossible for them to get a TV deal?"

"Not impossible, no." Sean tightened his lips. "He made the deal with Maureen over his research into the Campton case before the podcast really blew up. After that, he was desperate to get the rights back."

I dipped an apple slice in the peanut butter. "But Maureen wasn't too keen on that idea, I take it."

"No. I tried to reason with her." Sean shrugged. "I mean, all she had to do was give him more credit and some percentage from the book's advance and royalties, and he was willing to give her a cut of any media production profits. It seemed like a win-win situation to me. But Maureen was . . . intractable. Once she got an idea in her head, it was impossible to change her mind."

178

Death and the Librarian

I thought about her absolute conviction that Allen Cardullo had killed Beverly Baron. "Even when lawsuits were involved?"

Sean grimaced. "It seemed so. I wasn't around when she was dealing with the Cardullo family, but I understand she fought the settlement down to the wire."

I chewed the slice of apple before asking another question. "So you really don't know anything about Terry's background? Or Mindy's," I added, as the image of Allen Cardullo's younger sister came to my mind. *She actually has dark curly hair too and is around the right age*, I thought. *So if you suspect Terry because of that, Mindy needs to be in the mix too. In fact, it's possible they're siblings rather than partners.*

"I really don't. Although, sometimes I wonder . . ." Sean flashed me a smile. "I know it sounds silly, but both of them are rather cagey about the past. I've tried drawing them out, but they don't bite."

"Some people don't like to share those things," I said, playing devil's advocate.

"True, but they seem especially secretive. Anyway"—Sean swung his legs over the bench and stood up—"let me allow you to eat in peace. I'm sure you need to finish lunch and get back to work."

"Okay. Thanks for talking to me again," I said, pausing before dipping a stalk of celery in the peanut butter.

"No problem. Good to see you, and thanks for letting me dig through the archives." Sean waved a goodbye and headed off.

I watched him stride up the lane toward the main road, then turned back to my lunch. Chewing on the celery, I considered his words concerning Terry and Mindy. If they were hesitant to talk about the past, was it because they were simply private people?

Or because one or both of them were Allen Cardullo's sibling?

Chapter Seventeen

Richard was home on Monday evening, so I set aside *Deadly Desires* to read the next day. We'd had so few evenings to spend together recently, I wanted to enjoy binging some episodes of the television series we'd saved to watch together.

I finally dove into the book on Tuesday, after Richard left for his work with the dance company. Sitting on the sofa, flanked by Fosse and Loie, I read as much of the book as I could.

It was well written, and as suspenseful as fiction, which I supposed hadn't hurt its sales. Yet the sense of reading a novel rather than a work of nonfiction made me question the validity of some of Maureen Dryden's claims and conclusions.

Her assertion that Beverly wouldn't have opened her apartment door to a stranger was an important tentpole of her theory, but I had to wonder if the young actress had really known Allen Cardullo that well. Even though it was clear he'd been enamored with her, the evidence that she'd had anything but a passing relationship with him was rice-paper thin. They'd worked on the same film, and there was a scene or two featuring them both, but that was all. A few people on set claimed to have seen them eating lunch together, yet someone on the wardrobe staff said that Beverly had to ask Allen's name when he'd appeared at her trailer with a bouquet of flowers.

"It was all circumstantial evidence," I told Fosse, who flopped over, exposing his cream-colored belly. "I mean, Maureen constructed a plausible scenario, using all the bits and pieces of information she was able to cobble together, but if you remove one piece it all falls apart."

It's like Jenga, I thought. *The structure holds if you don't tug on an essential component hard enough to dislodge it.*

As I flipped to the center section to study the photos once more, my cell phone buzzed. I grabbed it from the coffee table and checked to see who was calling before answering.

"Hello, Kurt," I said. "What's up?"

"Many things, including taxes and the cost of eggs," he replied in that tone that occasionally made me want to kick him in the shins.

"Alright, let me rephrase that—why, sir, are you calling?"

Kurt chuckled. "Because, madame, I'd like to talk to you."

"You are talking to me."

"I mean, face to face." The hint of frustration in Kurt's tone told me he wasn't as cheerful as his original greeting might have implied.

"Okay, I'm off work today if you want to stop by," I said.

Death and the Librarian

"I'd prefer it if you'd come to Highview. You know how it is, I'm getting older. Sometimes it's not that easy to leave the house."

I snorted. "Come on, you could probably outrun me in a marathon. Older, my foot."

"That's not very kind, my dear." Kurt's trademark sarcasm sliced through his words. "I'll be eighty in a few months, you know. I may still look young and vigorous . . ."

"I wouldn't go that far," I said. "But I suppose I could cut you some slack and drive to your house if you insist."

"Good. I'll see you shortly then," Kurt said, and hung up.

I grumbled to the cats, who were nonplussed by my displeasure. Deciding that my worn cotton shorts and faded concert T-shirt were good enough for this command performance, I slipped on a pair of sandals and grabbed my purse off the side table. "Back soon," I told Fosse and Loie. "In time for your afternoon treats, anyway."

I texted Aunt Lydia before I left to make sure she didn't need the car, answering her question about where I was going with a vague mention of errands. Since I didn't know what Kurt wanted to discuss, I didn't want to worry her. They got along these days, but she still eyed him with suspicion when it came to his dealings with her family.

Kurt's home was located on a mountain road just outside of town. It wasn't that far a drive, but the washboard dirt and gravel road slowed travel speed to a crawl in places. I was happy to see the sign for Highview mounted on one of the stone pillars that flanked a black metal gate. I lowered my window and leaned out to press the buzzer on one of the pillars. When I spoke my name into the intercom the gate swung open.

Unlike the county road, Kurt's driveway was paved, its blacktop surface mottled with shadows cast by a canopy of leafy branches. Azaleas and rhododendrons created a screen of green at the base of the hardwood trees that lined the driveway.

I rounded a corner and slowed the car, taking time to admire the beautiful home coming into view. Set in the middle of a large clearing surrounded by woods, the three-story central section was constructed from gray fieldstone, while the two-story wood-framed wings were painted a pale jade green. Tall windows were sunk into the stone façade, their wavy glass proof of their age. Shorter windows flanked by black shutters gleamed against the wood siding, and a lacy veil of ivy covered the largest of the stone chimneys.

I parked in the circle of blacktop at the end of the driveway and walked over to a roofed porch featuring Grecianstyle pillars. Climbing the few stone steps to the forest-green front door, I admired the colorful cottage garden brightening the space between a whitewashed picket fence and the porch before pressing the doorbell.

Kurt opened the door and ushered me inside. "Let's sit in the study," he said, leading the way down the wide central hall, which was filled with art and antiques, and up a staircase to the second floor. At the top of the stairs, a decorative wood railing spanned an open portion of the upper hall. Kurt strolled past this balcony and stepped into a room at the end of the hallway.

Death and the Librarian

As I entered the room, I cast a glance at a large oil painting hanging in the one wall space not occupied by wooden bookcases. It was a landscape in which the predominant feature was the rounded, azure tops of the Blue Ridge Mountains.

I strolled across the muted blue and rose-gold Persian rug to examine the painting up close. It was painted in a realistic style but still held a hint of mystery. I wouldn't have been surprised to catch a glimpse of a fairy perched in one of the graceful trees surrounding a quiet field.

"It always makes me want to stop and study it more closely." I turned to face Kurt. "You won't ever sell this one, will you?"

"I will never part with any of Andrew's works." Kurt's gaze lingered on the landscape. "I just wish Lydia would sell me some others."

"Good luck with that." Sinking into the buttery leather cushions of a wingback chair, I looked around the study, which I always thought would be better described as a library. Dark wood shelves filled almost every inch of wall space, from the top of built-in lower cabinets to the high, coffered ceiling. Lining the shelves were books of every size and description.

Grabbing the back of the wooden chair tucked under an oak rolltop desk, Kurt rolled the chair around so he could sit and face me.

"Alright, now that we are comfortably situated, why don't you tell me what you called me here to discuss? I don't want to waste too much time. I don't have to worry about the twins, since they're visiting my parents this week, but I do want to get home in time to prepare dinner. Richard's schedule allows him to be home in the evenings right now and I want to take advantage of that."

Kurt's piercing gaze swept over me. "Ella and Nicky are out of town?"

"Richard and I thought it best," I said, studying his face to see if I could observe any reaction to this statement.

"I see. That's probably a smart move." Kurt rested his elbows on the wide arms of his chair and clasped his hands in front of his chest.

I met his hooded gaze without wavering. "Because my research and inquiries into the Eddie Jaffe case might incite retaliation?"

Kurt's expression turned stony. "There are many things better left alone. Sometimes the wisest course is to leave the past in the past."

I pressed my palms into the soft leather of my chair arms. *Time to jump into the fire.* "Does that mean you don't plan to tell me what you know about Eddie Jaffe's disappearance?"

"How can I, when I don't really know anything?" Kurt lifted his hands before dropping them down onto his thighs.

"I'm not sure I believe you," I said, sliding to the edge of my chair. "Maureen Dryden had some information that tied back to you. To your former name, at least. Why would she be so interested in that smoke if there was no fire?"

Kurt leaned into the curved back of his chair and surveyed me with a look that could freeze mercury. "I have no idea where Ms. Dryden heard my old name. Perhaps she came

Death and the Librarian

across it while researching the drug trade in this area back when Jaffe was peddling a few ounces of this and that. I suppose I was rather well known for my own business dealings."

"Business dealings?" I raised my eyebrows. "Okay, let's call it that. The thing is, since both you and Eddie were in the same line of work—"

"Hardly the same, but go on."

Crossing my arms over my chest, I held his imperious stare. "I have to say, I find it odd that you didn't run into each other once or twice."

"I never said I didn't see him here or there. Simply that we weren't acquaintances, much less friends. In other words, he wasn't someone I would choose to hang out with," Kurt said.

"Which means you weren't at the gathering in the woods the night Eddie Jaffe disappeared?"

"Why would I be there?" Kurt straightened in his chair. "As I said, I had no reason to pal around with him. My understanding is that he and his girlfriend and maybe a few others were having a rather raucous get-together that evening. Not something I'd want to get mixed up with."

"Raucous? Well, I guess that's true enough, based on the girlfriend's recollections. By the way, she's still alive. She lives at a nursing home in Smithsburg.

"Does she?" Kurt shook his head. "Rather surprising. I'd have expected her to die young, the way she looked when she was hanging out with Jaffe. Bit of a mess, if what I heard was true."

"But you were never officially introduced to her," I said, not phrasing it as a question.

Victoria Gilbert

"Not that I recall. Although, it's true that there are a few blank spots in my memories around that time." Kurt flashed a sardonic grin.

"So you could've been at that clearing in the woods that evening and simply forgotten it?" I asked, lowering my hands into my lap.

"Possibly. Although, I must reiterate—it would've been extremely odd for me to party with Jaffe or any of his pals. So I'm almost certain I wouldn't have been there." Kurt's lips curled back, exposing his large white teeth.

There it is, he's morphed into the Wolf, I thought. While I knew Kurt's nickname when he was younger was the Viking, I thought my name suited him better. "Did you ask me here to warn me off the Jaffe case or the Dryden investigation?"

"How about both?" Kurt rose to his feet and crossed the room to stand over me. "While I'm glad you have enough sense to make sure Ella and Nicky are safe, it could still be dangerous for others in your family, your friends, or, for that matter, you."

"How do you know I've been threatened? Did you slip me that note?" I asked, standing up to face him. Of course, I still had to tilt my head and look up.

"Note? What note?" Concern replaced the haughtiness in Kurt's expression.

"The note someone shoved in my pocket after the dance performance on Friday night. It was a pretty blunt warning that I should stop helping the authorities with their investigations, or my family and I might be in danger." I poked Kurt's forearm. "You were there. I saw you."

188

Death and the Librarian

"I was there, but I didn't pass you any note. Do you really believe I'd threaten you, or Richard, or the children?" Kurt encircled my wrist with his strong fingers. "Is that what you really think, Amy?"

Twisting my wrist free of his grip was impossible. "I thought you might send a warning, just to get me to back off. Not that you'd necessarily carry through."

"But I didn't give you that note. Which means there's someone else out there who could very well harm you and those you love." Kurt released my wrist and stepped back. "So why are you persisting in aiding these investigations? Leave it to the proper authorities."

I rubbed my wrist. "I doubt it matters anymore. I've already shared quite a bit of information with Brad, so if someone is opposed to my interference, they're probably already angry with me."

Kurt turned on his heel and crossed to stand in front of Andrew's painting. "I could've been that person, yet you came."

"Like I said, I didn't believe you'd hurt me, even if you had warned me off." I gazed at his back, noting the tension lifting his shoulders. "Can you at least tell me why you don't want me researching the Eddie Jaffe case? That one's so old, and there's almost no concrete evidence, so I doubt anything you could reveal would matter, in terms of proving anyone's guilt or innocence."

Keeping his back to me, Kurt continued to focus on the painted landscape. "Have you ever heard of an impossible choice, Amy? Like in that Stockton story about the lady and the tiger, or in Styron's *Sophie's Choice*?"

Victoria Gilbert

"Of course. Basically, there's no good option."

"Have you ever dealt with such a thing?" When Kurt turned to face me, pain was etched into every line on his face.

"No, thank goodness."

"It's a dreadful thing," Kurt said, in a weary voice. "Knowing that whatever you do, it's the wrong choice. Realizing that picking any of the myriad options may bring pain and destruction."

I stared at him, baffled. "Is that why you won't tell the truth?"

Kurt simply closed his eyes for a moment. "I think you should go now, Amy. You know the way out. Only"—he opened his eyes and fixed me with a steely stare—"be careful and stay alert. Don't take anything for granted."

Even your innocence? I thought but still nodded my head. "I'll see you around, then," I said, leaving the room without waiting for his goodbye.

Chapter Eighteen

Late Wednesday afternoon I got a text from Sunny asking if I wanted to stop by the farm after work to pick up some apples.

We have extra Lodi apples. Come get some. Great for pies.

I texted back that I'd stop by around five-thirty. Richard and I loved the organic fruit and produce from Vista View, and I knew I could also share some apples with Aunt Lydia, who was an expert at making all types of pies.

Vista View was owned by Sunny's grandparents, who had raised her after her mother dropped her on their doorstep and disappeared. But now that Carol and P. J. Fields were in their eighties, Sunny had taken over the management of the farm. She'd hired a couple of local workers to help out with the more difficult and time-consuming tasks but still had a great deal of responsibility, handling all the financial matters as well as advertising and sales. Much of the produce from Vista View was acquired by local restaurants as well as sold at local farmers' markets.

Fortunately, I'd driven to work, so I was able to head to the farm from the library rather than making a detour to my house. Vista View was located off another one of the gravel mountain roads just outside of Taylorsford, although this road was in better shape than the ones that led to Delbert's or Kurt's homes.

I turned at the wooden sign that marked the entrance to Vista View. It featured a vivid graphic of a cornucopia filled with vegetables and fruit, hand-painted by Sunny several years earlier. The sign was beginning to fade, which Sunny bemoaned as one of the many items on her never-ending to-do list.

Driving up the gravel lane that led to the Fields farmhouse, I admired the neatly cultivated field of vegetable plants to my left and the meadow of orchard grass on my right. Since Sunny and her grandparents didn't believe in raising animals for meat, they also made money selling hay to area horse farms.

I parked my car in a small gravel lot near the wooden-framed yellow house, between Sunny's Volkswagen Beetle and a battered vintage truck P. J. or one of the farm workers used to make deliveries. Walking across the front yard, I dodged a clutch of Carol's free-range chickens to reach the simple front porch. Its delft-blue trim, matching the house's shutters, was starting to flake. *Another chore for Sunny's list,* I thought, shaking my head.

Sunny appeared at the front door, which was open to allow the breeze to flow through the screen door. "Glad you could make it. We've had decent sales on the Lodi crop this year, but not enough to get rid of all of them."

Death and the Librarian

"They don't store well?" I asked, as I entered the front hallway.

Tightening the scrunchie that fastened her low ponytail, Sunny led the way to the kitchen. "Unfortunately not. We can't hold them over the winter like some of the other varieties, and I hate to see them go to waste."

"I'll put them to good use," I said, stepping into the large country kitchen. "Or, more accurately, Aunt Lydia will."

Carol Fields stood behind the chrome-ringed yellow Formica table that filled the middle of the room. Short and plump, she looked like the perfect stereotypical grandmother. But that impression didn't reflect her earlier life, when she and P. J. had fully embraced the hippie movement and had even turned Vista View into a commune for flower children for a period of time.

"Here you go, Amy. A whole bushel-full." P. J. Fields entered through the back door, carrying a large basket filled with chartreuse-colored apples. Sunny had inherited Carol's fair complexion, light hair, and blue eyes, but she'd gotten her slender frame and height from her grandfather. He was only a little stooped now and still strong for a man his age. "I'll help you carry them to your car, so let me know when you're ready to leave."

"No, set that down on the table. I'll help Amy take it to the car," Sunny said, concern coloring her voice. I knew she worried about her grandparents doing too much heavy lifting, but, as she said, they were too stubborn to entirely give up a habit of manual labor. She sighed as she took a seat at the table.

193

Carol shoved a short strand of white hair off her forehead before crossing to one of the kitchen's aqua-blue counters. "I heard you were helping Brad and his team on this latest murder case," she said, grabbing a bright-red metal tumbler from the dish rack before turning back to me. "Would you like tea or lemonade?"

"Just water, thanks," I replied, sitting down across the table from Sunny. "I am, although it's mostly background research. I was looking for information on the Eddie Jaffe cold case, mainly to see if there could be any connection between that and Ms. Dryden's murder. There was hardly anything in the archives, which surprised me at first. But then I heard from a few older Taylorsford residents that there wasn't much of a furor when Eddie Jaffe went missing."

"That's true." Carol set the tumbler in front of me and sat down in the chair next to mine. "I guess P. J. and I were in our mid-twenties at that time." She cast a questioning glance at P. J., who'd set the bushel basket of apples on the end of the table and taken a seat next to Sunny. "Is that right, dear?"

P. J. closed his eyes for a moment, obviously calculating the dates in his head. "It was 1966, so we'd have been around twenty-five. Which means we weren't really involved much in town business when Jaffe went missing."

"Yeah, we were still running the commune at that time. We stayed pretty isolated from what was going on in Taylorsford," Carol said. "I did hear that Eddie Jaffe had disappeared, but that was all."

"We figured he'd just moved on." P. J. hooked his thumbs through the straps of his faded denim overalls and leaned

Death and the Librarian

back in his chair. "I met him once, when he was painting a barn down the road, but he wasn't one for friendly conversation. I even tried to invite him to one of our communal meals . . ."

Carol shot him a sharp glance. "You did? I don't remember you mentioning that."

"I probably didn't. The guy basically told me he had no interest in our hippie-dippy community, as he called it." P. J. shook his head. "Never saw him after that. When I heard he'd skipped town, I wasn't too upset."

"Did either of you know Sheryl Abernathy?" I asked, leaning forward and resting my arms on the table.

"Knew of her." Carol scrunched up her button nose in concentration. "Her older sister, Diana, was a hairstylist in town. Of course, I never paid to get my hair cut at a place like that, but I heard she was pretty good."

"Sheryl was Eddie's girlfriend, right?" Sunny asked.

"According to her, yes. But I'm not sure Eddie was that attached to her." I traced one of the lighter-yellow spiral patterns in the Formica tabletop with my finger. "She was with him at some clearing in the woods, right before he vanished."

"The infamous clearing," P. J. said, sharing a look with Carol.

"Was this some well-known hangout?" Sunny asked, bumping her grandfather's shoulder with her own. "Someplace you guys used to sneak off to when you were young?"

"Not us," Carol replied firmly. "It's across town, not far from Amy's house, so we wouldn't have used that place for anything. I mean, we had the farm—acres of land and woods to play in. No need to trek up some mountain trail."

"We heard about it, though." P. J. released his grip on his overall straps and placed his hands on the table. "We had some folks who were living on the road stop by here for a night or two, you know. A few of them said that clearing was a good place to score drugs."

I slid forward in my chair. "From Eddie Jaffe?"

"They didn't mention any names," P. J. said. "Not surprising, considering the circumstances."

"But we put two and two together. We'd heard Eddie Jaffe was doing a bit of dealing on the side." Carol shrugged. "We never wanted to buy from him. We used more reputable sources."

"Reputable?" Sunny's golden lashes fluttered over her wide blue eyes. "Strange word to use, Grandma."

Carol slapped her palm against the table. "Now, missy, don't be getting on your high horse. You know our history, and that we left all that behind years ago. Long before we took you in, as a matter of fact. Besides, we never dabbled in the really hard stuff, even if some of our other commune members did."

"Okay, okay," Sunny said, waving her hands. "I wasn't trying to diss you. It just struck me as funny."

"Anyway, as far as the Jaffe case is concerned, I've always said he probably disappeared because he was being threatened by other dealers or something." P. J. tapped his fingers on the table. "There were some of those you didn't want to cross, no way, no how."

Death and the Librarian

Like Karl Klass? I wondered. But I wasn't going to bring up that name around the Fieldses. "I probably should get going," I said, pushing back my chair. "I want to split these apples with Aunt Lydia and then help Richard with dinner."

"Sure thing." Sunny rose to her feet and circled behind P. J. to grab the basket.

"Here, I can hold one side and you the other," I said, hurrying over to her. As we each gripped one of the wooden spool handles and hoisted the basket off the table, I thanked P. J. and Carol and wished them a good evening.

Sunny and I trundled down the hall and out onto the porch, the basket swinging between us. "I don't know how Grandpa can lift this by himself," she said as we crossed the yard to reach my car.

I smiled. "I think it might be sheer willpower."

"Wouldn't surprise me," Sunny said. "The grands have as many bushels of that as they do apples."

We placed the basket on the back seat of my car and I closed the door with a slam. My older car needed a little extra force sometimes so the door wouldn't fly back open. "I'll have to be careful not to hit any major potholes." I opened my driver's side door, ready to climb into the car.

"That won't be easy." Sunny, shading her eyes, stared off at the woods that separated Vista View from a neighboring property. "Who's that?"

"What?" I followed her gaze and realized she was reacting to a shadowy figure moving behind the first row of trees. "One of your farmhands, maybe?"

"No, they've already gone home. In this hot weather, they arrive at work early so they can leave before it gets too sweltering in the afternoon." Sunny pursed her lips. "I think it's a trespasser. Probably one of those neighbor kids who like to steal apples."

When she took off at a sprint, I tossed my purse onto the passenger seat of my car, shoved the door shut, and followed after her. But my short legs were no match for Sunny's long limbs. She'd reached the tree line while I was still huffing up the hill that led to the woods.

"Hey, you there!" she shouted as she plunged into the woods. "This is private property!"

When I reached the edge of the woods, I heard her pounding footfalls as she ran after the stranger, who was crashing through the undergrowth like a frightened deer. Following the sounds, I peered ahead, hoping to catch of glimpse of Sunny's gleaming hair so I could run in the right direction to catch up to her. But I wasn't watching the ground and the toe of my shoe caught on an exposed root, sending me flying forward.

I landed on my hands and knees, jolts of pain zipping up my legs and arms. Sitting back with a thud, I took several deep breaths to calm my racing heart. After a few moments, I examined my hands, which were crisscrossed with scrapes, and then my knees. The cotton slacks I'd worn to work were ripped open at my right knee, and blood seeped out under the cloth flap.

I let loose a string of swear words. As they echoed off the trees, I realized that the woods had gone quiet. I couldn't hear

Death and the Librarian

any footsteps or rustling of vegetation. *Where did that trespasser go?* I thought, grabbing a slender tree trunk to help pull myself upright. *More importantly, where is Sunny?*

I trudged ahead, determined to find her. My knees were aching, and my hands felt raw and gritty, but I knew I had to locate my friend. She'd probably chased the trespasser away, but what if she'd fallen too? There were rocks scattered amid the undergrowth, hidden stones that could cause serious damage if someone tripped and hit their head.

Dampness spread down my right leg, letting me know that my knee was still bleeding profusely. I ignored it and walked on, batting aside arching branches of wild shrubs and vines. Reaching the far edge of the woods, I noticed that the tall grass that swayed between the trees and one of the farm sheds was beaten down into an impromptu path. *The stranger and Sunny must've headed toward that building,* I thought, increasing my stride to follow them.

The shed was a simple wooden structure with a roof badly in need of new shingles. Its main door hung drunkenly off one set of hinges, making it easy to push it open.

"Sunny? Are you in here?" I called out, as stepped over the threshold, pausing inside to allow my eyes to adjust to the dim light.

A groan rose from one shadowed corner. I rushed over, shoving aside a metal seed spreader to reveal Sunny lying on a thin bed of straw. She looked up at me, her eyes slightly unfocused. "I'll live," she said.

"You'd better," I replied. "What happened? Did that trespasser do this to you?"

Sunny placed one hand on her head, her fingers moving through her hair as if searching for an injury. "Not bleeding, at least. But you are," she added, pointing at my knees.

"Minor stuff. Cuts and scrapes. I'm more worried about you. Did someone knock you out?"

"Not entirely. Just enough to keep me from chasing them." Sunny struggled to a sitting position. "I was never completely unconscious."

"Good. Less likely to have suffered a concussion then," I said, although I was certain she'd need to be examined to rule that out. "Did you see the person? Can you describe them?"

"No. I chased them in here, and before I knew it, they'd hit me from behind. But they did grab me as I was falling and dragged me over to this corner. Anyway"—she shuddered—"I felt their hands on me."

"A man's hands?" I asked, offering my own hand to pull her to her feet.

Wobbling, Sunny leaned against one of the rough wooden posts holding up the roof. "I'm not sure. They were wearing heavy gloves, so the actual size of their hands could've been masked by that." She brushed at her jeans, filling the air with the scent of moldy straw.

"Hold on, there's something . . ." I reached out and plucked a folded piece of paper from the pocket of the loose cotton shirt she was wearing over a tank top. "Looks like another note."

"From the same person?" Sunny blinked rapidly. "Sorry, things went a bit blurry."

"We need to get you to the hospital," I said.

"First, the note. What does it say?"

Death and the Librarian

I unfolded the paper. Like the message I'd received, this was typed. I read through it with a frown.

"Come on, read it out to me," Sunny said.

"Okay." I took a deep breath and read the note aloud. "Tell your librarian friend this is what was meant by harm coming to her family and friends."

"It's referencing that note shoved in your pocket at the theater." Sunny straightened her back against the post.

"It seems so. They wanted to show me they could make good on their threats." I frowned. "That also means they've been keeping close tabs on me. Which is pretty unsettling." I tucked the note into the pocket of my slacks. "But first things first. Do you have your phone on you? I left mine in my purse, which is in my car."

"I'm afraid not." Sunny put a hand to her head again. "There's a lump, but no blood. I think I can walk back to the house with your help. We can call 911 from there." She looked me over. "For you and me."

"I doubt I need that. But you should definitely get checked out. Okay, put your arm around my shoulders and let's try to hobble to the house."

Shuffling like two newly created zombies, Sunny and I finally reached the front porch, where I called out for help. P. J. and Carol appeared almost immediately, their expressions filled with dismay.

"I'll take her," P. J. said, pulling Sunny into his arms. "Call 911, Carol."

She bobbed her head and ran back inside to make the call while I slumped down on one of the porch rocking chairs.

201

"What in the world happened?' P. J. asked, guiding Sunny to another rocking chair.

Sunny let out a soft moan as she sat down. "I saw someone in the woods. Thought it was one of those kids who like to wander around the farm without permission, so I chased after them."

"And I chased after Sunny, only I tripped and fell," I said. "By the time I was able to catch up to her, she'd tracked the trespasser into one of your sheds."

"They hit me." Sunny sighed. "It was dark, and I think they were wearing something to conceal their face. Anyway, I couldn't see who it was."

"Why would they hit you?" P. J. asked in a strained tone.

"I think it was a warning," Sunny replied. "They also left a note."

I pulled the folded piece of paper from my pocket and handed it to P. J. "I got a note similar to this at Richard and Karla's dance company premiere. It seems like whoever this person is, they want to force me to stop looking into the Dryden or Jaffe cases by threatening those I love."

"Who's talking about threats?" Carol bustled out onto the porch and immediately started examining Sunny and me. "The EMS team is on its way," she added, as she clucked over my blood-soaked pants leg.

"No one, no one, don't worry," Sunny said.

"Too late for that," P. J. stared down the driveway as a siren wailed in the distance.

I sank down farther in the rocker. "I suppose I should call Richard so he doesn't wonder where I am."

Death and the Librarian

Sunny waved her right hand. "Lend her your cell phone, Grandma."

"It's upstairs in the bedroom," Carol said.

"Better get it and let Amy call Richard before he's told anything by someone else." Sunny cast me a faint smile.

"Oh yes, please," I said. "I'd hate for him to hear it from Zelda."

Chapter Nineteen

When emergency services arrived, lead EMT Hannah Fowler was able to dress my wounds and declare me fit to drive home, while Sunny was taken away in an ambulance. Carol and P. J. followed the ambulance to the hospital, promising to call or text me with updates on Sunny's condition.

Richard was ready to drive to Vista View as soon as I called him, but I told him it wasn't necessary, and I had to drive the car back anyway. I asked him to wait at home for me. He argued over this, of course, but finally accepted the wisdom of my decision.

Before I could leave Vista View, Brad pulled me aside to find out what had happened.

"I have a deputy headed to the hospital to take a statement from Sunny," he said. "But I'd like to hear your side of the story too."

"First, there's this." I handed him the note that had been shoved in Sunny's shirt pocket.

All the color bled from his face as he read the message. "It's like the first one you received, only more threatening."

Death and the Librarian

"And this time, they actually hurt someone," I said. "Apparently, whoever wrote the note wants to prove they're willing to do whatever it takes to dissuade me from helping either investigation."

"It seems so." Brad slipped the note into a small evidence bag and tucked it in his pocket. "Which doesn't rule out any of our suspects."

"I guess you haven't been able to track this last attacker yet?"

Brad pulled his hat down lower on his forehead, shading his face. "No, although there is evidence of a vehicle driving into the field of the farm next door. My suspicion is that they left their car there and then scaled the fence between the properties. It isn't that difficult since it's a wire fence weighed down by honeysuckle vines. Not really a hard thing to climb over."

"Can you tell anything from the tire treads?" I asked, flexing my fingers. Hannah had cleaned my palms and applied a soothing ointment, but my hands still felt raw and stiff.

"Unfortunately not. The perpetrator was smart enough to drive across grass, rather than dirt, so there aren't any viable tracks." Brad leaned against the side of my car, his gaze fixed on his steel-toed shoes. "I wish I had more to go on, so I could eliminate some of the suspects, but we haven't been able to narrow it down yet."

I stared at him, noting the tension deepening the lines bracketing his mouth. "I think we can rule out Delbert, at least in this instance. He certainly wouldn't be running through the woods or overpowering Sunny."

"I'd already taken him off the list, at least for Ms. Dryden's murder. He wasn't seen at the inn that night and I doubt he has any knowledge of drugs that could knock someone out." Brad toyed with the top button of his shirt. "The thing is"— he looked over at me with despair clouding his eyes—"this morning Allie said she was on duty, but when my mom tried to contact her because Noah had a slight fever, her department's desk sergeant said she wasn't working today."

I laid my hand on his slumped shoulder. "I'm sure that doesn't mean anything. Maybe she just wanted to do some secret shopping for your birthday. Isn't that coming up soon?"

"It is, but . . ." Brad rubbed his forehead. "I don't know. This whole thing is so bizarre. A murder with a possible connection to a decades-old cold case? It's been making me lose weight and sleep."

"I can understand that," I said, lifting my hand. "But maybe we're over-complicating things. Ms. Dryden's death could have nothing to do with Eddie Jaffe's disappearance." I laid out the information I'd discovered about Allen Cardullo's family. "If anyone had a reason to retaliate against Maureen Dryden, it was them."

"You think Terry Temkin or Mindy LaSalle, or both, could be related to Cardullo?" Brad straightened and shot me an incredulous look.

I shrugged. "It isn't impossible. Their ages and general appearances fit. I think it's worth investigating, just to be sure."

"Okay, I'll have my team dig deeper into their backgrounds," Brad said, his expression lightening.

Death and the Librarian

He thanked me for my help and walked away, leaving me to ponder his obvious concern over the possibility that his wife could be involved in a murder case.

Surely, life wouldn't be that cruel, I thought, as I climbed into my car.

But I knew better. Driving home, with the bandage on my knee crumpling slightly as I used my right foot on the pedals, I admitted that life could be more unapologetically cruel than I could possibly imagine.

* * *

Once I got home, Richard insisted on me staying off my feet. Moving aside the coffee table, he pulled up a hassock and forced me to sit on the sofa with my right leg propped up while he made us something to eat.

"Hannah, who's a trained EMT, said it was nothing to worry about," I told him, as he continued to fuss over me.

"Sure, because it's not her loved one." Richard handed me a tray that held a bowl of salad topped with grilled salmon. "What do you want to drink? If they have you on painkillers, you can't have alcohol."

"I'm not on any prescription drugs and, yes, I can and would like some wine." I picked up my fork and poked at the salad. "This looks good. Are you going to join me?"

"In a minute. Let me grab that wine and then I'll bring in my own tray." Richard hurried off into the kitchen.

While he was out of the room my cell phone buzzed. I picked it up from the side table.

"Good news," I said, as Richard returned with his tray, which included two glasses of wine as well as his salad. "Carol says Sunny only has a very minor concussion. The doctors are keeping her overnight to monitor her, but she should be fine to go home in the morning."

Richard sat down, balancing the tray on his lap. "Glad to hear it," he said, handing me one of the wineglasses.

I waited until we finished our meal before bringing up Brad's obvious concern over Alison's possible involvement in the Dryden case. "I find it hard to believe that Alison would do such a thing, but there are some suspicious circumstances," I said. "Like Alison being absent from her department today, even though she left Noah and Zoe with Jane Tucker as if she was headed to work."

"Still, drugging and smothering someone? That takes a certain mindset. I can't see Alison staying cool and collected in such a situation." Richard twirled his fork through the remains of his salad. "She strikes me as someone who might attack an enemy in a fit of rage, but a planned murder? It seems unlikely."

"That's how I feel too, although you have to admit that she probably has access to confiscated drugs through her work as a deputy. Which also gives her the training needed to handle dangerous situations. And"—I cleared my throat—"I hadn't told you this yet, because I wasn't sure she was telling the truth, but it seems Mindy and Terry claim to have seen Alison slipping out of the inn using an emergency exit. Mindy says Alison avoided any contact with the deputies on the scene and snuck off via the road behind the inn."

Death and the Librarian

"Hmm, maybe." Richard stood up, tray in hand. "I'll take this into the kitchen and come back for yours, so"—he inclined his head as I started to rise to my feet—"stay right there."

I took a swig of my wine before he returned to collect my tray. As he left, promising to stack the bowls and utensils in the dishwasher, I received another call, this time from Brad.

"Hey, Amy, how are you?" he asked.

"Fine. My knee and hands ache a little, but nothing too extreme." I took another sip of wine. "Did you have something else you wanted to ask me?"

"No, I just wanted to pass on some information. It's something I think you should know, and maybe a lead you could help me check out."

"Oh, what's that?" I asked, silently pointing to the phone as Richard returned and sat beside me.

"Delbert called me this evening. I thought it was kind of strange, since he doesn't talk to me that often. He's in contact with Allie a lot more. Anyway"—Brad audibly exhaled—"he said he'd remembered something else from that evening in the woods, the night Eddie Jaffe disappeared."

"Really? Did he actually catch a glimpse of anyone who was partying in the clearing? Other than Sheryl Abernathy, I mean." I set my empty wineglass on the side table.

"More?" Richard mouthed at me.

I shook my head. I'd discovered as I'd gotten older that drinking too much in the evening disturbed my sleep.

"No, other than that brief encounter with Abernathy, he didn't see any of the participants. But he did notice someone when he was heading out of the woods and into the field next to your house. It was a young girl. She appeared to be loitering near the head of the trail."

"The girl Sheryl mentioned!" I said, unable to quell my excitement at this development.

"Maybe. Anyway, Delbert said he didn't think it was that strange at the time, because it was close to the girl's house. He thought maybe she was just taking a breather after being out for a walk."

"Wait a minute." I bolted upright, my sudden action sending a frisson of pain through my knee. "A girl who lived close to the trail?"

"That's the thing. It was your aunt, Lydia Talbot, or Lydia Litton as she was known then. Delbert didn't speak to her, but he said she was pretty unmistakable, with her pale hair and skin and all."

"But what would Aunt Lydia have been doing wandering around at night? She was only fifteen at the time," I said, before the memory of my mother's words drifted through my mind. *What if she was following Andrew Talbot, as Mom claimed she did incessantly that summer? Does that mean Andrew was one of the partyers?*

"Delbert didn't know the answer to that," Brad said. "He just thought I should be told about another person seen in the general area that evening."

"So you want me to do what? Question Aunt Lydia concerning the night Jaffe disappeared?" I caught Richard's concerned gaze out of the corner of my eye. "That's a long time ago. She might not even remember it."

Death and the Librarian

"Perhaps not, but it seems prudent to ask. I thought you would be the best person to broach the subject, at least at first." The apologetic tone of Brad's words made me realize how unhappy he was to drag my aunt into the situation.

"Alright, I'll see what I can find out. But I'm not going to interrogate her. If she doesn't want to discuss the matter . . ."

"That's when my department will step in. Not in a contentious way, of course," Brad said, his voice softening. "We simply need to know if she saw anyone, or anything, suspicious that evening."

I once again promised to talk to my aunt, then wished Brad a good evening and ended the call.

"What was that all about?" Richard's fingers tightened on the stem of his wineglass as he eyed me with curiosity.

"It's something about Aunt Lydia," I replied.

"I gathered that much, and that Brad wants you to talk to her." Richard finished off his wine and set the glass on the end of the askew coffee table.

"Yeah, which I'm not looking forward to." I swiveled on the cushions to face Richard. "Apparently, Delbert Frye now claims to have seen Aunt Lydia the night Eddie Jaffe went missing. He says she was standing near the head of the trail that leads up to the clearing. Of course, it was pretty close to her grandmother's house, so Delbert suggested maybe she was simply out for a walk. But I don't know."

Richard lifted his eyebrows. "Is there any other reason she'd be in that area at night?"

"Maybe one." I grimaced as a twinge of pain shot through my knee. "According to my mom, and things I've heard from

Zelda over the years, Aunt Lydia was obsessed with Andrew Talbot in the way only a young girl can be. She knew him even before she moved in with Great-grandmother Rose, because he used to visit Kurt here. I mean, when it was Paul Dassin's house."

"She loved him all along? That doesn't really surprise me. Even though she's quite happy and devoted to Hugh now, I can still see the longing and loss in her eyes when she talks about your uncle." Richard laid his hand on my upper thigh. "Do you think she was trying to follow Andrew that night?"

"It's possible. Mom told me that Aunt Lydia used to trail after him the entire summer before he went to college." I gnawed on the inside of my cheek. "And Sheryl Abernathy mentioned a girl when I spoke with her at the nursing home. She called her something like 'that horrible girl,' and said she ruined everything. Sheryl even intimated that maybe Eddie ran off with this girl. But of course, that's not true, not if it was Aunt Lydia she saw."

"From what I understand, Sheryl was pretty out of it that evening. Maybe she just caught a glimpse of Lydia on the trail and conflated that with Eddie's disappearance."

"That could be true. Sheryl also said something about telling the girl to head back down the trail, so it sounds like she chased her off."

Richard absently rubbed his jaw. "Lydia wouldn't have seen who was in the clearing if that's true. She may not even have known whether Andrew was there or not."

"True. Perhaps she simply heard some rumor about a gathering in the woods that evening and somehow connected it with Andrew,"

Death and the Librarian

"Or she overheard him talking to someone about using that spot as a meeting place." Richard sat back, leaning against a pillow propped against the sofa arm. "Lydia is smart and determined. It wouldn't surprise me if she put two and two together from random conversations or gossip."

"I can see it." Making a face, I slumped against the sofa cushions. "Brad wants me to talk to her. Sort of a preliminary interview. If she admits being there, he'd have a deputy question her, but I think he wants to avoid jumping into that pit if there's nothing to Delbert's story."

"Can you blame him? Richard gave an exaggerated shudder. "I know I'd never want to get on Lydia's bad side."

"I knew you were a smart man," I said, with a smile. "Yeah, I'm not sure I want to bring this matter up with her, but I suppose I have to."

Richard slid closer and put his arm around my shoulders. "I've always known that you're brave, but this definitely proves it."

Chapter Twenty

I took over Sunny's shifts at the library on Thursday and Friday, despite her protests.

"I'm perfectly fine," she told me in a phone call.

"Well, a couple of little birds, whose names happen to be P. J. and Carol, told me that the doctor suggested you rest at home until next Monday. So just do that. The twins are still at my parents' house and, in fact, I'm going ask them to keep them until the weekend after this one, which means I can take over your shifts without any problem."

"But Saturday too? That's too much to ask," Sunny said. "Especially since you also got hurt."

"Don't worry, it's no worse than when we used to fall off our bikes as kids. No stitches or anything. Also, Samantha and some of the volunteers are going to work on Saturday, so I'll get that day off. As well as Sunday, of course, since we're closed."

"Alright, at least I can mollify Fred. In our video chat last night he was threatening to fly back here and guard the door to the house if I didn't take the doctor's advice."

Death and the Librarian

"Good for Fred," I said, with a little chuckle. "Do you know when he's actually coming back?"

"He thinks it will be sometime next week," Sunny said, her voice brightening.

"You'd better get well before he gets back. Or you won't be able to have a grand reunion."

"Oh, there are ways—" Sunny said before I cut her off.

"Enough of that. You take care, okay? Love you," I told her before we ended the call.

I waited until I got off work on Thursday to approach Aunt Lydia about Delbert's latest revelation. It took me that long to come up with a way to broach the subject without getting immediately shut down.

Having sent a text earlier in the day about finally delivering the apples I'd gotten at Vista View, I knew Aunt Lydia planned to be working in her extensive flower, herb, and vegetable garden in the late afternoon. So I went to my house and changed clothes before grabbing the bucket that contained half of the apples I'd brought home.

After I gave the cats some kibble, I headed out the back door off the screened porch, carrying the bucket to Aunt Lydia's backyard through the rose-covered arbor.

"Hello, it's me," I called out. "Where do you want the apples?"

My aunt, wearing a floppy straw hat that shaded her face, looked up from the herb bed she was weeding. "Just sit them by the back porch steps," she said, rising to her feet from the padded kneeling bench my mom had given her for her last

Victoria Gilbert

birthday. She brushed her palms together to remove some fine dirt, then wiped her hands on her garden apron.

"Not wearing gloves?" I asked, widening my eyes. "What about your manicure?"

"I have a nail appointment scheduled for tomorrow," she replied, her blue eyes glinting with good humor. "Might as well give them something to do."

"I'm sure they'll appreciate that," I said, not tempering the sarcasm in my voice.

"How's your leg?" Aunt Lydia asked, gesturing toward one of the white benches scattered around her garden. "We can sit down if you'd like."

"Sure, but honestly, my knee is fine. Like I told Sunny, it's no worse than some of the bumps and scrapes I got as a kid."

"Is Sunny feeling better?" My aunt led me down one of the white pea-gravel paths that separated her rock-bordered beds. She stopped at a bench that faced an intricately carved concrete birdbath. "I know you said she was resting at home through the weekend."

"She's doing well. Of course, it's difficult for her to stay still for any length of time." I sat down beside my aunt.

"Ah, yes, I think *rest* is a foreign word to Sunny." Aunt Lydia took off her hat and used it to fan her face and neck.

I turned to study her elegant profile. Her bone structure and patrician features allowed her to remain beautiful at any age, but I knew from photographs that she had been stunningly gorgeous when she was young. Kurt's words about

216

Death and the Librarian

Andrew loving beautiful things echoed in my mind. "You've lived here a long time," I said.

She shifted on the bench to meet my gaze. "Yes, but where did that non sequitur come from?"

"I mean, I know you were living here when the area beyond my house was a field. But the trails were already there, right?"

"Of course. One led to a mountain clearing and the other skirted the edge of the woods where the deciduous trees gave way to pines. Just like they do now." Aunt Lydia narrowed her eyes. "Why are you interested in such a thing?"

"I just wondered." I squirmed on the sun-warmed bench, wondering if I'd already destroyed my chance to speak to her about the night Jaffe disappeared. "That clearing was the last place Eddie Jaffe was seen. At least, as far as anyone can tell."

"That's common knowledge," my aunt said cooly.

"Yes, but there's some wrinkles in the case. I don't think I told you that I spoke with Eddie Jaffe's girlfriend. Or at least, that's what she claims to have been. Her name's Sheryl Abernathy and she's living in a nursing home in Smithsburg." I crossed my hands primly in my lap. "Brad Tucker actually asked me to speak to her, just to see if she was someone who needed to be interviewed by his deputies."

Aunt Lydia's lips tightened into a straight line. "Did he ask you to speak to me as well?" she asked, after a pause filled with the whirr of insect wings.

"Yes." I laced my fingers together. "He received some information from someone who was in the area that evening—"

Victoria Gilbert

"Delbert Frye." My aunt spat out the name through clenched teeth.

"That's right. He contacted Brad recently and mentioned seeing someone standing in the field, near the head of the trail. A girl with blonde hair and pale skin. So we just wondered—"

Aunt Lydia stood up so quickly she knocked her hat to the ground. "If it was me? Because, of course, I lived close by, and I fit that description." She paced over to the birdbath. "Very well, as you guessed, I was there."

"Why? Were you out for a late walk or something?" I asked, hoping to give her an out if she wanted to take it. "I know living with your grandmother was tough, and you might've needed to escape the house from time to time."

"That was true enough, but actually, I was hoping to see Andrew." Aunt Lydia flicked her fingers through the birdbath water. "I expect you've heard from your mother or Zelda that I was infatuated with Andrew, even as a girl of fifteen."

"They may have mentioned something about it."

"I'm sure." My aunt's slender frame was outlined by sunlight, giving her an ethereal appearance. She strolled back to the bench and picked up her hat. "I was a silly little fool back then," she said, sitting down with the hat in her lap. "I admit that. Andrew was all I thought about, partially because other things were too painful to contemplate."

"How did you know Andrew would be at the clearing that night?"

"I didn't. Not for sure." Aunt Lydia rolled the brim of the hat between her fingers. "I'd only heard rumors that he'd

Death and the Librarian

meet some people up there from time to time. So when I saw him earlier that day and he mentioned he planned to stay at Paul Dassin's house that night rather than head home . . ."

"You decided to see if you could find him," I said, keeping my gaze focused on a monarch butterfly flitting amid the lavender blossoms of a butterfly bush.

"Yes. I even walked up the trail a short distance, but then I ran into someone. It was a skinny young woman with a wild mane of black curls. She stopped me from going any farther." Aunt Lydia sighed. "I knew she'd been drinking because I could smell it on her. I think she'd done some drugs too. Her eyes looked funny."

"She admitted to me that she was pretty messed up that evening."

Aunt Lydia frowned. "Not surprised. Anyway, that intimidated me. I didn't want to walk into a group of people who'd lost all sense of reality. So I stayed where I was, even after she headed back up the trail."

I brushed a sweat bee away from my face. "Delbert must've run across her not long after that. He said they met at the trail, but after their brief encounter he just walked off into the trees to collect more wood."

"I suppose. I never saw Delbert. At least, not on the trail." Aunt Lydia rocked her upper body back and forth ever so slightly. "I waited; in case Andrew came by when he was leaving the gathering. Even though I didn't actually know he was there." She laughed mirthlessly. "The stupidity of young love."

I cast her a sidelong glance. "You never told the authorities you were there, did you?"

"Of course not. My grandmother would've killed me."
My aunt met my gaze with a wry smile. "I seriously believed
that at the time. Anyway, I wasn't going to take any chances."

"Did you see anyone else there, other than Sheryl and
Delbert?"

"Maybe." Aunt Lydia sat back and stared up into the clear
sky. "You have to understand that I was tired and more than
a little scared. So my memories are fuzzy. But I think I saw a
young man, older than me but still a teenager. I looked up the
trail at one point, and it seemed he was standing there, in the
distance, watching me. But then I blinked and he was gone.
I guess, if he *was* there, he ran back to the clearing."

"Was it Eddie Jaffe?" I asked quietly.

"It could've been. He had longish fair hair. I'd never met
Jaffe so I had no point of reference, but when I saw his photograph after he vanished, I thought maybe that *was* him." Aunt
Lydia closed her eyes and lowered her head. "Later, I convinced myself that he was a figment of my imagination. I'd
been hoping to see Andrew and conjured up a vaguely similar
figure."

We sat in silence for a while, allowing the breeze to tickle the
back of our necks as the mingled scents of flowers and herbs
perfumed the air. A few bees buzzed somewhere close by.

"He did love you, though, eventually," I said. "Andrew,
I mean. When he returned to the area after college, he pur-
sued you. At least, that's what I've always heard from Mom."

"Yes." Aunt Lydia's expression softened. "I had more sense
then. I didn't follow him around anymore." She smiled. "I
forced him to chase me."

Death and the Librarian

"You should tell Brad that you were on the trail that night." I rose to my feet and stood in front of her. "You don't have to say why. Just mention leaving the house and taking a walk to get away from your grandmother. He'll understand that. He knows what Rose was like."

"True. He joined the sheriff's department not long before she died and had some dealings with her as a newly minted deputy." Aunt Lydia looked up at me, determination hardening her features. "That was when she was really far gone, but I'm sure he'd believe me if tell him there were times I had to get out of that house when I was a young girl."

"There you go—you can tell him what he needs to know without sharing all your secrets."

"A good compromise," my aunt said. "I will do that. Tomorrow." She took hold of one of my hands. "I'll fulfil my civic duty, but promise me that you'll keep my other secrets."

"Of course." I squeezed her fingers. "Now, I'd better head back to the house. I'm sure Richard's home by now and probably wondering where I am."

"Nope," called a voice from the rose arbor. "I noticed the bucket of apples was gone so I figured you'd popped over here." Richard smiled at us, bringing a sense of lightness I hadn't felt since I'd approached my aunt earlier. "Hello, Lydia. I hope you're doing well."

"Quite well, thank you." My aunt stood up and placed her hat back on her head. "Good to see you, Richard, but I should get back to my weeding. Despite all my hopes and prayers, the weeds won't pull themselves." She turned to me. "Thanks for the apples, dear, and . . . everything."

221

I smiled and offered to help with the garden maintenance soon. "Once I'm not working so many hours," I said, then wished her a good evening.

"Come and pick up a pie tomorrow after work," she said as I turned and walked toward my own yard.

"I hope you didn't feed the cats," I said when I reached Richard. "Because I already did that before I left the house."

Richard pressed a hand to his heart. "You mean to tell me those pleading looks and pathetic noises were all a ruse?"

"Absolutely. And you fall for it every time." I poked his chest with my forefinger. "You're too easily duped by those little monsters. Just because they're cute."

"It's true, it's true. But I confess there are three things I can't resist," he said, leaning in to give me a kiss. "The cats, the kids, and you."

Chapter
Twenty-One

Friday morning, in the middle of processing the interlibrary loans that had been delivered the day before, I received a text from Sunny.

Want to meet at the Heapin' Plate for lunch? I have to get out of the house.

I clucked my tongue over this request. She really couldn't sit still. But knowing she might attempt a more demanding physical activity if I refused, I agreed to meet her at noon.

Leaving the library a little before twelve, I headed to the Heapin' Plate, which was only a block away. As expected, the restaurant was busy. I paused in the doorway, searching for Sunny. Located in a historic turn-of-the-century building that had once been a general store, the restaurant had retained its original pressed-tin ceiling and marble-topped walnut counter but was decorated in a vintage 1950s style.

Sunny waved me over to one of the round, chrome-edged tables. I crossed the black-and-white tiled floor, weaving my way past other tables and their metal ladder-back chairs, all filled with patrons. I wasn't surprised by the crowd. The owner, Bethany Virts, was an excellent cook, and the Heapin' Plate was one of only a handful of restaurants one could walk to from the center of town.

"You look good," I told Sunny, as I sat down across from her. "Are you feeling back to normal now?"

Sunny pushed her long hair behind her shoulders with both hands. "Pretty much. I still get headaches off and on, but my balance and vision are fine."

"Glad to hear it. You see, resting at home yesterday didn't do you any harm." I laid down my menu as a waitress appeared at our table. "I'll have the summer salad, with the house dressing, and I'll just stick with water," I told her, wrapping my fingers around a glass dappled with condensation.

"Same," Sunny said. After the waitress headed to the kitchen Sunny added, "For your information, I was incredibly bored yesterday. I couldn't read very much because my vision was still a little wonky. Then the grands kept fussing over me like I was an invalid." Sunny rolled her eyes. "That's why I had to get out today."

"Understood. I guess the sheriff's department doesn't have any leads about your attacker," I added, in a lower voice. There were a lot of people around and I didn't trust any of them not to eavesdrop. "At least, I haven't heard anything from Brad yet."

"Neither have I, although he did call this morning to see how I was doing." Sunny tapped her fork against the red tabletop. "It's still an ongoing search."

After the waitress returned with our salads, we concentrated on eating and sharing small talk rather than discussing

Death and the Librarian

the investigation into Maureen's murder and our subsequent threatening encounter on the farm. The crowded diner was no place to share confidences, although everyone at the table next to us had no compunction over loudly discussing the latest gossip about a town council member's affair

Sunny arched her eyebrows and motioned toward that table with a tilt of her head. "Now we know everything," she told me with a twitch of her lips.

"Best place to catch up on local news," I said at normal volume. "Who needs a town website or county newspaper when you can just come to the diner and hear it all?"

The neighboring table paid no attention to our comments. Her smile broadening, Sunny finished off her salad and pushed slightly away from the table. "That was good. The company is nice too."

"I agree." I slid my empty salad bowl to the side. "This is on me, by the way."

"No, I can pay for my own meal." Sunny lifted her purse from the floor.

I set down my glass firmly enough to make the remaining ice cubes clink. "I didn't get you any flowers after your injury, so let me do this."

"Well, in that case . . ." Sunny placed her purse in her lap.

A chair scraped the tile floor behind me. "Fortune must be smiling on us," Terry Temkin said.

I turned my head slightly to see Terry and Mindy standing side by side.

"What good fortune is that?" Sunny asked, eyeing them with suspicion.

225

Mindy ran her fingers through her blonde curls, drawing my attention to her darker roots. "We've wanted to speak to you both for several days, just to clarify a few things. And here you are."

I surveyed the crowed dining room. "This isn't the best place to talk."

"If you're done eating, we could go outside," Terry said.

"Alright." I shared a glance with Sunny, who nodded. "But not on the street. You can meet us on the sidewalk out front, but then we'll head to a small garden close by."

"A public space?" Mindy asked.

"No, but I have permission to use it," I replied. This wasn't strictly true. It was Kurt who'd bartered with Bethany, trading the more esoteric spices he could obtain in the city for the use of her garden. But I'd met him there a few times and felt I could claim to be his guest.

Sunny stood up and grabbed the bill the waitress had dropped on the table. "I'll take care of this," she said, silencing my protests with a chop of her hand. "You guide them around to the garden and I'll meet you there."

Once we were outside, I led Mindy and Terry down the narrow alley flanking the side of the diner. "The garden's in the back," I called over my shoulder. "We can talk more freely there."

The open space behind the diner consisted of a small square of grass surrounded by flower and vegetable beds. A wooden bench placed at the edge of one of the beds was weathered as gray as driftwood. "Please, have a seat," I told Terry and Mindy. Noticing Sunny jogging in from the alley, I added, "You too, Sunny. I'll stand."

Death and the Librarian

"You should sit. I don't mind staying on my feet," Terry said, as Mindy and Sunny settled on the bench.

"Very gallant of you, but I feel like standing," I said.

"As you wish." Terry took a seat beside Mindy.

"So what did you want to talk to us about?" Sunny asked, side-eyeing the two podcasters.

Terry and Mindy shared a significant look. "Okay, here's the thing," Terry said. "We want you to know that we should no longer be considered suspects in Maureen's death."

I paced the small square of lawn. "Why is that?"

"Because the detectives finally found the witness we'd told them about from the start," Mindy said. "That person confirmed that we weren't inside the inn when Maureen was killed."

"I saw you there," Sunny said, her expression mulish.

"Sure, we saw you as well. You were with a group of people in the large corner booth," Terry said. "And we were in the restaurant, at a table and then the bar. But before Maureen even headed up to her room, Mindy and I took our drinks out onto the patio."

Mindy flashed a smug smile and chimed in. "We couldn't prove that, even though there was a man out there smoking a couple of cigarettes. He was there long enough to see that we never left the patio until the maid announced Maureen's death."

"Fortunately, one of the deputies finally tracked him down yesterday, and he's willing to vouch for us," Terry said. "Which means we both have solid alibis."

I stopped pacing and turned to face the bench. "The sheriff knows this, I suppose?"

"Of course." Mindy lifted her chin and fixed me with a cold stare. "He didn't seem too thrilled, I guess because of our statement about seeing his wife sneaking away from the scene of a crime, but he accepted our testimony. One thing I'll say for Sheriff Tucker—he doesn't let any personal biases interfere with an investigation. Anyway, our witness corroborated our alibi, so we'd appreciate it if you would stop researching our pasts or whatever else you were doing to help solve the case. It isn't necessary anymore."

"Yeah, cease and desist," Terry said.

Mindy turned to Sunny. "And you—make sure the story you tell the authorities is clear. You *did* see us at the Taylorsford Inn that night, but you didn't have eyes on us the entire time."

"That is true," Sunny said, lowering her head to stare at the purse clutched in her lap. "I should have clarified that in the beginning."

"That would've been helpful." Terry swept a dark curl away from his forehead. "But no harm done, now that we have our witness. So I'm willing to let bygones be bygones." He rose to his feet.

Mindy stood up as well. "As long as you don't go around insinuating that either of us had anything to do with Maureen's murder, that is."

I raised my hands, palms out. "No worries. If Brad Tucker has struck you off the suspect list, I'll focus my efforts elsewhere." *Like Alison and Kurt*, I thought, tension cramping my stomach.

"Thanks. We're staying in the area to collect information for our podcast and we'd like to do that without a shadow hovering over our heads," Terry said.

Death and the Librarian

"I'll amend my statement with the sheriff's department." Sunny stayed seated as the other two stepped away from the bench.

"Thank you," Mindy said. "It will take a weight off our minds, for sure."

"What about Sean?" I asked, my words halting Mindy and Terry's forward momentum.

"What about him?" Mindy's dark brown eyes narrowed to a squint.

"Was he with you, outside on the patio?"

"No, he stayed inside. Near the bar, I think," Terry said smoothly. "I'm not entirely sure about that, but he was in the restaurant crowd when we went back inside after hearing about Maureen."

"He was pretty drunk, but you wouldn't know it to look at him," Mindy said. "I mean, he seemed perfectly normal. Very calm, as always. But not much fazes him, from what I've seen."

"Of course, we barely know the man," Terry interjected. "Come on, Min, let's go. We've got some interviews set up this afternoon and I want to make sure the equipment is working properly."

Mindy nodded in mute agreement, and they both left the garden, walking fast.

"That was weird," Sunny said, as they disappeared from view.

"I guess they want to able to talk to people without being suspected of murder." I shrugged. "I can understand that."

"What does it mean for the case?" Sunny slung the strap of her purse over her shoulder.

229

"I'm not sure," I said, although I had some ideas. "But I think I should take my research in other directions, if I even want to do any more research, that is."

"I guess you need to get back to work, huh?" Sunny held up her left arm and pointed to the watch on her wrist. "You might actually be a few minutes late. Sorry."

"No problem." I gave her a wink. "That's why I'm the big boss."

"What am I, then?" Sunny asked, linking arms with me as we stepped into the alley.

I cast her a grin. "The bigger boss, of course."

Chapter Twenty-Two

On Saturday morning I made the decision to go into work, even though I was scheduled to be off. Richard was going to be busy, giving Connor Vogler an extra one-on-one lesson. Connor had decided to enter an international dance competition, and Richard wanted to support him.

"We're going to fine-tune his audition piece," Richard told me over breakfast. "I hope you don't mind. I should be back in the afternoon and then maybe we can tackle the garden together."

"That's fine," I said. "There's an errand I need to run this morning anyway. Once we both take care of business, then we can enjoy the rest of the day. Maybe not in the garden, though. I was thinking more about something like a date." I pointed my fork at him. "You remember what that is, right?"

"Of course," Richard said, with a grin. "Alright, how about a movie and dinner? We can drive over to Harburg. They have a multiscreen cinema and good restaurants. Emily Moore recently gave me a recommendation for a Mediterranean place. She says it's very authentic."

"That sounds great." I smiled. "We might as well take advantage of the twins visiting my parents. We haven't really done that yet."

"Good point." Richard stood and collected the plates and utensils.

"Just set those in the sink. I'll deal with them since you probably need to leave sooner than I do," I said.

"I won't argue with that." Richard deposited the dishes, then turned and brushed a kiss against my forehead. "Looking forward to our date."

"Me too," I said, giving him a quick hug. "We can pretend to be young lovers."

Richard's eyebrows shot up. "What? We aren't?"

"Oh, go on, you," I said indulgently. He blew me a kiss before leaving the room.

After Richard left, I gave the kitchen a brief cleaning, or what my mom would call "a lick and a promise." Then I showered and changed into a lightweight pair of linen pants and a copper-colored short-sleeved silk blouse. As I dressed, I pondered the thought that had popped into my mind in the middle of the night.

I'd made a stupid research mistake—I'd searched for information on Maureen and her colleagues, as well as the Eddie Jaffe case, without checking one of the databases we'd subscribed to for many years. The service provided digital access to older newspapers from all over the country. It was a resource that wasn't used that often, but it could be invaluable in certain circumstances.

Death and the Librarian

Like when you need to check the background of individuals who may not be that active on social media, I reminded myself as I walked to the library. If they or their families had ever done something noteworthy or, more sadly, had been involved in some type of tragedy, it might have been covered by a newspaper from their local city or town. It was worth a try, anyway.

Samantha was surprised to see me enter through the staff workroom. "I thought you were off today," she said. "We're really fine. Zelda and Bill are here, and a few more volunteers will be in this afternoon."

I pressed one finger to my lips. "I'm not really here. I just need to do a little research in one of our licensed databases and thought it would be easier to access here than at home. I'm going to use the workroom computer if that's okay with you."

"Sure. I don't need it for anything." Samantha looked me over. "Are you still helping the sheriff with the Maureen Dryden investigation?"

"Sort of. It's also to satisfy my own curiosity," I said.

"I asked because one of the people connected to that case came in early to use the archives. It's that Sean fellow who was here a little while ago. I thought it would be okay to let him in to work without supervision, since you approved that before."

"That's fine," I said, sitting down in front of the computer workstation. "As long is everything is locked up when he leaves."

Victoria Gilbert

Samantha nodded. "I told him to just close the archives door and come around the building to enter through the front doors when he was done. Then one of us can go out and check things over and lock up."

"Sounds like a plan." I gave Samantha a smile before turning back to the computer.

The newspaper database wasn't the easiest resource to search, but I'd mastered all of its eccentricities over the years. Despite their proclamation of possessing an airtight alibi, I started with Terry and Mindy, searching for any connection to Allen Cardullo. I didn't find anything but did note one peculiarity—neither of them was mentioned in any articles until their college years. First, when Terry became a local DJ, and then when he and Mindy started their podcast. But of course, they were still young, so it was possible they hadn't done anything newsworthy before that time.

Switching my focus to Sean, I discovered nothing until one short article caught my eye. It included a photo of three young men in uniform who were receiving an award for valor for rescuing a shipmate who'd fallen overboard during a storm. One of the men was identified as Sean Gordon.

I peered at the grainy photo, further degraded by being digitized from a print copy. The young man listed as Sean Gordon bore some resemblance to the man I'd met, although in the photo he had a beefier build and his hair, cropped short, was basically hidden by his dress uniform hat.

If he lost weight and let his hair grow . . . I shook my head. It was impossible to tell. I rolled my task chair away from the desk and closed my eyes for a moment. Allen

234

Death and the Librarian

Cardullo had a half-brother in the military, which might also fit in with Mindy's comment about Sean remaining unfazed by critical situations, but is that enough to link the two men?

I printed the article and shut down the computer. Even if it was a long shot, I knew I had to tell Brad. He should have his detectives dig a little deeper into Sean Gordon's background. I sent a text to Brad asking for time to talk face to face. I wanted to share the article and photograph and knew it would be practically unreadable if I tried to email it to him. In addition, I believed I could express my admittedly confused thoughts on the situation better if I could talk to Brad in person.

I stood and wandered out of the workroom to stand next to Samantha at the circulation desk.

"All done?" she asked.

"For today." I fiddled with the pens stuffed in a wire holder next to the desk computer. We always kept inexpensive pens and pencil, as well as paper scraps, on hand for the patrons who inevitably forgot to bring them to the library.

"I heard about some trespasser on the Fields farm. Did he or she really knock Sunny out?" Samantha's deep brown eyes radiated concern.

"Not entirely. She only had a mild concussion, thank goodness. It was scary, though." I bit back a comment about the threatening note, aware it was something I shouldn't share too widely.

Samantha sighed. "I don't know what the world is coming to. People killed in hotel rooms and some stranger invading

Victoria Gilbert

personal property and attacking one of the owners. You don't think of those sorts of things happening in a town like Taylorsford."

"They happen everywhere, it seems." My cell phone buzzed in my pocket. "Sorry, I need to check this."

I immediately recognized Brad's number. Turning my back to the desk, I answered. "Oh, hi. I guess you got my message?"

"Yes, and while I'd like to talk to you as soon as possible, I can't possibly manage it today," Brad said. "Can you give me a hint as to what this is all about?"

"It has to do with looking a little more closely at one of Maureen Dryden's associates," I said. "I found an interesting article and photo from our national newspaper database. It might mean nothing, but I thought you'd want to check it out."

I could hear Brad tapping something against his desk. "Which one was it?"

"Sean Gordon," I said. "I'm not sure if it's even a match, but there are some interesting connections . . ."

"Okay, let's meet at the Taylorsford Inn tomorrow night around five," Brad said. "I'm sorry it's so late on a Sunday, but I need to reinterview some staff members to double-check their statements. Also, the bartender who was on duty the night Ms. Dryden was killed has been out of town, but she promised she'd be working the night shift tomorrow."

"That's fine. Tomorrow night at five at the inn," I repeated to make sure I'd gotten it right. "Okay, Brad, thanks. I'll be there."

Death and the Librarian

"Good. Talk to you then," Brad said, ending the call after a quick goodbye.

I tucked my phone back in my pocket and turned just in time to see a tall man with shoulder-length hair walk out of the stacks and hurry toward the main doors. "How long has he been there?" I asked Samantha.

"I'm not sure. He finished his work in the archives a little while ago and Zelda locked up behind him, but she said he was going to browse the shelves before he left." She gave me a quizzical look. "Why?"

"Oh, nothing," I said, silently cursing my carelessness.

I didn't know how much Sean had heard, but I was afraid any portion of my conversation with Brad was too much.

* * *

As it turned out, we didn't have a date night after all. Richard had just walked in the door when he received a call from Suzanna, one of his company dancers.

"There's been a car accident," he told me with a stricken expression. "She says she isn't badly injured, but I could tell she was simply trying to put up a brave front. Sorry, sweetheart, but I think I should go to the hospital and figure out the real situation."

"Of course," I said. "Did Suzanna call Karla too, or should I do that?"

"She already sent her a text, so I imagine Karla is on her way to the hospital now." He glanced down at his phone. "And there's a text from Karla, confirming that."

"Go, go, go," I said, ushering him toward the door. "You won't be able to relax until you know Suzanna is actually okay."

"It's true," he replied ruefully. "Especially considering how even minor accidents can ruin a dancer's career." He leaned in to give me a peck on the cheek. "Sorry again for ruining our plans."

I waved him off. "I'd think less of you if you didn't go. Don't worry, I'm going to make some popcorn and watch a cheesy movie on TV. You know, basically be a slob, lying around in my pajamas and drinking too much wine."

"Not *too* too much," Richard said, with a faint smile. "I don't want you to be comatose by the time I get home." He opened the front door. "Alright, I'm off. I'll call or text from the hospital once I know more."

"Okay. Take care, and give Suzanna my best wishes for a quick recovery," I said, before closing and locking the door behind him.

Fosse and Loie followed me into the kitchen. "It's just you and me, kids," I said, opening the pantry door to grab a bag of cat snacks. I dropped a few treats on the floor in front of each of them. "Here, have a blast."

While the cats gobbled up the treats, I wandered over to the refrigerator, opened the door, and stared at the contents before closing the door again. I grabbed an open bottle of red wine from one of the counters and carried it and a stemless wineglass over to the kitchen island. After pouring a full glass, I pulled my phone from my pocket and called my mother's number.

Death and the Librarian

"Hello, Amy, what's up?" she asked. Her tone was cheerful, which was heartening. Apparently the twins hadn't caused too much trouble recently.

"Nothing much. I just wanted to talk to the kids. Can you switch to video?"

"Sure." The screen flared and opened on Mom standing in front of her own kitchen island. She turned her phone to show me Ella and Nicky, who were perched on stools on the other side of the island.

"Mommy!" Ella shouted, leaning over the island so far that the flour dusting a large piece of parchment paper floated up like dust. "We're making a pizza!"

"Wow. I wish I was there," I said, swallowing back a sob as I looked at my children's bright faces.

"We want you here too," Nicky said. "Can you come and visit?"

"Not right now. There's things Daddy and I have to take care of." I cleared my throat. "Are you having fun with Grandma and Grandad?"

"Oh yes," Ella said, while Nicky bobbed his head in agreement. "We've been swimming every day and we're turning into dolphins, right, Grandma?"

"It's true. They've both come a long way. I think they'll be ready for more advanced lessons soon," my mom said, pride radiating from her voice.

"Grandma says she'll take us scuba diving when we get older," Nicky's conflicted expression matched my own trepidation over this news. I'd always worried over my mom's numerous dives, especially when they involved cold and dark water. Despite being an excellent swimmer myself, I'd never wanted to dive. My claustrophobia made even the idea of it nerve-racking.

"We'll see," I said. "You have to get better with your regular swimming before that."

"I want to be a lifeguard," Ella announced, leaving white streaks as she wiped her hands on her navy-blue tank top.

"I bet you've been doing a lot more laundry than usual," I told Mom dryly.

"Oh my, yes." Mom flipped the phone around so she and I could look at each other. "I think it's great that Ella and Nicky are so active, but they go through clothes like a hot knife through butter."

"Trust me, I know." I forced a bright smile. "Listen, Mom, would you mind keeping the kids until next weekend? Then when you bring them back you can spend a few days here again."

My mother's searching expression told me she wasn't entirely convinced by my smile. "Is something wrong there, Amy?" she asked, in a low voice.

"No, no. It's just that there's been a lot of stuff happening, with the recent murder and all. I don't think Ella and Nicky need to be around that sort of thing."

"Because you're mixed up in the investigation again?" Mom's gusty sigh filled my ears. "For goodness sake, Amy, when are you going to steer clear of such activities?"

I almost said something about her diving in dangerous waters as part of her former occupation as a marine and

240

Death and the Librarian

environmental scientist, but common sense silenced me. "It's mostly research, on my end. But it does make my schedule a little unpredictable. So I really do appreciate you and Dad taking care of the kids right now."

"It's not like we mind. We've been having fun, haven't we?" Mom turned the phone back on the twins.

"Lots!" Ella said, before adding, "We do miss you and Daddy, though."

"Yeah, we both miss you," Nicky said fervently. "We love Grandma and Grandad, but we wish we were all together."

"I miss you both too. Lots and lots," I said, blinking the tears from my eyes. "So does Daddy. And Aunt Lydia, and Sunny and Loie and Fosse too. We all miss you bunches and bunches."

"Sorry, Mommy. We'll send you kisses." Ella blew a noisy kiss toward the phone. Nicky followed suit.

"Alright, you guys, I'd better go so you can finish your pizza. Love you!" I said, determined to finish the call before I started crying in earnest. "Love you too, Mom. Richard or I will call again soon."

"Okay, dear. Be careful, and don't worry. We'll take care of the twins." My mom gave a little wave. "Lots of love to you and Richard, and we'll see you soon."

After the call ended, I dashed to the hall bathroom for a handful of tissues.

"Don't look at me like that," I told Loie, who was staring at me with slitted eyes. "You don't have any kittens. You don't know what's it's like."

Loie flicked her tail and gave me another sphinxlike stare before stalking off, while Fosse pressed his body against my leg and offered a comforting purr.

"At least someone understands me," I said, reaching for my wineglass.

242

Chapter Twenty-Three

Fortunately, Suzanna's injuries would not affect her dancing career. Richard made sure of that, consulting with her doctors to ensure nothing was done that might cause her problems in the future.

"So now you're a consultant," I said, when he explained how some of the procedures had to be adapted to allow Suzanna the chance for a recovery that included the full range of motion needed by a dancer. It would require a longer recovery time, but Suzanna was okay with that as long as she could dance again.

"Definitely not," Richard said, drying his damp, just washed hair with a towel. "I have too many jobs as it is."

"That's true. I think you should look out for your dancers and not go into anything medical, at least not professionally." I leaned in closer to the bathroom mirror to apply some lip gloss. "So, how about we have that date today? I do have to meet Brad at five, but we could catch an early movie and then enjoy a late lunch."

"I won't argue with that." Richard draped the towel over the pewter-colored bar that matched the other fixtures in our bathroom. "But listen, Amy—shouldn't I accompany you to the inn? I'm not sure I like you going out alone in the evenings these days."

"Don't be silly. I'm meeting Brad. What could possibly happen? Besides, you were up so late last night, you should rest today. Well, after our date." I stepped back and brushed my silver-streaked deep brown hair. "It seems like I have more gray strands every day. Should I color it? Sunny and Zelda say yes, but I'm afraid it would be one more thing to keep up with."

"You should do what you want. I'll love you with brown hair, white hair, or even no hair." Richard leaned over and kissed my shoulder.

I studied our reflections in the mirror. Richard, standing behind me, was tall and lean, while I was short and curvaceous, but at that moment we looked good together. Maybe it was simply because we were comfortable with each other, but we projected the aura of a perfect match. "I know it took both of us a while to find one another, but I'm glad we did. It was worth the wait."

"Absolutely." Richard wrapped his arms around me. "I don't really believe in fate, except where you're concerned. Meeting you was one of the few things I'd call destiny."

I raised my eyebrows. "Wow, you are waxing poetic this morning."

"And what's wrong with that?" Richard slid his hands up my arms and took hold of my shoulders. Turning me around to face him, he kissed my lips. "Poetry shouldn't be restricted to any specific time or place," he added when he released me. "Just like any art form."

Death and the Librarian

"You've always been such a romantic," I said with a smile.

Richard's lips curved upward. "Are you complaining?"

"Not at all. I appreciate my good fortune and applaud your romantic nature, even when your other love draws you away from me."

Richard's eyes widened. "Other love? What other love?"

"Dance, of course." I pressed my hand to his chest. "She's a demanding mistress."

"True." Richard tucked a lock of my hair behind my ear. "Does that bother you?"

I shook my head. "No. It's who you are. You'd lose a part of yourself if you ever gave it up. I don't want that to happen. I hope you'll be choreographing from your walker, if it comes to that."

"If it comes to that, I will," Richard said, before kissing me again.

* * *

We had a lovely afternoon, acting like teenagers snuggling close in the movie theater and then enjoying a delicious Mediterranean meal at the restaurant Emily Moore had recommended. It was so nice that I hated the fact I had to leave the house to meet Brad at the Taylorsford Inn.

"I promised," I said, as I changed into jeans and a black T-shirt, feeling my brightly colored sundress wasn't appropriate for a clandestine meeting. "Besides, it shouldn't take much time. I only have to tell Brad a couple of things and share that article with him."

"Alright, I'll stay here and keep the cats company," Richard said.

I gazed at the bed, where he'd stretched out on his back. Fosse was draped over one of his legs and Loie had curled up in the bent crook of his arm. "Looks like you've already started."

"Yeah, I may have to stay here."

"It wouldn't be the worst thing if you did. Maybe you can take a nap." I grabbed my purse from the top of the dresser. "I'm heading out. Be good, you guys," I said, addressing the cats. "You too," I told Richard.

"I'm hardly likely to misbehave when you aren't here," he said as I walked out the bedroom door.

I waved at him over my shoulder, then clattered down the stairs and headed outside. Although it was still light outside, I'd decided to drive rather than walk. I didn't think this meeting would take very long, but I didn't want to be wrong and end up walking home in the dark.

The parking lot at the inn was full, forcing me to parallel park on a side road. As I entered the lobby, I kept a lookout for Brad. I wasn't exactly sure where he planned to meet me, but assumed it would either be the lobby or the restaurant.

There was no sign of him in the lobby, so I headed for the restaurant.

"Do you have a reservation?" asked the young man at a podium just outside the entrance. He looked me up and down, obviously not impressed with my clothing choices.

"Um, no. I'm meeting someone here," I said, surveying the dimly lit restaurant. It looked crowded.

"Their name?" the host asked.

"That's not . . ." I took a breath. "Can I sit at the bar?"

Death and the Librarian

"Yes, that's fine," the young man, in a tone that conveyed it really wasn't. "Over that way."

I followed the sweep of his arm to locate the long, shadowy stretch of walnut and brass that filled the far wall. "Thanks," I said, walking away.

The bar was built in an old-fashioned style that suited the inn's vintage atmosphere. The walnut shelves, loaded with a wide array of bottles in a rainbow of colors, were backed by a foxed mirror that reflected hazy images. I sat down on one of the wooden stools and rested my sneakers on the brass foot rail. Leaning forward, I glanced up and down the row of stools, hoping to see Brad seated nearby.

There were a lot of patrons crowding the bar, keeping the bartender on her toes, but Brad was not one of them. When I spun my stool around to look out over the restaurant, I couldn't catch a glimpse of him either. I frowned. As tall and broad-shouldered as he was, I didn't think I could easily miss him.

He must be late, I thought, turning back to the bar. *Maybe something came up he had to deal with urgently.*

"What'll you have?" the bartender asked.

"Just a glass of unsweetened iced tea," I said, earning a supercilious smile from the young woman. It was obvious that she didn't appreciate someone taking up space at the crowded bar without drinking alcohol.

Lower tips, I thought, thanking her when she plopped the glass down on the paper coaster.

I sipped my tea slowly, hoping to stretch out the one glass until Brad appeared. From time to time, I turned to examine the restaurant patrons again, noticing at one point that Sean

Gordon was standing beside a table in the corner. Squinting, I realized he was talking to Mindy and Terry, who were seated at the table.

Great, the guy I want to talk to Brad about is here. I tapped my foot against the brass rail and watched the clock above the bar. After fifteen minutes, and several sharp looks from the bartender, I pulled out my phone and checked my calls and messages. There was nothing from Brad, which I found strange. *But if there was a bad accident or some violent crime he had to attend to, he might not be able to contact you*, I told myself. *Just be patient.*

After thirty minutes, I had to make a quick trip to the bathroom. When I came out, I noticed someone I hadn't expected to see. Not Brad, but his wife, Alison.

She was seated on the bench near the small counter set up for collecting and paying for takeout meals. I crossed to her, hoping she could tell me where Brad might have gone.

"Alison," I said, as I reached her. "How are you?"

"I'm fine." She stared at me, fine lines furrowing her brow. "Just getting some takeout for me and the kids. Well, and Brad's mom, who's staying with the children right now."

"Is Brad on duty?" I asked, trying to keep my tone nonchalant.

"He wasn't supposed to be." Alison pursed her lips. "But there was an accident on Route 24, just outside of town, and he got called out to deal with that."

"Oh, I see." I thrust my hands into the pockets of my jeans. That explained his absence but also meant we'd have to reschedule our meeting for another day.

Death and the Librarian

"Why are you here?" Alison peered around me. "Is Richard with you?"

"No. I was supposed to meet an old friend here, but apparently they can't make it," I said, employing the tactic of telling a lie with truth embedded in it so it sounded authentic.

The waitress at the counter called out Alison's name.

"Sorry," she said. "I need to get this. Nice to see you, Amy. Sorry your friend bailed on you."

"It's fine. We'll meet up another time." I gave her a nod in acknowledgement of her brusque goodbye.

Walking back to the bar, I pulled out my phone again and sent a text to Brad, informing him that I was aware of his situation. I also sent Richard a message to let him know I was on my way home. Setting the phone on the bar, I finished off my now lukewarm tea and signaled the bartender for the check.

I left as soon as I settled up. Hoping to earn some goodwill for the future, I included a larger tip than my bill warranted. As I slipped of the stool, I felt a wave of nausea sweep over me and paused, gripping the edge of the bar.

"You okay?" the bartender asked.

"Sure, just a little lightheaded," I replied, blinking and squaring my shoulders. "I mean, it was tea, so I can't be drunk." I flashed her a brief smile and walked away, fighting the sensation that my toes and fingers were tingling.

I must be more exhausted than I realized, I mused as I crossed the lobby and pushed open the entry doors.

The warm summer night air felt like a heavy blanket thrown over my shoulders. *Must be the humidity*, I thought, as

I slowly made my way to my car. Although it wasn't that hot, sweat beaded up on my forehead and the back of my neck.

I hoped I wasn't getting sick. This would be the worst possible time for something like that to happen. Turning the corner to enter the side street, I stumbled and almost fell forward, barely catching myself in time.

My car was only a few yards away, but it felt as if I was fighting a strong headwind to reach it. My steps slowed to a shuffle.

"I'm afraid you're in no shape to drive," said a voice behind me.

I fell against the side of my car. Fumbling in my purse for my keys, I looked up into a blurred face. The man looked somewhat familiar, but my brain couldn't make the proper connection to identify him.

That hair, I thought. *I remember that hair.*

"It seems I'm going to have to give you a ride," the man said, placing his hands on my shoulders. "Can you walk?"

"Sure, sure," I muttered, but when I took a step forward, I fell against his chest.

My knees buckled and my keys fell from my fingers, clattering against the sidewalk. I looked up at the man, but as my vision narrowed to a tiny circle, I gave up trying to match the blurry face with a name.

"You'll have to come with me, Amy. Sorry, but you brought this on yourself," said the man as he slid his hands under my armpits to hold me upright.

Then I passed out.

Chapter Twenty-Four

I woke up in the dark.

Blinking, I placed my hands on either side of my throbbing head. I was resting against something rough and hard. My fingers slid back to touch the surface under my head. It seemed to be some type of wood.

"How did I get here?" I asked aloud, my voice croaking. My throat felt raw. I worked up enough spit to moisten my tongue and ran it over my chapped lips. *Where am I? I went to the inn to meet Brad, but what happened after that?* I rubbed my temples, straining to remember anything from the evening before.

When I cleared my mind enough to realize I was lying on a wood plank floor, I became determined to sit up and examine my surroundings. Despite the fact that every muscle in my body ached, I used my hands to push off the floor beneath me, acquiring a splinter in my palm in the process.

My stomach rolled as I shifted to a sitting position, my back pressed against a solid wood post. I stretched out my legs, which were tingling as if the nerve endings were exposed.

Victoria Gilbert

"I was at the inn. I was supposed to meet Brad at the inn," I spoke aloud, while peering into the gloom to try to discern my location. "This is definitely not the inn."

As my eyes slowly adjusted to the dim light, I was able to see that the room was empty, except for a stack of firewood piled against one of the walls. It was a small, windowless space with one door. A scattering of straw covered a portion of the plank floor.

A shed of some kind, I thought, eyeing the wood pile with suspicion. I shivered. It was the perfect haven for black widow spiders. Or snakes. I pulled my legs back and hugged my knees to my chest. *Please don't let there be snakes.*

A sliver of light fell through a chink in the door, making me assume it was morning. Or at least, sometime during the day following my trip to the inn. I patted the pockets of my jeans with one hand, feeling for my cell phone.

"Where is it?" I asked the silent room. Squeezing my eyes shut, I tried to remember where I'd last used the phone. I knew it had been in my pocket when I'd left my house, but after that . . . I ran my fingers over my pockets again. My keys were gone too.

My eyes flew open as the realization that I must've been drugged and kidnapped washed over me. But how, and by whom?

And why? I puzzled over this question for several minutes, my inability to concentrate blocking any sensible answer.

The dust in the air swirled around me, causing me to sneeze and cough. But its movement, like the light spilling through the chink in the door, meant that some outside air

252

Death and the Librarian

was slipping through the rough plank and post walls. *At least I won't suffocate*, I thought, with a grimace. It was little enough good news, but it did lift my spirits.

I stared at the door. I'd probably have to crawl across the room, but it was worth the splinters if I could reach it and force it open. There was no way to know what was waiting for me outside, of course. My kidnapper could be there, keeping watch. But I'd deal with that problem once I was free.

Fighting the swimming sensation in my head, I dropped onto all fours and crept forward. I'd only made it halfway to the door when exhaustion forced me to pause and rest for a moment. *This is ridiculous*, I thought. *Why am I so weak?*

It had to be the drug my kidnapper had used on me. As I gathered my strength to continue my crawl, the memory of a question posed by a library patron flitted through my mind. They'd been researching date rape drugs for an article meant to warn women against such things.

"Rohypnol," I said, "Just like what was used to incapacitate Maureen Dryden."

While I couldn't remember anything, it was clear that my clothing hadn't been disturbed, which reassured me that I hadn't suffered a sexual attack. But then again, neither had Maureen. The so-called date rape drug had simply knocked her out long enough for her killer to smother her without resistance.

Same person, I thought, resuming my crawl to the door. *It has to be the same person. Maybe they thought I was getting too close to revealing their identity. But I'm not convinced I was, so how were they?*

Victoria Gilbert

Reaching the other side of the room, I wriggled my fingers into the crack between the doorjamb and the edge of the door and pulled. There was immediate resistance and the sound of metal banging against the wood. *A padlock,* I thought, with dismay.

I sank back into a sitting position and stared blankly at the door for several minutes. Then, feeling desperation fall like a blow across my shoulders, I scoured the interior of the shed with my gaze. There was nothing I could use as a tool to loosen or break the lock, except for a few larger branches in the woodpile.

It probably wouldn't work, but I had to try something. I refused to sit back and wait for my kidnapper to return, knowing, if he or she was following precedent, their next step would be to kill me. Gritting my teeth, I reached for the door again to help me stand. I did make it to my feet but had to lean against the door to steady my wobbly legs.

The woodpile seemed to have moved farther away. *That's not true,* I told myself. *That's just your blurry vision playing tricks on you.*

I turned so I could use the planks and posts to support me as I staggered along the shed walls. When I reached the pile of firewood, I hesitated, once again fearing the likelihood of spiders or snakes lying in wait.

But I had to do something, whatever the risk. I couldn't leave my children without a mother or abandon Richard and my family and friends. I couldn't give up, no matter how poor the odds.

I gingerly reached into the pile to pull out the sturdiest piece of timber. Yanking it free caused a landside of lumber.

Death and the Librarian

Small logs rolled onto the floor with a rumble. I had to fall back against the wall to avoid them smashing my toes.

Using my thick tree branch as a cane, I slowly made my way back to the door. As I studied the situation, determining my next step, I heard the rattling of the padlock and stumbled back.

The door swung open, revealing a tall figure outlined by light. I shaded my eyes with one arm and blinked against the sudden brightness.

"And what do you think you're going to do with that?" Sean Gordon stepped into the shed. "I doubt you have the strength to bring me down."

Sean? My thoughts whirled, trying to make sense of this revelation. *It was Sean who'd drugged and kidnapped me? But why?*

Images from another day, long before the drug had wiped my memory, floated to the surface. I'd been behind the library desk, on the phone with Brad, when I'd seen Sean stroll out of the stacks. I'd wondered then if Sean had overheard my conversation, setting up a place and time to meet to discuss . . . him.

Obviously, he had.

"Why?" I asked, my voice crackling like breaking glass.

Sean pressed his palms against the doorjambs on either side of the door, effectively blocking any exit. "Because you kept digging into the past," he said. "And you were just about to share something with Sheriff Tucker that I really didn't want him to know."

I leaned heavily on my makeshift cane. "You're Allen Cardullo's older brother, aren't you?"

255

"Half-brother, to be exact. Hence the different name and appearance. But he was truly my brother, no halves about it. My mother, who divorced my father when I was just a toddler, married my stepdad when I was three, so when Allen was born a year later, I always saw him as my brother. He was my family, just like the twins."

"You were in the navy when everything happened—Beverly Baron's death and the suspicions about him and Maureen's book . . ."

"A book that drove him to suicide." Sean's expression hardened. "That's right, I wasn't able to help him then. I couldn't get leave to go home, so he was left to deal with everything without me."

"So you decided to get revenge for him now?" I tightened my grip on the branch. If Sean was admitting to killing Maureen, he certainly didn't plan to let me live. I had to figure out how to use my only weapon in the most effective way possible.

Sean dropped his arms to his sides and moved closer to me. "It took time. I had to get out of the service and obtain the proper degree before I could have any hope of approaching Maureen for a job."

"That was the plan all along then. You became her research assistant to get close to her. You were waiting for an opportunity to murder her."

"Murder?" Sean's eyebrows arched over his hazel eyes. "More like exact justice. But yes, I needed to wait for the right opportunity. When Maureen dropped those names at the arts festival lecture, I knew it was my best chance. The people she

Death and the Librarian

mentioned, and in one case, also a family member of one of them, would muddy the waters of any investigation. Besides"—he lifted his hands in a dismissive gesture—"I had no reason to kill her, as far as anyone knew. I thought I could easily leave town while the investigation went cold."

"Your family's civil suit was settled out of court. Wasn't that enough?" I asked, hoping to stall any future action on his part.

Sean's laugh held no humor. "For peanuts, and Maureen would never admit her culpability in Allen's death. My parents wanted her to issue a statement, informing the public that most of her best-selling book was conjecture, not fact, but she refused."

"Did you slip me that warning note? And hit Sunny before shoving another note in her pocket?" I asked, lifting the branch slightly off the ground and swinging it almost unperceptively

"Yes to the second one. I don't claim the note you received. That must've been someone else who didn't appreciate your snooping."

"What did you want from Sunny?"

"To warn you by injuring her, of course." Sean's lips twisted into a mocking smile. "I didn't want to kill her, or believe me, she'd be dead."

My grip tightened on the branch as Sean took on the pose of a fighter, his legs spread apart and his feet firmly planted on the ground. "Now, I'm afraid that's all I plan to share right now. I think it's time to silence you for good."

At these words, I sent up a prayer and gathered all my strength. Swinging the branch back, then forward, I used its momentum to deliver a crushing blow, straight into his crotch.

Victoria Gilbert

He screamed and fell backward through the open door.

I dropped the branch and stumbled outside as he writhed on the ground. Forcing my rubbery legs to move as fast as possible, I dashed past him, seeking freedom.

Only to be stopped by the appearance of two people I never expected to see in this location.

"Sorry," Terry Temkin said, grabbing one of my arms while Mindy LaSalle gripped the other. "It's not going to be that easy."

Chapter
Twenty-Five

I struggled futilely against their hold on me. "What are you doing? I asked, as they marched me over to where Sean had pulled himself up to a sitting position, his back pressed against a boulder.

"You had a glimmer of the plan but didn't understand the entirety of it," Mindy said, jerking my arm until I was afraid she'd pull it from its socket.

"You were all in on this together?" I sputtered. "But you said you only met shortly before the festival."

"We lied, of course." Terry tightened his fingers, his nails digging into my skin.

I turned to look at him, examining his patrician profile and dark, curly hair. "Are you actually Duncan Cardullo, Allen's younger brother?"

Terry's sardonic smile made me look away. "Guess again. I'm actually Terrell Temkin. It's simply that I've been involved with the Cardullo family for a long time."

"Ever since we started dating in middle school," Mindy said.

Victoria Gilbert

I glanced at her. "You're Daria, then?"

"Yes, Allen's younger sister. My twin, Duncan, isn't involved in this. He's too much of a wimp, I'm afraid. Fortunately"—Daria tilted her head in Terry's direction—"my boyfriend is more willing to seek justice."

Terry nodded. "Allen was like an older brother to me too. My own family was a disaster, but the Cardullos always offered me a safe haven. I was close with all of them, and just as determined to avenge Allen as Daria and Sean."

Standing between them, I forced my mind to process this new information. "Who passed that warning note to me at the theater?" I asked.

"Me," Terry said, raising his free hand. "We truly hoped you'd back off at that point. Then things wouldn't have come to this."

Sean rose to his feet, his expression still betraying his lingering pain. "Daria and Terry and I planned Maureen's murder for years. We thought we'd covered all the bases, but then you had to stick your nose in."

"You told me you had an alibi," I said, looking from Terry to Daria and back again.

"And we did." Mindy's smirk made me wish I could slap her. "I drugged Maureen's drink while neither she nor the bartender was looking. Then Terry and I went outside and waited on the patio, where our witness was obligingly smoking a couple of cigarettes."

"While you'd already headed up to Maureen's room?" I asked Sean.

Death and the Librarian

He looked me over, his eyes dead as fallen leaves. "Bingo. You do have a knack for this. Too bad your amateur sleuthing will end here."

I glanced at Terry before looking back to meet Sean's gaze. "All your arguing was a ruse."

"That's right," Terry said. "We knew you were there, at the restaurant and then outside the archives. So we put on a little show."

Mindy squeezed my upper arm. "There's no television offer. There never was. We just wanted you, and the authorities, to think Terry and I might have a motive to kill Maureen, taking the heat off of Sean. Of course we also gave that false eye-witness testimony about the sheriff's wife. We did see her leave the building but not in the way we described. She wasn't hiding, and she left before the news of Maureen's death broke. She even waved at us, and said something about her car being parked on the side street near the patio. But our story was better—it cast suspicion on someone other than Sean, or us."

"Mindy and Terry were willing to be seen as possible suspects to muddy the waters further, although it wasn't really a risk. They knew they could prove they weren't viable suspects later, once the witness from the patio gave his statement," Sean said.

"Maureen's death had absolutely no connection to the Eddie Jaffe case," I said, talking more to myself than the others. "That was another misdirection."

Sean crossed his arms over his chest. "One I was more than happy to utilize."

I stood still for a moment, allowing all of this information to sink in. "Did you have to resort to murder?" I asked at last. "Why not simply expose Maureen's mistakes and wrong conclusions? That could've been enough to destroy her career. You didn't have to kill her."

"But don't you see?" Sean's words took on a plaintive tone. "It wasn't only that her false accusation drove Allen to suicide. It was also that her words twisted the investigation, making most people blame Allen and subsequently ignore any other suspects. So Beverly Baron's real killer was never discovered. Whoever it was, they've been able to escape justice to this day."

I stared at him, observing the pain etched in the lines of his face. "Did you know her? Beverly Baron, I mean. Had you met her before she died?"

"Once," Sean said, eliciting a gasp of surprise from Daria. "I met up with Allen in Los Angeles while I was on a short shore leave. It was a party thrown by a cast member from Beverly's last film." Sean's eyes grew misty, as if recalling the scene. "She was the most beautiful woman I'd ever seen, but she was also sweet and kind. We talked briefly, and then she asked if she could contact me when I went back to my ship. I shared my info, thinking she'd never follow through, but she did." He rubbed a hand across his eyes, as if wiping away the sweetness of that memory. "We corresponded by text and video chat for several months before she died."

"I never knew that," Daria said, anger replacing the plaintive note in her voice. "Why didn't you tell us that?"

Death and the Librarian

"Need to know," Sean said. "You didn't, and anyway, avenging Allen should've been enough for you. The fact that I had two reasons to hate Maureen was irrelevant."

"Not exactly, man," Terry said peevishly.

I could sense that Terry and Daria had been distracted by this revelation. Their grip on my arms had lessened. I considered my next action. It would be difficult to escape all three of them, but I needed to try.

The first thing was to get some sense of my location. I lowered my head slightly and surreptitiously examined the area outside the shed. Behind the small building, a thick grove of trees rose up the mountain slope, but off to one side, I noticed the roof of a log cabin.

It looks familiar, I thought, casting a sidelong glance to my left. Sure enough, another, larger shed sat at the end of a narrow lane.

I swallowed back a shriek as I realized I was standing on part of Delbert Frye's property. Sean must've found this remote location when he was attempting to interview Delbert. He saw this abandoned shed and brought me here, along with a padlock, certain no one, not even Delbert, would find me.

"It doesn't matter," Sean said, after concluding some conversation with Terry and Daria that I'd ignored. "The important thing now is to decide what to do with our overly curious little librarian."

"Just give her a super-strong dose of the knockout drug and leave her in the shed. By the time anyone finds her she'll be long gone," Daria said. "And so will we."

263

"I suppose that's best," Sean said, examining me in a way that chilled my bones despite the humid summer heat.

There was no time to consider alternatives. I had to act soon. Fortunately, fate was on my side.

"The rest of the Rohypnol is in the car," Sean said. "Hold her here while I go get it." He loped off in the direction of the other shed, where he must've parked his rental vehicle.

I waited until Sean was some distance away, then gave Daria a swift kick in the shin. She squeaked and dropped my arm. Taking the opportunity, I swung my other arm upward, driving my elbow into Terry's Adam's apple.

Choking, he stumbled backward. Free from their grip, I spun around and sprinted across the field to reach the edge of Delbert's property.

I'd planned to run to the cabin, but Terry and Daria were blocking that direction. Instead, I headed for another house whose layout I knew from past experience.

The wire fence that separated Delbert's land from the ski-chalet style home that had once belonged to my ex-boyfriend, Charles Bartos, had collapsed under the weight of honeysuckle vines, allowing me to clamber over it without too much difficulty. I was also thankful for the tall orchard grass that had overtaken Charles's former yard. It was tall enough to screen my progress from Daria and Terry, who I could hear crashing through the thick grass behind me.

I headed for the back deck of the house, knowing that it would be easier to open the door that led to the kitchen than the solid front door. But I hadn't considered the shape of the deck, which hadn't been maintained or stained for years.

Death and the Librarian

Many of the boards were broken and the rest were soft with rot. I picked my way over to the door, glancing over my shoulder to make sure Terry and Daria weren't on my heels. Reaching the kitchen door, I was relieved to see that the window in the door was already broken, allowing me to reach in and turn the lock without the sound of crashing glass.

Slipping inside, I crossed the large central room of the chalet, staying low so I couldn't be seen through the floor-to-ceiling windows that overlooked the woods and mountainous terrain beyond.

Glancing up at the cathedral ceiling, I noticed the network of spiderwebs festooning the exposed wooden beams. I kept moving, past the open kitchen and into a large bedroom.

I'd been here once before and remembered the expansive stretch of cabinets and closets that covered one wall. Crafted from pale wood, the various doors and drawers were fitted together with the precision of storage space on a yacht. Fortunately, the floor-to-ceiling windows that filled the opposite wall were now covered by blackout drapes. I locked the bedroom door behind me. It wouldn't keep out intruders forever, but it would buy some time.

Slipping inside one of the empty closets, I left a tiny crack of the sliding door open so I could keep watch and listen for anyone attempting to break open the bedroom door.

It was odd to be back in this house after so many years. Even stranger was the thought that it was Charles's old home that was protecting me now. *An ironic twist*, I thought, as I leaned against the back of the closet. The exhaustion brought on by the drug and my recent exertion made me want to slide down the wall and sit on the floor, but I knew I'd better not. I had to be ready to run or, if necessary, attack.

There were no clothes left in the closet, but there were wire hangers. I slipped a few off the hanging pole and quickly disassembled them, opening up them up to create a sharp-edged hook. I twisted a couple of the other opened hangers around the bottom of the jerry-rigged spear to give it more strength. I stared at my handmade weapon with approval. It might not kill anyone, but it could certainly put out an eye or two.

The thud of footsteps on hardwood floors alerted me that someone else was in the house. I imagined Daria and Terry had finally been able to track me here, probably with Sean in tow. I tapped the wire hanger spear against my palm. There were three of them, but I had a weapon and, from what I'd seen, they didn't. Except for the drug, which would be difficult to administer if I fought back hard enough.

I'll make it tough to kill me, I thought, as the bedroom door rattled on its hinges. *Not like poor Maureen, who was knocked out so she couldn't fight back.*

A thud followed by a shout put me on high alert. I cracked open the closet door a little wider, gripping my weapon in my right hand. Scuffling and more exclamations of pain or anger seeped through the bedroom door. I listened intently, trying to discern what was actually happening.

The bedroom door flew open, banging into the adjacent wall like a crack of thunder. I prepared myself for battle, determined not to give up without a fight.

Death and the Librarian

"Amy!" a familiar voice called out. "Are you in there?"

"Yes, yes, it's me," I said, dropping my handmade spear onto the floor as I dashed forward and threw myself at Brad's broad chest.

He huffed and grabbed my forearms, pushing me back. "Let me take a look at you. Are you okay?"

"I am now," I said.

Chapter Twenty-Six

As Brad guided me out of the bedroom, I saw Daria, Terry, and Sean standing in the middle of the empty living room, all three in handcuffs and under the watchful eyes of Brad's deputies.

"How did you find me?" I asked. "I mean, I'm grateful you did, but how?"

"The bartender at the Taylorsford Inn remembered you," Brad said, keeping his hand under my elbow. "You left your phone on the bar, and when she called the first number in your contacts, she reached Richard. He rushed to the inn, feeling something was wrong, and discovered your car and dropped keys on the side street. That's when he called us."

"But how'd you know to come here?" I stepped out onto the front porch, shading my eyes to look out over the numerous sheriff's department vehicles and a waiting ambulance.

"Some of my men had been keeping closer tabs on Sean Gordon ever since you mentioned him to me on the phone. When we realized you'd probably been abducted, the bartender recognized Sean from a photo. She said he was

268

Death and the Librarian

hovering around the bar when you went to the restroom, then left without buying anything and disappeared right before you returned."

"That must've been when he spiked my drink," I said.

"I imagine so. Anyway, a couple of my deputies noticed Gordon leaving the inn this morning in the company of Terry Temkin and Mindy LaSalle—"

"It's actually Daria Cardullo," I interjected.

"Ah, makes sense, but we'll get to that later. Anyway, two of my deputies followed them to this general location. They hung back, but when they saw Gordon go to his car and extract something that looked like a small medical bag, one guy called for backup, while the other immediately set off, tailing Gordon and his collaborators. They both caught up to the three suspects before they could harm you again, thank goodness."

"I'm definitely thankful for that." I observed another car speeding up the overgrown driveway. "You told Richard I was here."

"Of course. He'd never forgive me if I didn't," Brad said, stepping aside as Richard came running toward us.

He flew up the stairs and threw his arms around me, hugging me tight to his chest. "You're okay, you're okay," he repeated several times.

"I am," I said, lifting my head to look up into his face. He appeared haggard, and I knew it was probably because he hadn't slept since he'd discovered my car and keys. "I'm still a little loopy from being drugged, but it's getting better. Unfortunately"—I glanced over at Brad—"I can't remember anything about last night, other than going to the inn to meet

269

you. And I drank iced tea. I remember that now because the bartender seemed peeved with me. I think I gave her a decent tip anyway, but since she really helped you figure out what was going on, I wish I'd given her a bigger one."

"Don't worry, I did," Richard said before kissing me.

* * *

After I gave my preliminary statement, promising Brad to stop by the station to fill in any details the following day, Richard and I left in his car. Hannah Fowler, who'd encouraged me to take the ambulance to the hospital for a checkup, relented when I said I'd have my regular doctor examine me in the next few days. I allowed her to draw blood, though, as evidence of the Rohypnol in my system.

We arrived home to Aunt Lydia and Sunny waiting on our porch. I received hugs from both of them, as well as a minilecture from my aunt about once again falling into danger due to my relentless curiosity and determined search for the truth.

"All's well that ends well," I said, which earned me a sharp look and a few more words of advice.

"I'm going to take her inside now," Richard said, placing his arm around my shoulders. "I think she needs some real sleep, and so do I. Thanks for your concern; we'll call you tomorrow."

He ushered me into the house, ignoring Sunny's questions and Aunt Lydia's protests.

"I didn't call your parents yet, and now that you're home, I wonder if we even should," Richard said, guiding me up the stairs while Loie and Fosse dashed ahead of us.

Death and the Librarian

"I'd say let's not. They don't need to worry. I'm sure they'll eventually hear something from Aunt Lydia or others, but let's leave it alone for now. They're enjoying their time with Ella and Nicky; we don't need to ruin that."

"Agreed." Richard and I entered the bedroom, where the cats had already laid claim to the bed. "I bet you want a shower."

"Yes, please. I feel like I've been rolling around in a barn," I said.

Richard leaned in and sniffed. "Sorry to say, you smell like it too."

"Gee, thanks for your compassion." I stepped back and yanked off my sneakers and socks. "I'll have you know I was quite brave and inventive, orchestrating my own escape and then preparing to fight to the death."

Richard smiled. "I'm not surprised. You're a little tiger when necessary. Thank goodness," he added, his expression sobering.

"I didn't want to leave the kids, or you, for that matter. I mean, how would you get along without me?"

"Badly," he said. "Now, get your shower. I think we should both take a nap and worry about figuring out something for dinner later."

"Delivery," I called out as I headed into the bathroom.

After a long shower, I threw on a well-worn sleep shirt and took some acetaminophen to combat my continuing headache. Richard had drawn the blinds and was already in bed by the time I walked back into the room.

Victoria Gilbert

Loie and Fosse remained curled up at the foot of the bed, requiring some maneuvering as I slipped in beside Richard. "Are you asleep?" I asked.

"I was," he replied groggily.

"Sorry." I rolled over and snuggled up against his back. "Tired as I am, I may miss dinner altogether, although come to think out it, I haven't eaten in a while."

"Neither have I," he muttered.

A few minutes later, I could tell by the way his breathing had changed that he'd fallen asleep. I wanted to do the same, but too many thoughts were swirling in my brain.

The Dryden murder case is solved, I thought, *but that doesn't answer every question. Like Sean said, Beverly Baron's real killer is still out there, walking around free as air. And then there's Eddie Jaffe's mysterious disappearance. Will that case ever be closed?*

Eventually, despite my overactive mind, I drifted off to sleep, not waking up until early evening. Rolling over, I realized that Richard was already out of bed. Throwing back the top sheet, I got up and padded into the bathroom. My reflection mocked me with the dark circles under my eyes and my pasty skin. I shrugged. A quick brush of my hair and a swipe of astringent across my face would have to suffice.

I headed downstairs, still in my sleep shirt.

"Oh, you're up," Richard was sitting on the sofa, flanked by Loie and Fosse. He laid down the book he was reading. "Good. I'll order something then. How's pizza sound?"

"Great," I said. "The one with all the veggies and extra cheese, please."

Death and the Librarian

"Your word is my command." Richard leaned forward and grabbed his cell phone from the coffee table. "Oh, by the way, your phone is here too."

"Thanks," I said, picking up my phone and sitting down beside him. I checked for calls or text messages, noting that Brad had replied *okay* to my text from the previous evening. There was also a phone message from Kurt.

"Amy," he said. "I heard what happened. Glad you're okay, and that the Dryden case is solved." After a slight pause the message continued, "I've been thinking and would like to talk to you in person sometime soon. I believe it's time to tell you the truth."

I pulled the phone from my ear and stared at the screen. Was Kurt actually offering to tell me something about the Eddie Jaffe case? As Richard called in our pizza order on his phone, I sent a text to Kurt.

I'd like to hear whatever truth you want to tell. Why don't you stop by the library tomorrow? I'll be working, but we can use the archives to talk, if you want. Maybe after lunch, so around two.

My phone buzzed before Richard had even completed his order.

That's fine, Kurt's text said. *Tomorrow at two then.*

I set my phone on the coffee table and relaxed against the sofa cushions.

"Pizza should be here in about twenty minutes," Richard said, casting me an inquiring glance. "Something on your phone that concerns you?"

Victoria Gilbert

"No, not at all. In fact, I think it's good news, for once."

Richard slid his arm around my shoulders. "We certainly could use more of that."

"Totally," I said, scooting over to lean into him. "Listen, once we have our pizza, should we call my parents and talk to Ella and Nicky? I'd really like to see their shining faces and hear their sweet voices today."

"That sounds like the best medicine ever," Richard said.

Chapter
Twenty-Seven

I went into work a little late on Tuesday, first making a stop at the sheriff's department to ensure they had all the details concerning my abduction. Of course, there were portions of Sunday evening I couldn't remember, but Brad said they would be able to piece together a coherent timeline based on the information on my phone, as well as statements from the bartender, Alison, and others who'd seen me at the inn.

Samantha greeted me at the desk, disapproval stamped all over her face. "You should've stayed home today," she said. "Going through that ordeal—you need time to recover."

"I'm fine." I offered her a warm smile. "I had to go the sheriff's office today anyway, so I figured as might as well get back to work."

"Well, no need to push it. The volunteers and I will cover the desk until Sunny arrives later this afternoon." Samantha pointed toward the workroom door. "You can concentrate on book ordering or other things you actually enjoy."

"I don't mind working on the desk," I said, "But thanks. I do have some paperwork to catch up on." As I turned to head into the workroom, I added, "Oh, Mr. Kendrick is stopping by around two. He wants to use the archives. He asked for my help, so I'll take care of him."

"Okay," Samantha said, in a slightly dubious tone. "I'll make sure to let you know when he arrives."

By the time two o'clock rolled around, I'd completed my orders for the month and even reviewed our quarterly statistics and the latest budget spreadsheets. The truth was, I was so anxious to hear what Kurt had to say, I had to keep my mind occupied with other things so I wouldn't explode with anticipation.

Right on time, Samantha opened the workroom door and announced Kurt's arrival.

I walked out to greet him, my key ring in hand. "Hello there, do you want to start your research out in the archives?"

Kurt, casually dressed in a white polo shirt and khakis, offered me a wide smile. "That will be perfect. Thanks."

"One question before we get to your information," I said as I led him out the back door and across the parking lot to the archives building. "Why were you at the inn that Sunday night? I found that strange."

"Meeting a client," he replied. "Someone looking for a Chagall painting. They invited me to the inn for a meal while we discussed the details. When they left, I lingered for a while, enjoying a good scotch."

"Okay, that makes sense." While I unlocked the door, Kurt slid his fingers over the plaque we'd installed in memory of two former Taylorsford residents.

Death and the Librarian

"Ada Frye and Violet Greyson," he said. "I hope they're together now, somewhere they can be happy."

"I'm sure they are," I said, opening the door. Light blazed as I flicked the switch. "Come on in."

Kurt followed me inside and waited in the middle of the room, looking over the space, while I closed the door. "So much history here," he said. "So many lives captured in all those boxes and files."

"I hadn't really thought of it like that, but I suppose you're right." I gestured toward the desk and office chair. "Please, have a seat."

"No, I think you're the one who should sit down." Kurt's piercing blue gaze held me in place like a pin impaling a butterfly.

"Why? Is your information so devastating it will knock me off my feet?"

Kurt's stoic expression was somehow more intimidating than his usual wolfish grin. "There is that possibility."

I strolled over the chair and rolled it away from the desk. "Seriously? I can't imagine anything that dire. Especially if it has to do with Eddie Jaffe's disappearance. Unless, of course, you killed him." I sat down and studied him. Kurt's shoulders were slumped and it seemed as if the lines on his face had been carved with a chisel. I hugged my arms, suddenly cold. It was the first time I'd seen him looking his age. "Did you?"

He turned to the side, displaying his rugged profile. "No. I did not."

"But you were there," I said, realizing this had to be the truth.

"Yes." Kurt walked over to one of the shelves and examined the rows of boxes. "I didn't want to be, but I was there."

I leaned forward, resting my forearms on the desk. "Why? Was it some sort of drug deal?"

"Not on my part. I wouldn't sell to someone like Eddie, and certainly wouldn't have purchased the junk he was peddling." Kurt turned and met my gaze.

The sorrow in his eyes shocked me. "Then why were you there? I caught my breath. "Because of Andrew?"

"Brava—you're always clever at putting the puzzle together," he said, approval dripping from his words. "You just needed more pieces this time."

"You accompanied Andrew to that gathering to protect him."

"In a way. Although I didn't accompany him. I showed up a little later, when I realized where he'd gone." Kurt raked his hands through his thick white hair. "I warned him not to get mixed up with Jaffe and his gatherings. I told him the people involved with those so-called parties could be dangerous and unpredictable. But Andrew had a side to him . . ."

"A wild, bohemian artist side? A need to take chances and explore new experiences?" I asked, thinking of the mystical qualities inherent in some of my late uncle's paintings.

"Something like that. He often allowed his emotions to overwhelm his common sense. And occasionally, even his sense of self-preservation." Kurt took a deep breath. "The day Eddie Jaffe went missing, Andrew told me about a gathering

Death and the Librarian

taking place in that mountain clearing. He wanted me to go with him, but I refused. I said it was a bad idea. 'We don't know who will be there,' I said. 'It could be infiltrated by narcs, or some of the partiers could be carrying weapons.' I tried to make Andrew see the danger, because I knew the sort of people Jaffe associated with. They weren't to be trusted."

"But Andrew decided to go anyway." I didn't pose this as a question.

"He was determined. Jaffe had promised some special experience—a new drug he'd acquired. When I heard that from one of my customers, who'd been invited and declined, I knew I had to go. If I was there, I could make sure Andrew didn't ingest something that could have deadly consequences."

The raw emotion in Kurt's voice reminded me how much he'd loved Andrew. *And still does*, I reminded myself. "You followed him up the trail to the clearing that evening."

"Yes. I knew he'd taken his car and that he usually parked it behind the library and walked to the house when he visited Paul. I think that was to throw off Lydia, actually. So I parked at the library as well, next to his car. I walked to the field and then hiked up the trail. At first, I felt reassured. The only people there other than Andrew were Jaffe and some skinny young woman who claimed she was his girlfriend." Kurt flashed a sardonic smile. "Jaffe didn't back up that claim, by the way."

"That was Sheryl Abernathy. When I spoke with her recently, she said she was too far gone to remember who else was there that night, except for Eddie, of course. She did

279

mention running into Delbert Frye when she stumbled down the trail to answer the call of nature."

"I never saw Delbert. He didn't come up to the clearing," Kurt said.

"I know. He told me that. But there was another girl . . ."

Kurt's lips tightened into a straight line.

"Sheryl blamed the girl for some reason. Claimed she ruined everything." I sat back, dropping my hands into my lap. "I know the girl was Aunt Lydia. She's admitted as much, although she said she only saw Sheryl briefly on the trail. No, wait"—I drummed my fingers against the arm of my chair—"she also caught a glimpse of someone farther up the trail staring at her. Or thought she did. She wasn't sure."

"That was Eddie Jaffe." Kurt's chest rose and fell with his deep sigh. "I don't think she ever saw Andrew, or me, though."

"She didn't. She said she never made it to the clearing, so if you both stayed there until she left . . ."

"We did. Lydia was nowhere in sight when Andrew and I descended the trail."

"So what happened? Did Jaffe take off through the woods or something? Sheryl said she passed out and when she woke up, no one was there."

Kurt paced the small area of open floor in front of the desk for a minute, then turned to face me. "Amy, what I'm about to say, you can't tell anyone. Not Sunny, or your parents, or Brad Tucker. Not even Richard. And certainly not Lydia. Do you promise to keep this secret?"

I narrowed my eyes and stared at him. "It's difficult to say yes when I don't know what this is about."

Death and the Librarian

"But you must. If you want to know the truth, you must." Kurt crossed to the desk and leaned over it, pressing his palms against the heavily varnished wood top. "Promise me, Amy."

"Alright," I said reluctantly.

Kurt straightened and squared his shoulders. "By the time I arrived, Andrew was already under the influence. Not from Jaffe's new drug, thank goodness. I'm not even sure there was such a thing. It could've been something Jaffe made up to lure people to his drug-and-drink gathering. Anyway, all of them—Jaffe and Andrew and the girl—had obviously been drinking. They'd probably popped some pills too. It looked like it. I stayed sober, because I knew I'd have to get Andrew home, or at least, back to Paul's house."

"Paul Dassin would accept him in that condition?" I asked.

"He would. He had a soft spot for Andrew." Kurt grimaced, as if this admission pained him. "Much more so than for me. At any rate, I knew I could leave Andrew on the porch at Paul's house and ring the bell and Andrew would be taken care of. I didn't want Paul to see me, but there'd be time for me to disappear before he got to the door."

"Is that what happened? Jaffe disappeared and then you and Andrew did, leaving Sheryl behind to fend for herself?"

"Not exactly." Kurt glanced up at the fluorescent light, where a moth beat its wings against the cylindrical bulb. "I only wish that was what happened. But it wasn't that simple."

I searched his face for answers, but his expression was unreadable. "You said you didn't kill Eddie."

"I didn't." Kurt rubbed his hand across his forehead. "That girl, Sheryl, did wander off at one point. When she came back, she never mentioned Delbert, but she chattered about a girl loitering about midway down the trail. So Jaffe went to take a look. He returned to find his supposed girlfriend unconscious. At that point, Jaffe went a little crazy. He told Andrew and me that we shouldn't go without female companionship simply because Sheryl had passed out. He suggested . . ." Kurt cast me an apologetic look. "He said he was going to go back and grab the girl and bring her up to the clearing for a 'little fun.'"

An expletive exploded from my mouth.

"I felt the same," Kurt said. "Jaffe had described the girl in detail, and it was pretty clear it was Lydia. She was always following Andrew around, so it wasn't that surprising. Andrew recognized it was Lydia from the description too. When Jaffe made his disgusting suggestion, Andrew lost all remaining remnants of his self-control. He wasn't in love with Lydia yet, but he always liked her and admired her beauty. Besides, he wasn't the sort of man to take advantage of a woman or, in this case, a young girl." Kurt paused for a moment, obviously regulating his own self-control. "I tried to talk Jaffe out of such a terrible idea, but Andrew didn't have patience with that. He launched at Jaffe and they began to fight. I pulled them apart once, but then they were right back at it. In the blink of an eye, before I could separate them again, Andrew pulled Jaffe to the cliff and then he"—a flush stained Kurt's face—"he pushed Jaffe over."

I froze, my hands clutching the chair arms as if they were my only salvation in a storm. "Andrew killed Eddie?"

Death and the Librarian

"Yes. I don't think he meant to. It was in the heat of the moment. Or perhaps it was an accident during their fight. I'm not absolutely sure."

"But there was no body or other evidence found on rocks or in the gulley," I said.

"Because no one reported Jaffe missing for several days. It was only when his landlady went to collect the rent and saw his tools and clothes in the apartment, while noticing Jaffe and his truck were gone, that anyone informed the authorities about his disappearance. That gave me time to go back and remove the body and anything that might suggest Jaffe had fallen to his death." Kurt smiled humorlessly. "I had a few trusted colleagues who were willing to help, for a not-so-small fee. We were able to retrieve the body and haul it away in his truck, then make both items disappear. As you probably know, forensic techniques weren't so great back then, especially if it was a small town or county force dealing with the case. The authorities never found any real evidence."

"And you've been keeping this secret ever since." I released my grip on the chair arms and rose to my feet. "You've been protecting Andrew, even after his death."

"Back then I was protecting him from any legal complications. Later, after he passed, I wanted to protect his reputation and the public's perception of him. I wanted his art to be his legacy, not Eddie Jaffe's death." Kurt looked me over. "And then there was Lydia."

"You didn't want her to know," I said. "Not about Andrew's actions, or what Jaffe might've done to her if you and Andrew hadn't intervened."

283

"Exactly. I had to protect her as well. I believed Andrew's life, as well as hers, would be better off if no one knew the truth." Kurt shrugged. "Eddie Jaffe's death was no great loss, not compared to the possible ruin of Andrew's life, or the pain Lydia, who was only fifteen, would have to bear for the rest of hers."

"Did Andrew remember what he'd done?" I asked, after a moment of silence.

"I don't know. He recalled blacking out from the drugs and alcohol. He even had a vague recollection of me carrying him down the trail on my back, loading him into my car, and driving him to my place. But whether he remembered all of the events of that night . . ." Kurt balled his fingers into fists. "He never talked to me about it afterwards, not even when I had to take him to recover his car a few days later. I always hoped he didn't remember. I wanted that to be true. But I don't know."

Kurt's conflicted expression matched my inner turmoil. I could understand how this might torment him. Andrew, who could never entirely kick his off-and-on drug habit, even after he married Aunt Lydia, may have been haunted by more than just his personal demons. That had to weigh heavily on Kurt, who remained his friend until Andrew died at age thirty-two in a horrible car accident.

"Don't worry, I said, my voice sounding hollow to my ears. "I won't tell Aunt Lydia. I won't tell anyone."

"Thank you. It is a relief to tell the story to someone, but I don't want it made public. It could do great harm, even now."

Death and the Librarian

"That's why you warned me off the case and were so adamant that I give up investigating Eddie's disappearance. You didn't want this truth to be revealed." I circled around the table to stand in front of him. "Even though it means the case will never be solved, and Eddie can never be properly laid to rest or mourned by any of his family members, or even someone like Sheryl. That was your impossible choice."

"With two bad outcomes." Kurt placed a hand on my shoulder. "I know I'm placing a heavy burden on you, Amy, but I was afraid you'd find out the truth through your own efforts, and you might reveal portions of it before you understood the whole story."

"I understand now. But it seems wrong, not being able to tell the truth. Still, I'll keep the secret, because I also feel it would be terrible for Aunt Lydia to suffer over Andrew any more than she already has." I offered Kurt a wan smile. "Knowing, that whatever I do, it's the wrong choice. That is indeed a dreadful thing."

"But we will bear it, nonetheless. Because there's no other option," Kurt said, lifting his hand.

I nodded. "Because it's for the people we love, so we must."

Chapter Twenty-Eight

"Does anyone need anything else?" Aunt Lydia asked, as she collected a few empty bowls from the linen-draped folding table.

"Heavens, no." My mom, relaxing in a chaise lounge, rubbed her stomach. "I'm about to bust as it is."

"Anyone?" my aunt called out to all of the people gathered in her backyard.

A chorus of "thank you, but no" filled the air.

"Sit down, Lydia," my dad told her from his seat in the folding chair placed next to Mom. "You've been running around all afternoon."

"Yes, come and join me," Hugh, who'd returned from overseas a few days earlier, patted the space next to him on one of the white benches. "I haven't been able to spend much time with you lately."

"I simply want to make sure everyone has what they need. That's what a good hostess does," Aunt Lydia said, raising her chin and looking down her aristocratic nose. But she handed

Death and the Librarian

the stacked bowls to Zelda and walked over to join Hugh nevertheless.

"That's one thing no one would ever question," Richard said, strolling out of the garden. He'd been playing hide-and-seek with Karla, the twins, and Brad and Alison's son, Noah.

"Did you find all of them?" Alison asked. Three-year-old Zoe, who was in her lap, started wiggling and repeating "down."

"Not yet, but Karla's still in the game. I just need to grab a drink before I jump back into the fray." Richard crossed to the table and pulled a bottle of water from a galvanized metal tub filled with ice and a variety of other drinks.

"They've probably disappeared into the woods, even though you and Karla said they should stay in the garden." Brad held out his arms so Alison could pass Zoe over to him.

Zelda, who'd returned from the kitchen, looked over the gathering of family and friends. "I'm surprised Sunny and Fred aren't here. I'm sure they were invited."

"They were," I said piling some silverware on the serving platter that had been set out to collect used utensils. "But they said they wanted to share Sunday dinner with P. J. and Carol and then 'catch up on things,' as Sunny put it. They may stop by later."

Zelda cast me a mischievous look as she walked past to join Walt at another bench moved out of the garden for extra seating. "Catch up on things? No doubt."

"It seems this woman will never learn to behave," Walt said as Zelda sat next to him. He threw his arm around her shoulders and pulled her close. "Not that I'm complaining."

Zelda playfully swatted his upper leg. "You'd better not."

"Not to bring up business, but how's the Dryden case going, Brad?" Walt asked. "Are you going to be able to wrap it up soon?"

"It's in the attorneys' hands now." Brad bounced Zoe on his knee. "Of course, we'll be providing any new evidence and working with the prosecution, but since all three of the culprits have basically confessed, it's a pretty open and shut case."

"I guess Amy will have to be called as a witness, poor lamb," Zelda said.

"That's what she gets for continuing to put herself in dangerous situations," Aunt Lydia said with a huff.

"Now, dear, that isn't entirely true." Hugh took hold of my aunt's hand. "Amy started out simply conducting some research, right, Brad?"

"True. We didn't think it would lead where it did." Brad set Zoe on her feet She toddled over to Walt and Zelda, who slid apart and lifted her up onto the bench between them.

"You two are like the quintessential grandparents," Richard said, tossing his empty water bottle into the bin we'd put out for recyclables.

"What are we, chopped liver?" My mom's cheerful tone took the sting out of her words.

Richard grinned. "No, you are the epitome. That's another top spot."

"Good save," Dad said.

"It's too bad Eddie Jaffe's disappearance couldn't be solved as well," Zelda said. "I guess that's going to remain a cold case."

Death and the Librarian

I shot a swift glance at Kurt, who was sitting in an Adirondak chair Richard had dragged over from our back porch. His stylish straw boater was pulled down low on his forehead and his stillness gave the impression that he'd fallen asleep.

But I knew better. His hands were lying loosely on his thighs, but I spied his fingers curling into his palms. "I guess we can't expect all cases to be solved," I said.

"Sad, but true," Brad said. "Sometimes you just have to accept not knowing."

"That's hard for a librarian." I glanced at Aunt Lydia, who was resting her head on Hugh's shoulder. *She's definitely better off not knowing,* I thought, while sneaking another look at Kurt.

He sat up, taking off his hat to fan his face. "Another excellent meal, Lydia. So good and so filling that I grew sleepy and drifted off for a few minutes."

"I thought we needed a little celebration. The recent murder has been solved and Amy and Sunny and probably a few others are now out of danger. Speaking of celebrations"—she released Hugh's hand and stood up—"I should go and bring out the cake you brought, Kurt. Thanks again for that."

He waved this aside. "My chef made it, not me. But you're welcome."

"I'll go get it," I said, motioning for my aunt to sit back down.

Kurt stood up. "I'll help," he said.

"Then I'd better go alert Karla and the kids," Richard said. "They'll need to wash their hands before eating cake, and you know they'll want to dive into it as soon as they realize it's on the table." He walked back into the garden, calling out for Karla, Ella, Nicky, and Noah.

I picked up the used utensil platter to carry it in with me.

"Anything else need to go inside?" Kurt asked, as he joined me at the table.

"The condiment tray," I said, tilting my head in that direction since my hands were full.

We carried the trays onto the sunporch, then Kurt balanced his on one hand so he could open the back door to the house for me.

"I assume you want this in the kitchen," he said, as we stepped into the hallway that ran from the front to the back of the house.

"On the kitchen table is fine," I said. As I set my platter on the counter next to the sink. I turned, resting my lower back against the edge of the countertop. "Thanks."

"No problem," Kurt said, examining me carefully. "How are you feeling? We haven't talked since Tuesday."

"I'm fine. How are you?"

"Same as always." He replied. "I've been carrying the burden much longer, and with many more regrets, of course."

I toyed with the neckline of my lemonade-yellow sundress. "He did really love her, didn't he? Andrew, I mean. He truly loved Lydia, right?"

"Oh, yes. There was no doubt about that. When he met her again after college he fell like a ton of bricks." Kurt's smile turned rueful. "I never stood a chance, you know."

"But you loved him anyway."

Death and the Librarian

Kurt lifted his hands. "What can you do? Love doesn't always evoke love in return. But that doesn't make it any less real, in terms of the unrequited lover. It still exists, outside the gift of reciprocity."

Silence hung between us for a moment.

"He must've cared deeply for you, or he wouldn't have maintained the friendship," I said at last.

Kurt's troubled expression brightened. "Of course. I think, in his way, Andrew loved me very much. And that's something I've always kept locked in my heart." He swept his hair away from his broad forehead. "It's been enough."

"That's admirable. I'm not sure I could've remained as devoted as you," I said.

A twinkle sparked in Kurt's eyes. "That's not to say I haven't indulged in numerous love affairs over the years. I'm loyal, but not a saint."

"No one would ever call you that," I said with a smile.

"Not if they've met me. Now"—Kurt strode over to the refrigerator—"let's deal with this cake. I can carry the box if you grab the extra small plates and forks."

I collected the plates and utensils and followed him back outside, where four children were eagerly waiting.

"Cake!" Zoe squealed when Kurt removed the lid on the box.

"I want a big piece," Ella said, her eyes as wide as saucers at the sight of the chocolate-on-chocolate confection. "Like this big." She spread her hands apart.

"That's a bit much," I said. "You have to leave some for others."

291

"Yeah, like me," Nicky said.

"And me!" Noah, who was the perfect mini-me of his father, raised a hand and waved it wildly through the air.

"Everyone will get some," Richard said. "Just be patient."

I laughed, amused by the obvious impatience displayed by the children. "Might as well ask them to build a pyramid."

Brad and Alison hurried to the table to take charge of Noah and Zoe, while Karla looked over at me and winked. Aunt Lydia rose gracefully to her feet and marched over. She picked up the cake knife and swiped through the air.

"I'm in charge of this," she said. "Everyone else please back off."

All the guests, even the children, obeyed this command.

"I still want a really big piece," Ella muttered, loud enough for everyone to hear.

"You'll get the piece I give you," Aunt Lydia said as she deftly wielded the knife. "And you'll like it."

Richard, who'd strolled over to stand beside me, whispered in my ear, "Now, that's how you handle things."

"I'm taking notes," I said, slipping my arm around his waist. "Maybe someday I can become just as intimidating."

Kurt, who was standing behind us, laughed. "Not likely, my dear. Only one in a million can command that kind of unwavering respect."

"Besides," Richard said, pulling me close to his side, "I prefer you just as you are. Props to Hugh, but much as I love her, I don't think I could deal with Lydia for extended periods of time."

Death and the Librarian

"She is unique," I said, watching my aunt cut perfectly symmetrical slices of cake and dole them out.

"Aren't we all, in our own way?" Kurt said.

I glanced over my shoulder and smiled at him. "Some more than others."

Acknowledgements

It's hard to believe that this is the ninth book in the Blue Ridge Library Mystery series. Of course, it wouldn't be possible without the talent and support of the following individuals:

My agent, Frances Black of Literary Counsel.

My editor at Crooked Lane Books, Faith Black Ross.

The Crooked Lane Books team, especially Matt Martz, Dulce Botello, Megan Matti, Stephanie Manova, Mikaela Bender, Thaisheemarie Fantauzzi Perez, and Doug White.

Cover designers C. Griesbach and S. Martucci.

My friends, family, and fellow authors.

Bookstores and libraries—the best institutions ever!

All the bloggers, podcasters, YouTubers, and reviewers who have mentioned, reviewed, and promoted my books.

And, as always, my wonderful readers!